BRUTAL OBSESSION

CARUSO COSA NOSTRA SERIES
BOOK 1

SHANDI BOYES

DEDICATION

To the women who want to be chased... and caught!

COPYRIGHT

Written by: Shandi Boyes

Cover: SSB Covers & Design

Photography: Ren Saliba

Editing: Courtney Umphress

Proofreading: Anisa Worthington

WANT TO STAY IN TOUCH?

Facebook: facebook.com/authorshandi

Instagram: instagram.com/authorshandi

Email: authorshandi@gmail.com

Reader's Group: bit.ly/ShandiBookBabes

Website: authorshandi.com

Newsletter: https://www.subscribepage.com/AuthorShandi

1

VALENTINA

I'm late. Again.

While I curse the stupid Maps app as if it's solely to blame for my tardiness, my inexpensive heels batter the uneven cobblestones in the heart of Carlisle. Their stomps mirror the discouraged honks of the early-morning commuters who loathe as much as I do that peak-hour traffic starts well before dawn.

The sun has barely risen, and its low hang creates shadows on historic architecture I'd slow to admire if I weren't on a time crunch.

Carlisle is a sunburned metropolis on the north coast of Sicily. Nestled between rolling lemon groves and the sparkling blue waves of the Tyrrhenian Sea, it's the perfect location for rest and recovery.

Well, that's what I told myself three months ago when I abandoned everything familiar for this country's promise of solace.

Willing the blue dot on my phone's screen to magically fix itself, I follow its directions to the wire. An additional thousand steps don't resolve my issue. The Maps app continuously leads me to a decommissioned council building instead of the hospital I'm seeking.

Carlisle's labyrinthine streets mock modern technology, but I doubt I'd fare better with paper maps. All the old buildings painted in white, terracotta, and pale-blue hues look *exactly* the same. I can't tell a family-run bakery from a gelato store.

Anger reddens my cheeks when my phone notifies me to turn left.

"There is no left! So how the hell am I meant to turn left?"

I'm already strangling my phone, but my clutch firms enough to crack the screen when a message from Dr. Russo's secretary pops up. If I don't arrive at Ospedale San Giorgio's in ten minutes, Dr. Russo's secretary will postpone our meeting until after Dr. Russo returns from a six-week international conference.

Determined not to let technology sabotage a mission over a year in the making, I quicken my pace. This morning's meeting isn't with the local council's corrupt building inspector. It's far more important than hiding the cracks of an unsteady foundation so I don't end up homeless. This could unravel my entire existence.

"*Dio mio*," I mutter, glancing at the time.

I wouldn't be on such a time crunch if I'd left earlier, but my hair loathes extreme humidity, and I didn't foresee a dead battery. I'm usually the first to arrive...

Actually, scrap that. Tardiness has become my middle name of late. It isn't my fault. Carbs are cheap, but they also demand weekly wardrobe tweaks. Since laundry day isn't until tomorrow, I'm down to the bare basics. My blouse is barely holding together. Three buttons are all that stand between disaster and me. My ample cleavage won't survive a fourth loss.

After regulating my breathing, which I'm praying will reduce the likelihood of being arrested for public indecency, I close the Maps app and scroll through the Photos app. Carlisle is a patchwork of identical buildings and picturesque coastlines, but if any of the business names match those I've passed three times this morning, perhaps sometime within the next century, I'll escape the maze endeavoring to swallow me whole.

I find the image I'm seeking as a horn blasts in the distance. I hardly notice it. I glue my eyes to my phone's screen, anxious to identify the name of the giant stone wall blocking my path.

I'm in such a hurry that I don't register the smoothness of the curb compared to the unevenness of the footpath, nor do I hear the truck hurtling down the main road at a reckless speed. My focus is fixed on the universally known hospital icon on the old-school map I snapped a picture of months ago, and relief surges through me when I realize it's mere blocks away.

I'm oblivious to the danger roaring my way, but thankfully, not everyone's brain is as sluggish as mine when denied a morning shot of espresso.

A rough, urgent hand snatches my arm and plucks me out of the path of danger with barely a second to spare. My phone slips from my hand, and before I can catch it, I'm flattened against the cool metal of a dark SUV.

The good Samaritan who saved me from a head-on collision with a truck shields me with his body as the speeding motorist thunders past us. Our near miss is so close that the air whistling from the undercarriage of the truck whips my hair back and rattles my core.

That was a close call.

Too close.

For several heart-thrashing seconds, only my pounding pulse and the fading echo of the truck's horn fill the silence.

Even with imminent disaster gone, the stranger doesn't release me from his protective cocoon. I don't mind. My skyrocketing heart rate is settling, but the spasms in the lower half of my body remain steadfast. They make me wonder if they stem from fear or if they're associated with something I've not experienced in a long time.

I wipe the fear from my eyes with a handful of blinks before peering up at the man who saved my life. Though his body is still squashed against mine, since he stands a good foot taller than me, I encounter no issues drinking him in.

The sophisticated scent of his cologne matches the striking features of his face, and his messy dark hair is tousled in a way that suggests he runs his hands through it multiple times a day. It's early, but his chiseled jaw already displays the start of a five o'clock shadow, and his sable eyes are intense.

When I huff, shocked someone can start their day looking this fantastic, my minty breath fans his cheek. Mistaking my sigh as a wordless request for space, he steps back, further highlighting his alluring package. He's not just attractive. He's also tall, broad-shouldered, and dressed in a tailored black suit. The collar of his crisp black business shirt is open. His watch looks expensive but understated, and his shoes have been polished to a mirror shine.

His commanding presence draws a crowd, but his intense gaze remains fixed on me. I won't lie. The interest his eyes hold as he travels them over my face and body makes me blush.

He's suited for the boardroom of a multibillion-dollar company or behind the wheel of a luxury superyacht, not rescuing a flustered woman from a traffic accident.

He probably dates women who glide through life with perfect hair and effortless grace, so someone who is perpetually late and a gluttonous breath away from a wardrobe malfunction should be an unlikely candidate for his attention.

But I get a second glance—more than once.

He eyes me with the same interest I give him, and his mutually needy stare announces my near collision with a truck isn't to blame for my spiking pulse.

That burden rests entirely on his shoulders.

We're from different realms, but I hide my insecurities with strong eye contact. He must find my endeavor to keep the playing field even humorous. The corners of his plump lips lift into a confident smirk as his thumb brushes the vein thudding in my wrist.

If he's trying to stabilize my blood pressure, he needs to take a step back—a *giant* step.

"*Stai bene?*" His accent is low and unmistakably Sicilian. He's a native, probably born here. His accent is more authentic than the one I've tried to imitate so the locals wouldn't categorize me as a tourist, despite that being the status of my visa.

Nodding, I swallow hard to loosen the lusty clutch curled around my throat. "I think so," I reply in English, hopeful it will announce I am, at best, a novice in Italian.

As he inches back, allowing enough space for my lungs to fully expand, a refreshing breeze tickles my chest. I glance down, and my eyes bulge. My blouse didn't survive his pluck-and-rescue routine. My fitted shirt-and-skirt combo was already struggling to contain my ample curves, and my near tumble made their efforts pointless.

Almost every curve I own is on full display.

Grimacing, I tug down the hem of my skirt with one hand and clutch my blouse together with the other. I've always worn double digits, and most days, I'm comfortable in my own skin, but tell me a girl who wouldn't feel awkward standing next to the World's Sexiest Man?

The stranger scrapes a hand across his bristled jaw, hiding his smile, when I fasten the *only* functioning button left on my blouse. It barely conceals the fleshy globes on my panting chest, but it's better than nothing.

Even though he appears amused, his tone showcases concern when he asks, "Are you trying to die?"

"I didn't see—"

"You didn't look." I steady my sways with the SUV's door handle when he brings back the seriousness of the situation. "You were about to walk straight under that truck." He shakes his head and mutters something I don't catch before he stoops down to collect my phone from the footpath. "You should pay more attention. Carlisle traffic doesn't stop for anyone."

"I'm lost," I confess. "My car wouldn't start, so I took the bus, three buses actually, because I have an important meeting I can't miss. The app must have gotten its town plans from the same place my ex got directions to my cl—" I stop when I realize how absurd I sound. He is the epitome of wealth and sophistication, and I'm rambling like a homeless person at Venice Beach. "Thank you. You saved my life."

His response is barely audible. "My mother always said variety is the spice of life."

His change in pitch piques my curiosity. The shrill of an alarm, however, brings to mind the reason for my distraction. I don't have time to dawdle—regretfully.

I extend my hand as if a handshake is sufficient payment for saving a life. "Valentina Raimondi."

The stranger shakes my hand but doesn't offer his name. Instead, he pries. "You're not from here, are you, Valentina?"

I bristle, defensive. Though I wasn't born and raised here, my mother is from Palermo, and my father is from this region. I am of Sicilian origin. My mother simply chose to raise me in the United States.

"I am," I reply, my composure more collected than it was moments ago. "My mother grew up not far from here."

He arches a brow, unfazed by the sarcasm in my voice. "And your father?"

After gritting my teeth, I steer clear of a topic I'll happily avoid for decades. "I apologize, but I must go. I'm late."

He glances at my cracked phone screen, knits his dark brows, then gestures to the SUV he had me pressed up against. "Hop in. You can't walk to the hospital from here."

Assuming he read my destination through my cracked screen, and not because he's a deranged stalker, I don't seek clarification on how he knows where I'm going. I pursue more precise directions. "The app says—"

"Your app is telling you to go through a wall. You need to go around it." He opens the SUV's front passenger door and then signals for me to enter.

Warning bells ring in my head, but the memory of the truck and the taste of fear still sharp in my mouth prompt me to nod. "All right."

As I sink into the plush leather seat, the handsome stranger jogs to the driver's door. With an animalistic grace that matches his commanding aura, he slides in, starts the engine, and pulls into oncoming traffic without waiting for an opening.

I'm shocked when the commuters he cuts off don't honk. He dictates traffic as if his SUV has government plates, and in a matter of seconds, the icon I was seeking earlier presents on each street sign we pass.

With a confidence that comes with insider knowledge, he makes fast work of the heavy traffic. He isn't immune to the road rage most commuters face at one stage in their lives, though. He curses a moped rider for cutting him off, then laughs when a group of teens chase his SUV down several streets, hopeful for a sneaky snap of him and the men in the convoy of SUVs tailing us.

Either a security team is following us, or the vehicles behind us are racing to the same location. They mimic the stranger's hair-raising maneuvers turn for turn—even the illegal ones he does when traffic becomes too dense.

After rubbing a hand over my hair to smooth the frizz, I ask, "Are you famous?"

I can't see his face, but I know he is smiling. I can feel it in my bones. "Not exactly. Carlisle was once a small town. Everyone knew everyone." The SUV's tires squeak when he turns down the cobblestoned street I inputted into the Maps app over an hour ago. "But now she's a wild thing. If you don't respect her, she'll eat you alive."

My agreeing huff flaps a wayward dark lock from my face. "I'm slowly learning that."

We fall into a companionable silence as the city awakens around us. Markets spill onto the streets, older men argue over chess in the local park, and children chase pigeons through the piazza. It represents a perfectly normal day, and I'm praying it stays that way.

After both an eternity and an instant, the still-unnamed man pulls up outside a gleaming glass building. "Here you go. Ospedale San Giorgio's. The main entrance is—"

"Past the fountain," we say in unison.

Relief and gratitude surge through me as I quickly gather my belongings. I've already taken up too much of his time, so I don't want to waste more. "Thank you. I can't bear to think about what could have happened if you hadn't been at the right place at the right time."

He shrugs off the admiration as another impish grin spreads across his face. "Just promise to pay attention next time and to not trust technology more than your head. If you can do that, we will be on our way to an equal scoreboard."

Scoreboard?

Running out of time, I nod and then crank open my door. "No more apps for me. I promise."

After straightening my barely held-together blouse, I slip into the rapidly warming sunlight. With my brain still on the fritz, I don't remember to turn around and wave off the stranger until I'm halfway to the entrance.

I startle when I realize he's already gone. His SUV has blended into the hustle of Carlisle's traffic, leaving me with nothing but the tingles his touch inspired and the memory of his concern when he contemplated my mishap not being an accident.

I'd love to investigate his concern more thoroughly, but a far more pressing matter demands my utmost devotion.

I square my shoulders and dash through Ospedale San Giorgio's double entrance doors. Although shaken, I'm committed to ensuring this morning's brush with death is the only one I face today.

2

GIOVANNI

Halfway back to Carlisle's town center, I murmur to myself, "What the fuck was that, Vanni?"

Carlisle is a small coastal community, though not so small that every face is familiar. Valentina should have been another shadowed figure in the morning rush. She wasn't. One glance of her beautiful face and cock-thickening body warranted another, and another, and another, until she became the *only* thing I could see.

I left her only five minutes ago, and she's occupied my thoughts every single second. It isn't solely the way she looked at me that repeats in my head, or the way her sexy voice curled around my dick in silent promise of the best blow job of my life. It's every pore, every seductive curve, and each fleck of honey in her light-brown eyes.

Her beauty isn't in the way social media tries to portray as attractive. It's unvarnished and real. She's a recently mined diamond still waiting to be polished. Her hair is a wild dark mane, one I can tell resists any attempts at taming. When the first light of dawn caught it, I pictured how soft it would feel while running my fingers through it.

That isn't me.

I don't admire from afar, nor do I simp over women.

I'm a Caruso.

We fuck—hard. Then we leave.

That is the *only* way we operate.

So why can't I stop mulling over the drastic shift in Valentina's attitude when we arrived at her destination?

Something changed in her the instant she stepped out of my SUV. Although shaken, her confidence was bright enough to cut through the morning haze. But when her feet touched the pavement outside San Giorgio's, her light faded, similar to a candle snuffed out by a sudden draft. It was as if San Giorgio's had stolen her spark and left only a shadow of the woman who immediately captivated me.

If time were in my favor, I would have scrutinized her change in composure to the same extent my hands would have explored her sultry body and face. Alas, I didn't even have the luxury of waiting for her to enter the hospital. The clock on the dashboard was screaming at me. Every second that ticked by underscored what was at stake. I told myself I had no choice, that the family's business and Carlisle locals need to come first. But as I weave through the narrow streets I'm trying to save, I can't shake the concern that I fucked up.

I'll come back. I will find her again. That isn't a question. It's a promise. Our introduction is merely undertaking a brief intermission so I can keep a promise I made many years ago.

It won't take much to find her once my meeting is over. I know her full name and last known location.

Valentina isn't as fortunate.

I didn't give her my name. I saw her curiosity when I accepted her greeting without an official introduction but acted ignorant. I'm not being arrogant when I say every resident of Carlisle recognizes my name. Although that makes me proud, I learned the hard way that being known carries as many burdens as it does comforts.

The Caruso name opens doors, but it can close them if you listen to the wrong tales. Since I didn't want to risk anything scaring Valentina away before I've had the chance to offer a proper introduction, I withheld a minor detail of my life.

While recalling how Valentina offered me her hand to shake, as if she knew I was picturing ways for that exact body part to help settle the debt she now owes me, I roll her name over my tongue.

Valentina Raimondi.

Her name suits her. It's unapologetically Sicilian, yet with a sexiness that conjures images of her fuckable curves and flawless face.

I've met plenty of beautiful women. I've dated models, actresses, and heiresses, but none of them has ever made me want to forget my responsibilities.

I don't do this. I don't get involved or let myself care. Loyalty, secrets, and the unspoken understanding that nothing lasts forever formed the foundation of the Caruso dynasty. Everything can vanish in an instant. I've spent thirty-four years learning that lesson, and during that time, I've carved out a place for myself in a world where trust is more valuable than gold.

Attachments are dangerous.

They make you hesitant.

They make you weak.

And yet, I acted today without considering how my gallantry would favor my family or myself.

That was unheard of only thirty minutes ago. For thirty-four years, I've looked out for no one but myself and my family. No one has ever had the privilege of slating their names next to my parents and brothers. Not even Dante's baby mama, whom I've not spent a single second looking for, even though she's been missing for six weeks.

If I hadn't been there, watching Valentina from afar, she wouldn't be here now. The thought adds to the anger still blackening my veins. As I roll up my sleeves, too hot under the collar not to react to my rising body temperature, the moment Valentina nearly stepped into the path of the truck plays through my head in crystal-clear detail.

Valentina's head was down, so she was oblivious to the danger barreling toward her. Without the instincts I've developed from living on the edge, I wouldn't have rushed to her defense before my head could object.

In three heart-thrashing seconds, I grabbed her arm, yanked her back, and then crowded her against my SUV. Despite the wind tunnel the truck's brutal speed caused, the wild flutter of Valentina's pulse against my pulse made my dick as unbendable as a steel rod. Then, when her eyes met mine, wide and unguarded... *fuck.*

Everyone knows the Carusos are direct. We're not known for subtlety or hesitation, but something about Valentina made me act differently. She's beautiful, yes, but it's more than that. Her commanding presence drew my eye long before she stepped into danger.

Even though I shouldn't care how close to death she was, I do. The anger clutching my throat hasn't loosened its grip in the slightest, and my jaw is tense enough to crack. I'm late for an important meeting, and although my commitments usually take precedence, the desire to beat the living shit out of the person responsible for my annoyance is too potent to ignore.

Confident my brothers will support my decision to right an injustice, I swing the SUV into a tight U-turn. Burning rubber fills my nostrils as I turn down a familiar street. I know the company I'm seeking. The logo on the side was subtle, but I'd recognize it anywhere. It's from one of my family's many businesses.

The knowledge enhances my fury.

My family rarely offers mercy. Our rules don't protect you solely based on your gender. If you double-cross us, expect to pay for your stupidity with your life. This is different, though. Valentina didn't steal a drug shipment or place pinholes into my brothers' condoms to try to force ties with a legacy in the billions. She was walking on the fucking street, as thousands of tourists and locals do every day.

That doesn't warrant a death certificate.

I work my jaw side to side while pulling into the dusty lot of a transportation company five clicks out of town. Once parked at the front, I get out and shut the driver's side door with a bang.

Heads turn as I walk toward where the trucks are stored. They know this can't be good. The Carusos only visit when something is awry. We don't do drop-in spot checks, especially not the person who heads the clan.

Although my visit will whistle through the gallows for months, my strides don't falter. My blood is too hot to let this go.

It only takes scanning half a dozen faces to spot the one I'm seeking. I didn't see the driver's face or plate while racing to beat him to Valentina. I was too busy sheltering Valentina to take in any identifiable features, but the guilt on this man's face tells the entire story. He knows who I am. Just like he knows why I'm here.

"*Signor* Caruso." Even with fear flaring in his bloodshot eyes, his composure is calm. I don't believe his red eyes are because he's been crying. It seems he enjoys the drugs this company transports more than a casual user would.

Dust kicks up when I bridge the gap between us. "You nearly killed someone back there."

The fool shrugs, feigning indifference. It's a pity his shaky hands betray his fear. "It wasn't my fault. She wasn't looking where she was going."

His lazy dismissal extinguishes the last of my patience. Fisting the front of his shirt, I yank him forward until his face is an inch from mine, and the popping of his buttons pierces through the noise in my head. He's taller than me and a good thirty pounds heavier, but backing down isn't in my vocabulary.

"Not only did you drive through Carlisle like you own the place, but you did it with *our* merchandise dusting your fucking nose." I flick his nostril with my spare hand. My fairy tap springs tears to his eyes and sprinkles the collar of his uniform with the white powder I'm skeptical he paid for. "When you wear this uniform, you represent *my* family. Today, you made us look irresponsible. That's unacceptable."

Color drains from his face when it dawns on him how serious I am. He tries to pull back, but my grip is ironclad, so he returns to being a coward. "I-I'm sorry, *Signor* Caruso. It won't happen again. I-I—"

Before he can issue another pathetic excuse, I strike him hard across the cheek. My backhanded slap sends him sprawling backward, and he lands on his ass with a thud. Seconds later, the crack of my foot breaking several of his ribs booms over the shocked huff of the people surrounding us.

Tears trickle down his cheeks as bewilderment and pain mingle on his face. His sudden remorse doesn't slow me down. I can't stop recalling the fear in Valentina's eyes before I plucked her from danger, and how different things could be if I'd hesitated for even a second.

"You don't get a second chance with stuff like this." I remove my gun from its holster, and the driver scrambles back, eyes wide with fear. "Let this be a warning." I crane my neck to the people doing nothing to help their colleague. "If you work for the Carusos, you represent the Carusos. I don't give a fuck what's going on in our personal life; *never* tarnish the Caruso name. If I *ever* hear about anything like this happening again, you'll answer to me. Trust me, you don't want that"—I return my attention to the driver sniveling at my feet—"because it will only ever end one way."

With a direct hit to the head, I remove the light from his eyes like he almost did to Valentina. Then I divert my attention back to the onlookers. I hold their gazes for a prolonged period, letting my threat settle, before I holster my gun and return to my SUV.

Partway across the dusty lot, Elio, the youngest of the five Caruso brothers, exits the lead convoy SUV. He could bark orders to those below him to clean up my mess, but that isn't Elio's way. He believes he's the only one qualified to fix my mistakes. If his belief was miles off the bullseye, I'd ensure he felt differently. Since it's not, I give him instructions on how I want this handled.

"Make this public. I want his death to be a warning."

A smirk lifts one side of my mouth when Elio asks, "A warning to stay away from Carlisle's latest repatriate, or the merchandise he sampled while waiting for it to be packaged for transport?"

Given that I met Valentina only thirty minutes ago, my reply is too swift not to be reckless. "Both."

After lifting my chin in appreciation for his support, I slide behind the wheel of my SUV and drive away. Anger still simmers beneath the surface of my skin, but there's an immense amount of satisfaction knowing the locals won't forget this encounter for years to come, which, in turn, means they'll also stay away from Valentina.

Carlisle is my hometown. My family's town. And today, I made sure everyone who represents our name remembers that for years to come.

As I pass the area where I first spotted Valentina, I force myself to focus on the task at hand. My blood is still hot with adrenaline, but I can't skip this meeting. The outcome of this deal is critical for Carlisle's future.

Dante usually manages this aspect of our business, but since he's distracted by the disappearance of his daughter's mother, his brothers are picking up the slack.

The streets of Carlisle's town center blur when I increase my speed. Sunlight spills over the rooftops, and the aroma of fresh bread mingles with the salty breeze wafting off the coast.

I know these streets better than I know myself. Every shortcut, alleyway, and shadow I've made a deal or ended a life in. I was born in a villa on the outskirts of town and was raised among acres of lemon orchards and marble halls. I learned at a young age that power is fragile. It's easily lost and never guaranteed, which is the sole reason I need to remain on the ball.

The Caruso name carries weight in Carlisle, and it's my job to keep it that way. Our reach stretches from the orchards to the harbor, and from the council chambers to the back rooms of the pubs where men whisper our name with both awe and dread.

We don't advertise our power like I just did. Everyone knows who pulls the strings, and they either play by the rules or find themselves buried under six feet of dirt.

I loosen my grip on the wheel when I pull my SUV through the manned gates of a warehouse with white walls gleaming in the early-morning sunlight. With Matteo's car already in the lot, the responsibilities I can't escape slam back into me.

After killing the engine, I adjust my blood-splattered tie and then exit the SUV like my day is just beginning. The air is pungent with the scent of a recently fired gun and the tangy aroma of blood.

Walking up the steps and past two guards, who nod in deference, I enter a concealed office at the back of the compound. Matteo, the very definition of a middle child, sits behind a big, bulky desk. Excluding a handful of crimson droplets on the cuffs of his dress shirt, his suit is as immaculate as his slicked-back hair, and his expression is a mix of impatience and concern.

He's younger than me by two years but in some ways more mature. He's always looking for a new angle to expand our network and make more money, whereas I'm happy to keep things local.

"You're late," Matteo says, not looking up. "The councilor is waiting. We could lose the advantage if we keep him waiting too long."

I shrug, unrepentant. "There was an incident in town."

Matteo rounds the desk, props his ass on the battered wood, then folds his arms across his tattooed chest. A knowing smirk curls on his lips, and it's now that I realize he must have witnessed the whole fiasco.

Of course he did. Matteo misses nothing.

He raises a brow as his eyes glint with amusement. "Saving her life wasn't enough? You had to drive her where she needed to go, too, Vanni?"

I shoot him a warning look. "She was shaken up. I couldn't leave her defenseless in the street."

He pushes off the desk and falls into step behind me as I lead our trek to the "boardroom" where our meeting will be held. "Most people would have walked away." He catches up to me before backhanding my chest. "By most people, I mean you. You don't even wait for them to finish shuddering before you skip out butt fucking naked." He tugs on the lapels of my suit. "Is there a knight hiding somewhere under that tailored suit?"

Grunting, I unlock the boardroom door. "Don't start. You said it yourself. The councilor is waiting, and Dante isn't himself. We can't afford *any* distractions right now."

"I think I could spare an hour or two for those tits—"

I silence him with my fist. My whack isn't as hard as the one that knocked the driver on his ass, but it warns Matteo that occupying Valentina's time is *not* up for discussion. Ever.

Matteo holds up his hands nondefensively. If only his words weren't so vocal. "Elio's warning was on the money. You don't just want our drivers acting like Ms. Daisy. You want to keep everyone's eyes off Valentina's rack."

The sting of knuckles on bone lingers on my hand, and I still have a heap of frustration to disperse, but now isn't the time for shenanigans.

Mercifully for Matteo, Councilor Messina has been tiptoeing the rope for months now, and it's finally time to remind him who really runs the show around here.

"Councilor..." My snake-like greeting doubles the putrid scent of fear loitering in the air.

Messina looks up. He's gagged, his wrists are tied behind his back, and his ankles are secured to the legs of a rickety chair. His face whitens when he stalks my entrance, and sweat beads on his cut and swelling brow. The bravado he wore in the council chambers while striking Carlisle locals' century-old dwellings from the ledgers is gone, replaced with fear and desperation.

He should be scared. Because he ignored Dante's warnings, there's only one conclusion for our meeting: It's time for him to go.

I pause a few feet away from the councilor's battered and bruised frame before tugging his sticky socks out of his mouth. Even though he's no longer gagged, silence stretches until it's uncomfortable.

Matteo's attention would have assured Messina that we're not here to discuss business. That chapter closed weeks ago. But there's no harm in letting him stew. He's mistaken the Carusos' ethics once before, so who's to say he won't do it again?

You'll never believe the secrets some men share when they think clemency is on the table.

I'm about to worsen the bruises and nicks mottled throughout Councilor Messina's body when he tries to take the coward's route. Bad choice. The driver's pathetic show of cowardice proves that tactic doesn't work for me.

"Th-this isn't necessary, Giovanni. We can talk. I'm sure we can come to some sort of arrangement."

"An arrangement?" With twisted lips and a raised brow, I feign interest in his offer. "Is that what you called it when you forced families out of their homes with falsified building defects?"

Messina swallows as his eyes dart between Matteo and me. "It was a misunderstanding. I never meant—"

I cut him off with a backhanded whack that sends two of his teeth scuttling across the concrete floor. My slap also adds depth to the split in his cheek and sends his sobs bouncing off the damp warehouse walls.

"The people you forced out of Carlisle were good, honest people. They had lived here for decades. That wasn't a mistake. It was a deliberate act of defiance against the Caruso name."

"No. Never—"

I hit him again. This time with a closed fist. The warehouse is eerily quiet, saved by the councilor's muffled sobs. The only light comes from the single overhead bulb, which casts shadows across the dirty concrete floor, but it doesn't hide how coarse his wrists are from the rope or the sweat and blood staining his suit.

Once the councilor's whimpers simmer to quivering breaths, I crouch down and level my gaze with his. "You know why you're here, so stop the crap. You and your friends on the council think you can sell Carlisle out from under its people. You think you can force people from their homes and hand their keys to foreigners wanting a slice of Sicilian paradise they didn't fight blood, sweat, and tears for!" My last five words are roars.

My family worked hard for everything we have, so it infuriates me that he believes something as pathetic as greed can take it away from us.

"You're selling our history, our fucking blood, for a quick profit. The government wants to run us out of town again, as they did in 1925, when the repression nearly wiped all the Cosa Nostra families from the map. But what you don't realize, Messina"—I spit out his name as if it arrived with a heap of vomit—"the Carusos are here to stay. My family built this town from the ground up. We protected it when the government turned its back and when the law was just another word for corruption. Not even the mafia wars in '64 and '81 kept us dormant for long. *Famiglia* comes before *anything*, and the people you ran out of this town are *our* family."

My nostrils flare when I lean in close. I've always found the scent of fresh blood fascinating.

My reply is void of emotion and deadly calm. "You're going to tell me everything about this latest ploy the council is running." He nods, the fight in him lost before I've even spelled out all my terms. "Then…" I make him wait to ensure he knows who the true owners of Carlisle are. "I'll let you choose how you go out."

"Gio—"

"Don't push my leniency, Councilor. You were only granted permission to pick your exit because an unusual spiritedness is coursing through my veins. If it weren't"—I fist his hair roughly enough to pull several strands from the roots, then yank his head back—"I'd spend the next several hours reminding you that mercy isn't a commodity reserved solely for the rich." Every second I spend here delays my return to Valentina, so I display unusual impatience. "Speak. *Now.*"

3

VALENTINA

I arrive at my appointment with Dr. Russo by the skin of my teeth. I'm out of breath and rattled, but not every gasp is because of my mad dash through the winding maze of Carlisle's town center. My mind is still processing this morning's antics, but for the most part, the electric rush I felt when the handsome stranger shielded me from harm is the cause of my current breathlessness.

When Dr. Russo's secretary tells me to have a seat, I observe my surroundings as if I'm seeing them for the first time. I wish that were true. The hospital has been a second home to me for the past three months. The antiseptic smell in the air and the muffled shuffle of nurses' shoes are awfully familiar.

Mercifully, the stranger's alluring scent is still embedded in my shirt. His warm and comforting fragrance screams of wealth. I bet his cologne isn't available at a standard department store. It reminds me of cedarwood battered with rain after an impossibly humid day. It's earthy and rich, but with the sophistication you'd expect a man of great power to wear.

For a moment, the stranger's cologne drifts me away from where I am. I feel safe surrounded by it. Protected, even.

I hold on to that belief for as long as possible because I'm confident my nightmares are about to return stronger than ever.

Today's meeting isn't about meet-cutes or the chance encounters people share over coffee while laughing about how fate brought them together. I'm at the leading oncology hospital for a reason.

My life's purpose hangs entirely on the outcome of this meeting.

As much as I want to believe in happy endings, right now, all I can do is fight to keep it from disappearing entirely.

When the secretary announces that Dr. Russo is on her way and that I can wait for her in her office, I'm forced back to my fragile reality. I barely register the secretary's sympathetic glance when I bypass her desk fifteen minutes after our scheduled meeting time.

I'm used to the sympathy and pity stares. They're everywhere—except in the eyes of the stranger when he peered down at me. His gaze was intense, almost challenging. It made me stand taller and had me desperate to prove that I'm more than the sum of my troubles.

It reminded me of who I am under the weight of worry and exhaustion.

I'd be dishonest if I said I wasn't praying for another impromptu meeting. The chemistry that blistered between us deserves to be explored. I just need to maneuver through this latest roadblock before I can think about adding another challenge to my life's plan.

Sunlight streams through the tall windows of Dr. Russo's office and paints the floor pale gold. After sitting opposite Dr. Russo's desk, I fidget with a thread in my now-indecent blouse while I wait.

Thankfully, Dr. Russo doesn't keep me waiting long.

Her expression is unreadable when she enters her office holding a clipboard. Her poker face has always been intense.

"Valentina, I'm so glad you could make it." Instead of sitting across from me, she slots her backside onto the desk near my shaky thigh. "I just wish I had better news."

My heart sinks to my toes.

This is what I've been fearing.

"Your mother's condition has advanced faster than we planned. The therapies we're offering aren't enough anymore. She needs specialist treatment, which she can only get with private care. It isn't something we can provide for her here."

Numb, I absentmindedly nod as she continues updating me. I hear the words she's speaking but struggle to process them. They're too brutal to swallow whole. I need to break them down into manageable pieces before I can consider digesting them.

I always knew this day would come, but nothing could have prepared me for the brutal stab of pain when forced to stare death in the face.

I'm not being facetious when I say losing my mother will destroy me.

My shoulders are hunched and my chin quivers, but I put on a brave front. "How much does the specialist treatment cost?" My shaky words expose my true composure. I'm scarcely holding it together. This can't be the end. I refuse to accept any outcome that will take my mother away from me.

Dr. Russo pauses before announcing a figure so far from my reach it might as well be a foreign language.

As the walls close in on me, I bite back a sob. Even as I struggle to breathe, clarity still seeps through the cracks of the carnage. "There must be something else we can do. Another trial? Different medication? I can't just take her home and watch her die." Tipping my head back, I peer at the ceiling and blink back tears. "I'm not ready. I have no idea how to be."

"I'm sorry, Valentina. I wish I could offer more, but I can't. If there were a suitable trial, I would put her name forward, but we're limited in what we can offer while she's under the care of the public health system."

Unable to comprehend what's happening, I nod in disbelief. We uprooted our lives because Sicily has free healthcare. It was meant to save my mother's life, not end it faster.

"How can that be?" The question cracks out of my mouth. "We came to Sicily for the *free* healthcare, so how can you deny her the care she requires? I thought you'd look after her here. I gave up everything in the US because I believed the promise of *free* healthcare."

Dr. Russo grips my hand before encouraging eye contact. Her eyes are full of empathy, but that won't keep my mother alive. I need answers. Solutions. I need a miracle.

"Her care is free, but she needs more than we can give her."

In her eyes, I see the words she can't speak.

My mother will die without the costly treatment suggested.

Mindful that I'm holding on by a thread, Dr. Russo throws me a life vest. "There are some private clinics that offer payment plans. You're working, right?"

When I nod, snot threatens to dribble from my nose. "I work nights at the pub, but I can barely cover the property taxes on our villa. It was decades in arrears when we came back, and now we're being fined for building defects I can't afford to fix. I have nothing left to give." I swipe under my nose to ensure nothing gross spills before aligning my eyes with Dr. Russo's. "I'm sorry. This isn't your burden. I just don't know how things operate here. I could probably ask for an extension for the tax arrears, but that would place us back under scrutiny from the council's building supervisor."

Unless I prance around in my underwear during his monthly inspections, the supervisor has it out for me. His grievances with our building aren't entirely unfounded. The flat we own is a dump in a crumbling block on the outskirts of town. Half the windows are boarded up, and the elevator is permanently out of order. But it baffles me that they expect residents to fix the problems while they issue citations well into the thousands. Every fine increases the debt we owe, and it has us on the brink of filing for bankruptcy.

Even after months of threats from the council to condemn our building, they continue to charge exorbitant fees that would make a New Yorker blush. I pay what I can when I can, but it's never enough. Every day is a stark reminder of our precarious financial situation.

Dr. Russo curls her hand around mine, drawing me from my thoughts. "You have nothing to apologize for. You're doing everything you can to ensure your mother receives the best possible care. That's why I felt compelled to tell you that the treatment she needs is no longer here. If anything, she's better off at home, away from these germs. It could give her an additional two to three months."

Her last sentence is a crushing blow. It ends my fight in an instant.

I want to be the daughter who can fix anything and refuses to give in, but I'm exhausted. Every day is a battle to stay afloat, and now it isn't solely money getting in our way; time is against us too. Guilt washes over me for even thinking about giving up, but the negativity is getting harder to avoid. I'm losing the person who made me who I am, and with every passing day, a part of me vanishes with her.

Too tired to continue fighting, I push words past the burden slowly suffocating me. "Thank you for being frank with me. I appreciate your honesty."

Dr. Russo's smile is tinged with sadness. "What are you going to do?"

"I haven't figured that out yet." My chest sinks when I breathe out deeply. "I'll work it out. I always do. I just need a few minutes to wrap my head around everything."

Nodding, Dr. Russo hands me a business card with her personal details scribbled messily on the back and a list of specialist services that accept payment plans. "If you want to talk, my cell is always on. Call anytime. Day or night."

I muster a moderately amicable grin. "Thank you, Doctor. For everything."

With mechanical efficiency, I dip my chin in farewell and then leave her office. I can't believe this is happening. We moved to Sicily for its free healthcare, but now that safety net has unraveled, leaving us in free fall.

After wandering the corridors of Ospedale San Giorgio's for over two hours, seeking a solution for our predicament, I force a smile before entering my mother's hospital room. She's perched on the edge of her bed, brushing her freshly shampooed hair. Her hair matches mine in darkness but has more kinks, and she painted her lips a hopeful shade of pink that hides how cracked they are.

When she detects she is being watched, she looks up and smiles. "Did you hear the news, *tesoro*? I might get out of here today."

I return her grin, unsuccessfully trying to mirror her cheer. "I did. It's great news. There's nothing like sleeping in your own bed."

She attempts to mask the hoarseness of her lungs with a strained laugh. "I feel better already just thinking about it. Maybe I'll even make it to the market this week."

Needing to conceal my watering eyes from the only person capable of using them to see through to my soul, I gather her tattered nightgowns from her freestanding closet and place them into the suitcase that barely survived its second continental trip. It's the suitcase my mother used when she left Sicily while pregnant with me and severely heartbroken.

I've never met my father, but from what I've gathered from the rare few who knew him, he is a horrible man. He beat my mother so badly when she was eight months pregnant that we nearly died. That's why it was such an uphill battle to get her to agree to come back to Sicily. She didn't want to run into him again, and the leading oncology hospital in the country was in his hometown.

"You should take him first," I whisper, staring at the ceiling.

When my mother's eyes land on me, the concern in them triggers a memory of the fun we had when her initial prognosis required her to occasionally use a wheelchair. "We'll go to the market together. I'll use your wheelchair as a ramrod. That way, we'll get all the good tomatoes."

Mom grins, but her shaky hand when she passes me the tinned cookies I arrived with last week exposes her as a fraud. She's as terrified as I am. I act ignorant, though. I discuss the weather and tell her how our neighbors asked about her last night because I want her to believe she's on the road to recovery.

I can't face the truth right now. It's a reality too cruel to consider. It is tearing me apart.

Shortly after, a knock sounds at the door, and then my aunt bursts into the room, forever cheery and loud. Her arrival breathes life into the oppressive gloom no number of steps will shake.

"Good morning, my darlings!" Aunt Maria's hands are full of fresh fruit and magazines for Mom, and her smile is warmer than the sun. She kisses Mom's cheek before offering her a peach. "I bought them at the market. It was full of gossip today. Apparently, a by-election is coming up. It was a snap decision after Councilor Messina unexpectedly quit. Some are saying he had a family emergency, but what would I know?" Her *pfft* sprays the air with spit, which she clears away with a frantic flap. "I'm not high enough up the food chain for that."

Aunt Maria dumps the basket of fruit onto the drawers I'm clearing before she twists to face Mom. Her expression is impassive, but she has a knack for reading people, even when they're pulling out all their best tricks to hide their pain behind a smile.

She waits until the front-page gossip of a glossy magazine distracts Mom before gently bopping my arm. "Can I have a word?"

"I—"

"This is no concern of yours, Miss Nosy," my aunt says, cutting off my mom. "Just because your birthday month is coming up doesn't give you the right to snoop on every conversation. Some things are better kept hidden... like the gift I was eyeing for you earlier."

Mom's face lights up with childish glee, and Aunt Maria responds to it with a wet, noisy raspberry.

While smiling with gratitude that I'll never be crowned most childish in our family, I shadow my aunt into the corridor.

The door scarcely muffles Mom's husky laugh when my aunt pounces. "What happened? You're pale. You're never pale. The only time I've ever seen your cheeks this white was when you FaceTimed to tell me about your mother's cancer diagnosis."

Tact dictates slowly ripping off the Band-Aid, but I misplaced my empathy somewhere between Dr. Russo's office and my mother's hospital room. "Dr. Russo said there's nothing more they can do. Mom needs specialized treatment, which isn't covered by the public healthcare system."

Her sigh rustles my hair, and then she pulls me in for a hug. "Oh, *tesoro.* I'm so sorry."

Tears threaten to spill as I offload some of my worries onto her shoulders. "I don't know what to do. The council keeps raising the interest rate on our overdue taxes, and the building is falling apart. I can barely keep up with the bills, so there's no way I can pay for private healthcare."

I inch back and stare at my aunt as if she grew a third eye when she says, "There's nothing we can't fix." She goes from semi-insane to a full-blown lunatic. "You and your mom can stay with me. My apartment isn't big, but you and your mother can share my room, and I'll sleep on the sofa."

"I can't ask you to do that." She's years older than my mother. That doesn't make her close to ancient, but my back can't handle the stiffness of a sofa bed, so I don't see her fairing any better.

"Why not?" she immediately fires back. "I'll be there if Concetta needs anything while you're working, and I won't have to commute across town after being on my feet for nine hours a day to babysit her. My offer will benefit me as much as it will you."

I don't consider her tiny kitchen, cramped living room, and single bed with as much time as they deserve. That's how lost I am. Two hours of aimless wandering didn't yield a single solution to our dilemma.

"Are you sure?" I ask after a beat. "I don't want to put you out."

Aunt Maria smiles while brushing a lock of hair from my face. "Family is family. You need help. Let me do that."

Relief cracks through some of the despair sitting heavy on my chest. "Thank you." I wrap her up in a hug so firm that I knock her back. "I'd be lost without you."

She squeezes the living bejesus out of me before she gestures with her head to Mom's room. "Let's go tell your mom the good news. She's been seeking ways to share a room with me since we were kids."

I cease following my aunt back into my mother's room when a familiar voice calls my name. Cranking my neck, I spot a nurse who's been working on my mom's ward for the past month. Luca is friendly but a little creepy. I've caught him watching me from afar more than once. His gaze always lingers too long and too low for my liking. I highly doubt he could tell you the color of my eyes.

Luca shuffles from foot to foot when I join him at the nurses' desk, and glances over his shoulder before speaking. "I hope this isn't too forward, but I wanted to talk to you about your options for your mother." I prepare myself for another lecture about palliative care, but he surprises me. "There's a clinic in Palermo that pays women to donate their eggs. It isn't easy money by any means, but it's good money. It could be enough to get your mother the care she needs."

I stare at him, stunned. This isn't a solution I've ever considered, and I genuinely don't know if I should consider it, but curiosity killed the cat. "How much, exactly?"

"Ten to twenty thousand a deposit."

"Thousand?" I double-check, certain I heard him wrong.

I didn't. Nodding, he hands me a leaflet for a specialist IVF clinic. "You'd have to go through some tests, but I've seen women pay for their treatments this way..." His nervous shuffling is back. "And new boobs. But you don't need them. Yours are..." His words stop when I not so inconspicuously yank together my blouse. Finally, his eyes lift to my face. "I thought it might be something you could be interested in, so I gathered a pamphlet for you. I'll put my number on the back in case you're interested." Faster than I can blink, he yanks the brochure out of my hold and scribbles his details on the back. "Call me if you want to go through with it. I have a contact there, so I could probably get you in sooner than the standard wait time."

I thank him, but my praise is weak. I can't imagine doing something so intimate and clinical for money, but I'm also desperate. This kills me to admit, but I can't give him a definite answer until I've had time to weigh the pros and cons.

I can't do that while being eyeballed like the last dessert at an empty buffet, so I tuck the leaflet into my pocket, tell Luca I'll think about it, and return to my mother's room to continue packing.

With my mother too frail to walk, and my faith in the Maps app too low to consider busing it home to check if the battery charger is functional, I use the last of our funds to take a taxi to my aunt's apartment.

The driver doesn't speak during the commute. He stalks us through the rearview mirror, and he eyeballs Mom like the disease stealing the life from her eyes also stole her beauty.

It hasn't. My mother is a beautiful woman. Men of all ages admire her, and during her youth, she often had more than one date a night.

The further we travel, the more I realize this ride is nothing like the one I took this morning. There are no leather seats or hints of quiet confidence from a powerfully rich smell. Just the rattle of loose change and the aroma of stale cigarettes.

Needing to distract myself from the surging fare, I peer out the window and watch the city slide by. The market stalls shut hours ago, and instead of chasing pigeons, the children are playing football in the street.

Everything is distant, as if I'm watching someone else's life from the outside. It's a scary outlook. This isn't meant to be my life. My mother left her abuser. She escaped the torment, so why is she being so cruelly targeted?

When I seek answers from the only person who can give them, I learn that the half-dozen stairs at the front of San Giorgio's must have exhausted Mom. Her head is resting on my shoulder, and the breaths of her faint snores dust my cheek with warm air.

I kiss her temple before breathing in the comforting scent of honey and amber. I feel like crying. Salty blobs have been threatening to spill from my eyes all day. But I can't release them yet. I need to remain strong for Mom.

Furthermore, crying won't help anything. It will just add another problem to my already overstuffed plate.

"One more step, Mom," I say, aiding her slow climb up the stairwell in my aunt's building that's painted the color of an old lemon. "We're almost there."

Aunt Maria is at her front door, ready to welcome us with open arms. She helps me settle Mom into her bed and is rewarded with my first genuine smile of the day when she fusses over every minute detail. Maria gives Mom the best pillow and wraps her in the softest blanket.

Although the apartment's sole bedroom is compact, it's clean, and the sunlight warming the aged walls provides a luxurious ambiance Mom hasn't experienced in months. The rays highlighting her petite features burst happiness through her eyes.

"Go fetch some milk from the corner store." My aunt presses a few coins into my hand. "I'll pop the kettle on. Your mom's been dying for a sneaky *granita di caffè* for a week."

Grateful for the excuse to get some air, even if it's only for a few minutes, I collect my purse from the kitchen and leave.

Freshly baked goods and sun-kissed skin permeate from the

busy supermarket. I place some discounted bakery items the store will discard tonight if unsold and a pint of milk in a basket.

When I get to the register, I pull out my phone and hope for the best. The cab fare took me down to my last ten dollars, but because I forgot about the bus fare this morning, I'm suddenly not confident I'll have enough funds.

The cashier barely glances at me when I tap my phone against the payment terminal.

My heart plummets to my stomach when the machine beeps and then flashes red.

Declined.

My cheeks burn when I try again and achieve the same result. Mumbling that there must be a bank error, I fumble for coins at the bottom of my purse. On the counter, I count out what little funds I have while striving to ignore the internal alarm announcing payday is still four days away.

I don't have enough, so I tell the cashier I'll return when the bank fixes its error to purchase the baked goods I have to leave behind.

Outside, the ghastly humid air adds to the sting of humiliation painting my cheeks red. The coins I gathered in a hurry feel heavier in my pocket than they should. They're a testament of how little stands between us going under. Even the smallest comforts, like a sweet pastry or a cup of coffee, are luxuries now.

Back at my aunt's, I sit in darkness and watch Mom sleep. She looks fragile in a bed designed only for one, and her breaths are shallow and uneven. I'd give anything to pound out my frustration with a five-mile run before downing shots like I've never had a hangover. Instead, I press my palms to my watering eyes and breathe through the burden drowning me on land.

The afternoon passes in a blur. I help my aunt with dinner and act as if it's normal for a child to spoon-feed her parent before I get ready for my shift at the pub.

As taught, I empty the pockets of my skirt before placing it in the laundry hamper. A trickle of hope peeks out from beneath the dark swamping me when I remember the pamphlet Luca gave me. I try not to grant his promise of a big payday any attention, mindful that nothing good comes easy, but the more I strive to forget it, the more the crumpled pamphlet beckons me to it.

Dr. Russo discharged Mom with enough medication to last her four weeks, but after that, we're on our own. I'll have to pay for the next round. It won't be the full rate since we're on benefits, but the number of prescriptions she needs is more than I can afford.

The numbers I mentally crunch drop my heart to my feet. Months of scraping by and watching hope still slip through my fingers snaps something inside me.

Before I can talk sense into myself, I snatch up the crumpled pamphlet and dial the number on the back. I can't save Mom with hope. I can't pay for her life-saving treatment with pride. I need money—*real money*—and if the only way I can get that is by selling a part of myself, then so be it. I'll do that.

In under a minute, I'm no longer the girl who came to Sicily for a fresh start. I'm a daughter and caregiver. I am whoever I need to be to save my mother's life.

Even someone who'll sell their soul to the devil, if they must.

4

GIOVANNI

As I navigate a well-known curve adjacent to Ospedale San Giorgio's, I grip the steering wheel firmly enough to whiten my knuckles. The route, road, and bleak white building are identical sentinels. I've driven this journey so often over the past month that it's become a ritual. I could do it blindfolded.

Each day I convince myself that today will be different, that I'll see Valentina's molten locks reflecting the morning light, and her curves moving through the crowd with that quiet confidence I can't forget. But every day, disappointment waits for me at the curb.

The footpaths outside San Giorgio's and the warehouse where Councilor Messina died remain lackluster and bland. The entrance doors of San Giorgio's slide open and shut thousands of times a day, but never for Valentina.

My frustration has grown over the past month, and the silence has exacerbated it. I've exhausted every resource to find Valentina. I contacted hospitals nationwide, bribed county clerks for records, and leaned on favors worth far more than a raid on every Raimondi property in the area.

Nothing I've done has worked.

It's as if she vanished from the face of the earth after exiting my SUV. I'd believe our meeting was a dream that dissolves when I wake if news of the truck driver's murder weren't still circulating the streets of Carlisle.

For an entire month—*thirty fucking days*—I've chased shadows. I should let it go. Every morning when I wake up, I tell myself to do precisely that. *Let it go, Vanni. Focus on what matters. Family first.*

What I say doesn't matter. I dedicate several hours a day to my search.

My father's empire, which was rebuilt after a second internal mafia war nearly destroyed the Cosa Nostra, demands constant vigilance. Deals in the billions, shipments, and rivals who'd give anything to catch me unawares all require attention. There's no time for distractions, yet I keep driving the same streets, unable to break the cycle of my obsession.

I stiffen my grip on the wheel when the city's skyline appears ahead. Horns blare, and Carlisle residents continue unaffected by my internal conflict.

I saved her.

Me.

That should mean something. You don't pull someone back from the brink of death and then walk away like it never happened. That morning plays in my mind a minimum of three times a day. Even after a month, I can still recall the softness of Valentina's curves and the way her breath hitched when her terrified eyes finally found mine.

It isn't solely her fear that keeps my search alight. Beneath sparks hot enough to scald and an attraction that made me rock hard, a previously unventured, yet worth fighting for, challenge awakened within me.

I'm fucking clueless why the hook sank in so deeply this time.

Valentina is a stranger. I have a name, a face, and a moment frozen in time. That's *all* I have. But it's enough to keep me stalking the streets at all hours, even while knowing I should let it go.

I have too many unanswered questions and only one person capable of answering them.

Was Valentina's ashen face that day a result of lingering fear? Or was her visit to the hospital as personal as it gets?

San Giorgio's is a leader in oncology care, but it can't give its patients the world-renowned treatment only money can buy. It's limited in how it can help by the same bureaucratic nonsense my family has strived to remove from these shores for three decades.

As I turn down the boulevard leading to the docks, my focus transitions from personal endeavors to business. Work calls. It always calls. The chain of command expects results, and I deliver them. That's who I am. Giovanni Caruso doesn't falter on a promise or lose focus.

At least, that's what I want my competitors to believe.

If they knew how many hours I've wasted chasing a ghost, they'd question everything. They may even try to use it against me.

Good luck with that. I play nice when it benefits me, but if push comes to shove, I won't hesitate to knife those in the back who have done me wrong.

My phone buzzes in the console of my SUV before it lights up the dashboard. It's a call from Nico, another brother and my somewhat right-hand man.

I jab the speaker button. "Talk to me."

"Shipment cleared customs." His gruff tone does little to hide his boredom. "We're good for tonight."

"Any trouble?"

"Nothing I couldn't handle. Though I'm surprised you missed out. You're usually always there with bells on for the beatdowns."

His scarred brow being scratched sounds down the line before he asks, "Did you get stuck in traffic again?"

"I'm pulling in now." Not wanting to out myself as a chump driving aimlessly through the city, hunting for someone who may not want to be found, I keep my reply short. "Should I pop the trunk, or are you dumping this one overboard after gifting him a pair of concrete boots?"

"Matteo's got it covered." Nico pauses. It's a telltale sign he's about to see straight through the bullshit I'm presenting to him. "Are you okay, Vanni? You seem distracted."

"I'm fine." My words snap out moodier than intended, and it doubles the length of Nico's silence this time around.

"Right," he finally says. "See you soon."

When the call clicks dead, I exhale slowly and unclench my jaw. Nico isn't stupid. He knows something's off. I've been distracted, and in our world, that can get you killed.

I need to bury this manic obsession before I make a mistake I can't fix.

Family first.

Always.

Sitting in my car, however, peering out at the city my family has controlled for over fifty years, I know it's easier said than done.

Hours later, the deal is done. A billion dollars in yearly revenue will keep the Caruso name gilded for another generation. I should feel triumphant, but the truth is, I'm restless. My satisfaction tonight is hollow since it's drowned out by a frustration that refuses to loosen its grip on my senses.

By midnight, I'm behind the wheel again. City lights bleed into a starless sky as I prowl Carlisle's empty streets. I should go home so I can sleep and reset for tomorrow's battles. Instead, I steer my car toward San Giorgio's again, forever a sucker for punishment.

It's madness. My obsession with Valentina is borderline possessive, but I'm unable to stop. Not until I see her... or better yet, bury the person keeping her hidden.

The streets are quieter now. Shadows pool in every corner, so I slow down to scan the faces of the patients and late-night visitors outside the ER.

A couple smokes near the entrance, and a nurse hurries to her car as though the injured man limping toward the hospital's emergency entrance might miraculously recover and chase her for her knockoff purse, but there's no sign of Valentina.

As if I've not already reached the limit of insanity, I park across the street with my engine idling and watch the city liveliness slowly taper into a vacuum of nothingness.

Eventually, I kill the motor and lean back to stare up at the glass structure that pierces dark, stormy clouds.

What the fuck am I doing? This isn't me. I don't wait or yearn. I take what I want when I want it. That's the code I live by. So why am I acting like a man who's never had his dick sucked?

I'm saved from an internal interrogation when my phone buzzes. It's probably Nico checking in, so I ignore it. I'm not in the mood to talk business. All I want is answers.

All I want is her.

Angered by thoughts that will get me lynched, I whack the steering wheel firm enough to fear the airbags will disengage before I fire up the ignition and speed out of the hospital's parking lot like my life depends on it.

I need to get *her* out of my fucking head, and I know the perfect place to achieve that.

Several miles later, the lights of Carlisle brighten as the entertainment district stretches ahead. Tourists and locals spill from bars and music halls, chasing the thrill sometimes only a seedy nightclub can offer.

Laughter tangled with bass lines carries through the air in a silent promise that anything is possible before sunrise, yet I move through the disorder with a completely different purpose.

I study every face, seeking that one in a million.

This wasn't the plan when I left San Giorgio's. I was meant to go home, get shitfaced with my brothers, and pretend the world doesn't exist.

A burning tide of anger crashes into me. My lifestyle has no patience for weakness. My father raised me on that truth, and I've enforced it myself more times than I care to admit. In our world, the second you let your guard slip, someone is behind you with a knife and a smile.

And yet here I am, losing focus over a woman I barely spoke five words to.

I'd stop the insanity if I could, but obsession is an incurable addiction. There's no quick-fix solution—*except* another hit.

The irritation prickling my skin eases as I visualize the reward of my hard work. Valentina's body will be the perfect canvas to rectify the injustices I've faced. I'll take my time with her, savoring every luscious curve while reminding her how she can't outrun her consequences any easier than she can outrun me.

Halfway down the neon-lit tide, my phone rings again. Not wanting to have my ass chewed out for being a lovesick chump, I jab the call button before telling Nico that business will have to wait until the morning.

"I'm fucking wrecked."

"Glad someone's finally admitting it," replies a voice I immediately recognize. It doesn't belong to Nico.

Although grateful Dante has finally reached out, something is off with his tone. "Camille..."

"Is tucked up in bed." His tone is nothing like it usually is when speaking about his daughter. It's urgent and brimming with angst. "You need to come home. *Now.* Dad's taken a bad turn."

His last sentence smacks into me, landing like a punch to the gut, and I forget everything not associated with the founder of my very existence. The deals. The frustration. Valentina. None of them matter right now.

"I'm on my way."

I slam my foot down on the gas pedal, and the SUV's engine roars as I tear through Carlisle faster than I ever have before.

VALENTINA

The day I've been waiting for and also dreading has finally arrived. Today is the day I trade a portion of my soul for the money I hope will save my mother's life. I aced the genetic testing that would have taken me back to square one if they'd found anything awry, signed the consent forms that announced more than my dignity is on the line today, and read every scrap of information I could find about the egg retrieval procedure. I know how they will use my eggs and the anonymity on offer, yet it still feels clinical.

I never thought I'd ever give away a part of me for money. This afternoon, I'm not solely donating cells. I am sacrificing a piece of my future I may never achieve.

Although it hurts to consider a part of myself existing with no awareness of my presence, prioritizing additional time for my mother is what truly matters. The benefits I might receive could exceed what I'm about to lose.

The treatment my donation will fund could save my mother's life.

That hope is the sole thing keeping my resolve intact.

Will I regret this down the track? Possibly. But I need more than air to ensure my mother will be here to celebrate any children I may have.

As I dress, I remind myself why I'm doing this. It isn't for me. It's dedicated to my mom, who raised me on her own and provided me with a fantastic childhood.

Though my wardrobe selections are minimal, I choose comfort over style, mindful that some discomfort is typical during egg dona-tion. I intend to look presentable, even if my shaky knees give away my true composure.

After changing into a loose-fitting skirt and top, I enter the bath-room recently vacated by my aunt and mom and attempt to tame my wild hair into submission. They believe that I'm traveling to Palermo for a job interview. They're clueless that the handful of pounds I put on is from the medication required to stimulate more eggs during ovulation. Someday, I'll tell them about the procedure, but not until my mother's latest health battle is over.

My reflection in the vanity mirror is pale. Dark circles now ring my caramel eyes from too many sleepless nights, and the fluid I'm retaining has blanched my rounded cheeks. The pamphlets I received during my first appointment at the IVF clinic state that the weight gain shouldn't last. It typically sorts itself out when the dona-tion cycle ends.

While pulling my hair into a low ponytail, I tell myself it's temporary. Everything is temporary—except the love I have for my family.

When I exit the bathroom, my steps falter. Mom is propped on the sofa. Her frame is so svelte that the cushions swallow her. Her skin is almost translucent, and her teacup clatters against the saucer when she brings it to her mouth.

It kills me to see her like this. She's so frail she has to be in pain. She's just putting on a brave face. How do I know this? I do the same for her.

"Don't fuss, *tesoro*," she whispers when I mop up the tea she spilled down the front of her shirt with a damp cloth. "I'm not going out today, so I can wear a tea-stained shirt." Her laughter is brittle, but it still warms my heart. "Go, darling. You don't want to be late for your interview."

After swallowing my apprehension, I brush my mouth against hers. "I'll be back tonight, Mamma. I promise." With a deep breath, I inhale the faint fragrance of her favorite soap.

My heart warms when she breathes in my scent just as readily before replying, "It's fine. You're young. Enjoy the city life before you're too old to truly relish it."

Nearby, my aunt hovers with her arms crossed and her eyes glistening with unshed tears. She tries to keep things light by bustling around the kitchen, but I see the worry etched on her face.

After a beat, she jumps onto the we're-fine train with my mother. "Go, Valentina. We have everything covered. Take the day to recuperate and revive."

"Thank you, Maria." I hug her goodbye, and after casting a final glance at my mother, I hurry into the corridor, desperate to outrun the fear that my campaign to save my mother's life is too late.

Having visited the clinic twice before, I'm familiar with the trip to Palermo. I know how to navigate its hilly streets without the use of the Maps app. Though the knowledge doesn't make my hands any less shaky.

This trip is far scarier than my previous two. During the first appointment, a phlebotomist took a blood sample for genetic testing, and during the second visit, an IVF specialist administered egg-stimulating medication.

This time, they'll walk away with something far more valuable.

The train to the town center becomes more crowded as the city awakens. This line stretches from patisseries with the rich scent of coffee drifting from their open windows to cliffside homes precariously dangling over the open sea.

When a group of rowdy teens joins me at the back of the train car, I guard my bag as if the folded leaflet from the clinic inside is the bank check I'm praying will be deposited into my account before close of business. Despite my best efforts to ignore what I'm about to do for that money, the thought persistently slips through the cracks. It circles in my mind like a vulture wanting to pick at a dead carcass and makes me want to vomit.

When the train arrives at my destination, I rush out the electric doors, desperate for air. I inhale a long and steady breath before reminding myself there's no use fighting the inevitable. Being willing to do anything necessary to save my mother's life isn't weak. It's the most admirable thing I've ever done.

With my head back in game mode, I pace toward the clinic. Palermo is louder, brighter, and more chaotic than Carlisle, but mercifully, the clinic is tucked away from prying eyes. Nestled between a bakery and a florist, it has multiple discreet and unmarked entrances.

As I walk past graffitied stairs that seem steeper than they have previously, my heart wildly thuds. I'm early for a change, but there's already a crowd forming. My face isn't easily recognized to the people of Palermo, but my aunt's comments about my resemblance to my mother at this age necessitate caution.

While making my way through the throng of people milling

near the clinic, I keep my chin tucked into my chest. I'm almost in the clear when an odd sensation compels me to stop. Goose bumps prickle the back of my neck before augmenting down my spine. They're subtle at first but stand taller with each passing second.

Slowly, I angle my head and slide my wide gaze over my shoulder. A familiar face in the distance catches my breath halfway between my throat and lungs. The stranger who rescued me weeks ago is getting out of a stylish black SUV that closely resembles the vehicle he pinned me against that morning in Carlisle.

Since I thought he was a local, I looked for him there and wandered through its twisting streets at all times of the day and night, hopeful for a glimpse of his ridiculously handsome face.

All avenues were fruitless. No one had any information. Yet, now he's here, in Palermo, as if destiny is giving me a second shot.

Excitement ignites in my chest. I desperately want to ask him why he's here and to confess that he hasn't left my thoughts for a single second, but just as I'm about to make my move, I notice he isn't alone.

A beautiful woman with long, glossy locks and a petite frame slips out of the SUV beside him. Every inch of her is flawless, and I shrink away, suddenly aware of my rumpled clothes, my tired eyes, and the anxiety of my sudden weight gain.

Compared to her picture of perfection, I look like a slob.

My heart sinks as I watch the dark-haired stranger take the brunette's hand in his. His fingers lace with hers with easy familiarity, like it's something they do regularly.

As they walk hand in hand toward the clinic, a million questions fire through my head.

Two stand out more clearly than the rest.

Is she his wife?

His girlfriend?

Looking for a ring never crossed my mind, and I didn't have

time to ask the right questions. I was too frazzled from the near miss and, if I were honest, my body's particular reaction to the stranger.

I've met many handsome men in my life, but there was something about him, something unique, that made me curious about the sparks that fired between us that morning.

Now, watching them, I feel foolish for even pondering more.

The stranger doesn't enter the clinic with the beautiful brunette. He guards the door protectively—o*r is it aggressively?*—and his aviator sunglasses covering his dark eyes reflect the screen of text he reads while waiting for her to return to his side.

Suddenly, his head jerks up from his phone, and he scans the crowd wedged between us. Afraid he might see me, I duck behind a pillar and watch him from afar.

War wages inside me for several long seconds. I want him to see me so I can prove that the chemistry I felt that morning wasn't a lie, but I shouldn't want that from a taken man.

I am the result of an extramarital relationship, so I'd *never* volunteer to be the other woman.

As that mantra rings on repeat through my head, I slip around the side of the building and find the secondary entrance I used during my last visit. It's quieter here and hidden from any eyes that might recognize me.

After letting myself in, I lean against the wall of one of many examination rooms off this corridor and steady my breathing. Inside, the clinic is bright and sterile, and cleaning products are acute in the air.

Once my lungs are functioning close to normal, I head to the receptionist area. I check in at the desk and hand over my paperwork before answering the secretary's questions with automatic precision.

The receptionist is kind and her smile is gentle, but I barely register her words. My mind is still outside, with the dark-haired stranger and the woman beside me who is impossible to ignore.

She's the woman I saw outside, and up close, she's even more intimidating.

When she eyes my paperwork as if privacy is merely suggestive, a dazzling grin doubles her beauty. "I hope they don't get us mixed up."

Confused, I peer at her with a screwed-up nose. Her glossy dark locks cascade flawlessly down her slim shoulders, and her handbag costs more than my entire wardrobe. We couldn't be more different if we tried.

It dawns that I'm the only one comparing us when she says, "Our names are so similar it's scary."

I lower my eyes to her paperwork, stomping on her privacy as she did mine, before gasping.

Her name is Valeria Raimondo.

"Were you born in Palermo?" Even though she's asking a question, she doesn't pause for an answer. "Your accent reveals you're not from around here, but you look familiar. Have we met before?"

"Um. No... I don't think we have."

I give her a weak smile, then retreat into myself. I feel like a troll standing next to a fairy tale princess and wondering what it would be like to be transported to an alternative universe where my life would be easier and better offers no comfort.

My hair is limp and lifeless, and my clothes are the cheapest in the store. We're worlds apart in terms of beauty, so I won't mention financial stability. I highly doubt Valeria is here to sell her eggs, and the knowledge worsens the swirls of my stomach.

I've had many inappropriate thoughts about her partner over the past month, but he most likely forgot about me the instant he dropped me off at San Giorgio's.

That hurts to admit, but it's clear now why he fled so quickly.

Why would he want to spend a second longer with me when he had the epitome of perfection waiting for him at home?

Graciously, I'm saved from my dour thoughts by the clinic's head nurse. "*Signora* Raimondo."

"Raimon*do* or Raimon*di*?" Valeria asks, giggling. Even her laughter conjures up images of angels serenading someone in heaven.

The nurse's brows furrow as she checks her paperwork. "Raimon*do*," she confirms two seconds later.

"Then that would be me." Valeria squeezes my arm with her perfectly manicured nails before she saunters away, leaving a trail of expensive perfume in her wake.

As the door to the examination rooms swings shut, I let out the breath I've been holding before searching for a vacant chair in the crowded waiting room. My stomach grumbles when I sit next to a couple who smell like fresh basil, tomatoes, and garlic. They must be here for a procedure that doesn't require fasting. I haven't eaten since last night.

Starving, I pray each time the head nurse appears for her to say my name.

Regrettably, she consistently calls in someone else.

I try to distract myself. I count the tiles on the floor and reread the pamphlet about my procedure, but my mind keeps drifting.

Thankfully, they mainly center on my mom.

She's so frail now that every hour away from her feels like I'm losing seven. As I glance at the clock ticking impatiently behind the reception desk, I recall the promise I made to her this morning.

If they don't call me in soon, I won't make the last train to Carlisle.

The thought of my mother needing me while I'm not in the same zip code hurts my heart. It's so firm that I get impatient. Leaping up, I make a beeline for the receptionist. She sees me coming but still answers her ringing phone. Her ignorance makes me furious, but before one-tenth of the death stares I'm shooting her way find their target, my name is finally called.

Well, it's close to my name.

"Raimon*di*?" I check, even though I'm confident Valeria left hours ago.

"Yes, sorry," the head nurse says.

I'm led to a small room, given a gown, and then guided toward a changing area at the side of the cramped space.

"Do you have someone to drive you home?" a nurse I've not met previously asks when I exit the changing room.

Preferring to lie without words, I nod.

"Fabulous." She instructs me to hop onto the bed I've been dreading for the past six weeks before she places an intravenous line into my arm. "The IV is for the sedation. We use a combination of medication, but most commonly we stick to propofol. It will provide deep sedation, so you won't feel any pain or remember the procedure."

"Great," I reply, my tone low but grateful. I'd prefer to forget than relive the procedure as I have my run-in with the handsome stranger over the past several weeks.

As the nurse increases the dosage, clouding my head with wooziness, I wonder what the stranger is doing. Is he assisting Valeria into bed for rest after her procedure? Doting over her as a partner should? Or was his sighting today just another thread in the tangled web of fate that keeps pulling us together and then tearing us apart?

I could hunt for an answer, but I'm too afraid I won't like the outcome of my hunt.

The nurse with oddly nurturing laugh lines returns my focus to her. "Are you ready, Ms. Raimondo?"

I attempt to correct her, to tell her she has me mistaken for the raven-haired beauty who left hours ago, but the sedative is too good.

Within seconds, I drift into a blissful abyss where there are no sick mothers or men who beat the women they claim to love. And there is definitely no such thing as cancer.

I wake slowly. The world is fuzzy and distant, and the ceiling above me is unfamiliar. When a nurse gently rubs my chest, waking me further, I blink before trying to gather my bearings. My head is groggy, but I recognize her face. She is the nurse who mistook me with Valeria.

After a quick swallow to soothe my dry throat, I take stock of my surroundings and the aches of my body. I'm sore but not in a heap of pain. The main discomfort is from the restraints on my ankles and at the opening of my vagina—and that's when the truth smacks into me.

I just donated a living part of myself for money.

While informing me that the procedure went well, the nurse helps me sit up before steadying my sways with her plump frame. "Would you like some tea? A sandwich, perhaps?"

Suddenly mindful of my ravenous state before my procedure, I dip my chin.

I scoff down the food she arrives with minutes later, grateful for something to distract me from my thoughts, then change back into my clothes.

"Once your support person arrives, you're free to go," the nurse says, clearing away my empty sandwich container and disposable cup.

Humiliation prickles my skin that I don't have anyone waiting for me, but I hide it well since my focus is elsewhere. "Um... about the payment? How long does it usually take for the receptionist to process the payment?"

She glances up from the clipboard, her expression unreadable. "The payment isn't approved until we know whether the procedure was successful."

My tongue thickens with worry. "Successful?"

"We need viable eggs. If the retrieval was successful and the eggs are suitable, we will process your request for payment. If not, we will schedule a second retrieval."

Disappointment overwhelms me. I hadn't realized the money was not guaranteed. If I had, I would have never signed up.

"Don't look so worried, sweetheart," the nurse says, squeezing my hand. "You're young, so I'm sure everything will be fine."

As my life crumbles, I gaze out the window. Tears prick my eyes, but I refuse to cry.

If I start, I may not stop.

When a white sedan pulls down the alleyway, I say, "That's my ride."

Frantically, I collect my things and then make a beeline for the exit. The nurse shouts for me to wait, but I'm already moving, eager to escape before anyone learns how stupid I am.

As I exit the clinic through the same side entrance I used earlier, guilt about what I've done bears down on me. It was necessary. My mother's treatment isn't optional, and neither are her prescriptions. But the way I rushed into the procedure and how I trusted the clinic's promises without making sure the money was guaranteed are my burdens to carry.

I slide down the wall until I'm crouching on the cold ground with my elbows on my knees. The pharmacist's voice this morning creeps above the sludge.

"You can pick up your mother's scripts tomorrow."

I nodded like I had everything under control. Now tomorrow is coming fast, and I don't even have half of what I need.

When the wind brushes my hair across my tear-free face, I tuck a loose lock behind my ear and then force myself to stand. I can't stay here forever, nor can I undo what I did. All I can do is figure out the next step and pray it won't involve something even more drastic.

I've heard kidneys fetch twenty to thirty thousand on the black market.

As I walk out of the alley, laughing like another donation is off the cards, I notice that the rain has eased. The city glistens as if Palermo itself is waiting for something magical to happen. I love the scent of fresh rain on heated pavers. It reminds me so much of my childhood and why I shouldn't be so hard on myself.

When someone you love is sick, you don't think straight or morally. You merely do what needs to be done.

I'm at the end of the alleyway when an SUV half a block down from the clinic stops me dead in my tracks for the second time today. It isn't just any SUV. It's the exact sleek dark vehicle the stranger exited earlier.

My thoughts tumble over each other with all the possible explanations for why the stranger hasn't left yet. Part of me, clearly the lovesick part, hopes he spotted me earlier and is waiting for me.

I doubt that is the case. More times than not lately, my reality has been the cruelest option.

Nonetheless, I can't move my feet. I'm stuck in place, watching the unmistakable silhouette of the stranger in the dimming sunlight as the evening crowd of Palermo mills around me.

After ending a call that carved a groove between his brows, he shifts his focus to the entrance of the IVF clinic. He stares for barely a second before his gaze jackknifes my way. When his wide eyes land on me, standing frozen mere feet away from the main entrance doors of a clinic predominantly used by couples, the world narrows to a single point.

His eyes light up with recognition, and a subtle smile touches his full lips. I should run or, at the very least, look away. Instead, I stand mute as my heart thuds so loudly I'm sure he can hear it from across the street.

The stranger blinks as if he's dreaming, straightens up when he realizes he isn't, and then pushes off the SUV. The air thickens with humidity as he bridges the gap between us with impatient yet controlled steps.

In seconds, Palermo shifts from a bustling hive of activity to two strangers bracketed by rain-slicked brickwork, neon reflections, and an electricity potent enough to reform storm clouds above my head.

I'm so caught up in the sheer relief in his dazzling dark eyes that it takes the urgent final warning of a train's horn to slap me out of my stupor. Its angry rumble announces that it is the last train out of Palermo tonight. If I miss it, I won't be able to keep my promise to my mother.

Promise is a big word. It either makes something or breaks *everything.*

I can't afford to let it break everything.

I'm barely holding on as it is.

The dark-haired gent's long strides falter when I murmur, "I'm sorry. I have to go."

"No!" His voice bellows over the sudden return of the noisy city. It is clear and commanding. He's used to giving orders and having people follow them. He isn't accustomed to being denied, but I have no other option. I can't push against the restraints if I want any chance of keeping karma on my side.

The conductor's last whistle redirects my focus away from the stranger's sudden fury and sees me sprinting toward the station's entrance.

My shoes slip on the wet pavement, but my speed remains unchecked. I hear the stranger chasing after me, his footsteps growing more insistent the longer we run, but I pretend not to because my emotions are too raw right now for any good to come from the carnage.

I reach the platform as the doors commence closing. With a final burst of energy, I leap inside the train car, nearly stumbling into the arms of a startled commuter.

The doors slide shut behind me, sealing me off from the world outside—and from him.

As the train jolts forward, carrying me away from the station and the stranger's lingering watch, I fight like hell to catch my breath. That was thrilling, but not in a way that's easy to explain. My panties are drenched, and a nice thrumming sensation is running rampant through my core, but I'm also sick with worry about how much I enjoyed his chase.

We all want to be loved to the point of insanity, but again, I shouldn't be wanting that from a taken man.

6

GIOVANNI

I ran. I really fucking ran. My shoes pounded the pavement as ruefully as my heart thundered against my ribs, and my lungs burned from the effort of my sprint. I haven't run like that since I was a boy dodging my brothers' lemon bombs in the orchard that surrounds our childhood home.

I'm not a boy anymore, and this isn't a game, but I'll admit the thrill of the chase is sending a hot buzz of electricity straight to my balls. Usually, I say jump and everyone asks how high. No one has ever challenged me like Valentina just did, so although part of me is furious she denied my direct order, my grin while chasing her through the streets of Palermo was anything but threatening.

I almost caught her. I'd reached the platform just as the train doors shut with Valentina on one side and me on the other.

"Stop the train!" I shouted, slamming my palm against the glass of the ticket box while ignoring the startled glances of the station staff and a handful of late-night commuters. "Open the doors! Now!"

A uniformed attendant approached me with his hands raised in a placating gesture. "*Mi dispiace, signor.* It doesn't work like that. Once the doors are closed, the train is gone. Next stop is Carlisle."

And in that precise moment, I realized my chase wasn't over.

I've found men who didn't want to be found, money that vanished into shadows, and traitors who thought they could outrun the consequences of their actions in Carlisle. Compared to those, finding one woman should be easy. Especially since I know *exactly* where the chase will recommence.

I turn on my heel, smile blazing, and sprint back down the entry stairs of the station. With the engine running and headlights slicing through the mist, my SUV waits at the curb. My driver, a nervous teen with more loyalty than sense, is already out of the car, holding open the back driver's side door for me.

After sidestepping him, I slot into the driver's seat. The leather is warm from our hours' long wait today, and the stitching on the embossed steering wheel scratches my palm when I grip it firmly.

The train from Palermo to Carlisle is fast, but I doubt it has anything on my determination.

"*Signor Caruso...*" The driver's brows crinkle as he shifts from foot to foot. His panic is understandable. Disappointing me usually only ends one way. With death. "Should I have stayed with Ms. Valeria?"

Valeria? *Fuck.* For a second, lifelong responsibilities derail my plans. Valeria's name evokes obligations and deals struck while pacing the hallway outside my father's deathbed.

He's dying. We all know it, though no one is game to say it aloud. The doctors stopped pretending months ago, and not long later, the house filled with the rancid scent of impending loss.

Our father made me the man I am today, and although at times his demands are tough, he's only ever wanted what is best for his sons.

His dying wish is to orchestrate one last act of control before the curtain falls.

"Giovanni, you're the eldest, so the family's future rests on your shoulders." If the burden of the business he built from nothing weren't already enough, he reminded me months ago that this has always been about more than power and money for him. It's a legacy. "It's my hope to see my sons wed before I go and to meet the grandchildren who will carry the Caruso name into the next century."

Since I've always seen that side of our business as clinically neutral as the rest, I went along with his plan. Given that I hadn't met Valentina yet, I told my father he could select my wife-to-be, as is custom with arranged marriages. I had only one term. No feelings. If there are no feelings, there's no mess. It's just business.

Valeria accepted my father's proposal because it aligned with goals she had for herself. We've known each other for years, and neither of us wants more than the arrangement that would see our families' dynasties reaching legendary status.

Seeing Valentina again has made it impossible for me to proceed with my father's plans. I want to grant him his dying wish, which would honor him and the legacy he built, but not this way. Not at the expense of my happiness.

Valeria is a beautiful, intelligent woman. She'll make a perfect Cosa Nostra bride. But there's no fire or spark between us. We're business partners, not lovers. She wants security, and I want the freedom to run my family's business without guilt. It is destined to fail within months of my father's passing.

The intensely hot sparks I felt while chasing Valentina through the streets of Palermo, however, could provide me with the best of both worlds.

I could have it all.

A fresh surge of adrenaline spasms through me. It thickens my cock and makes me impatient. "Go to the clinic and request that they cancel Valeria's procedure."

"Sir..." the driver murmurs again, his shock too high not to revert to English. "You want me to do what?"

"Tell them to cancel the procedure," I repeat, slower this time. "I'll send another car for you and Valeria."

The driver hesitates as a mask of confusion slips over his face. "But, *signor*, Ms. Valeria—"

"I'll send another car!" I shout with a finality that brooks no argument. I'm not requesting he do this. I am demanding he do it.

He scrambles to obey. While fumbling for his phone, he inches back from the car. I slam the driver's door shut, then flatten my foot on the gas pedal. The driver's face blurs when I tear out of the parking spot with my tires screeching and my heart pounding.

I'm no longer chasing a train or a woman.

I am pursuing a legacy that could validate decades of dedication.

As I race toward the highway, I force the high-horsepower motor to its limit. The train will reach Carlisle in a little over an hour. If I push it, I can be there before Valentina's shoe even graces the platform.

Rain slicks the streets of Palermo, but my speed remains unchecked as I hit the call button on the dashboard. Nico answers my call two rings later.

"I got it handled. The shipment cleared customs without any issues."

After feigning surprise, I get to the point of my call. "Can you do me a favor?" Confident he'll comply with my request, I continue without pause. "There's an IVF clinic in Palermo. It's on the corner of—"

"The clinic you were taking Valeria to today?"

Again, I hum. "She's there with one of our drivers. Can you send a car for them?" Guilt is responsible for my following words. "Make sure they look after Valeria. I canceled the procedure, but she may still be a little... *tender*."

There's a pause, then a low whistle. "You sure about this, Vanni? Dad won't like it. He's been telling everyone about your upcoming events."

"The plan is still on… It just won't be Valeria's ass heating the driver's seat." My last sentence is a whisper.

A grunt of shock follows another pause. "You found her?"

I don't answer him. I don't need to. Nico understands me better than anyone, so he already knows I'm on the hunt.

"Consider it done, but I'm leaving the cleanup to you. This is above my pay grade."

Laughing, I let him know I'll take care of it, disconnect our call, and then focus on the road. The city falls away behind me as I speed down the open highway. The rain has lessened, but the air is thick with humidity and the smell of wet earth and diesel.

As I drive, my thoughts drift back to the morning I spotted Valentina. Something shifted inside me that day, and I've been chasing that feeling ever since.

Since the highway is clear, I test the capabilities the salesman promoted while directing me toward this SUV. The speedometer climbs to an unsafe speed remarkably fast, and the motor shows the steady semblance of power my family will forever strive for.

My brothers would call chasing a woman I hardly know madness. My enemies would call it weakness. I don't give a fuck what either of them says.

I'm doing this for me.

Fingers crossed Valentina feels the same pull, because if she doesn't, I'm not opposed to showing her how the Carusos survived so many wars.

No isn't in our vocabulary.

7

VALENTINA

Since my cell's battery died halfway into my trip, I sit by the window with knees drawn up and my forehead an inch from the rain-dotted pane. The last train to Carlisle speeds through the rain-soaked countryside, slicing through the air like a bullet. The swift, reckless motion turns the passing scenery into a blur of lights and streaked glass.

The pace is exhilarating, but it also slumps my shoulders.

Chasing this train by car would be futile. Not even the most determined driver could achieve such speed. So even though I'm picturing the stranger behind the wheel of his SUV with his jaw set and his eyes burning with that daring glint that makes my heart race, the scenario I've tried to ignore the past hour isn't likely to occur.

He'll never beat me to Carlisle... *though I do hope he gives it his all.*

My inner monologue makes me annoyed and hopeful all in the space of a single breath.

I don't want him to chase me, but a sensation miles above fear trickles through my veins when I replay the scene in Palermo. It's the same needy pulse that thrummed through my lower stomach when his eyes locked on mine through the train's glass doors as they slid shut.

The wildness in his eyes makes me wonder what would have happened if he'd caught me. Would he have kissed me? And would I have let him?

The uncertainty has me flustered and—God help me—playful. Those are two responses I didn't anticipate today. I should be exhausted and wrung out, but instead, I feel alive and electric, as if the world is suddenly brimming with possibilities.

Closing my eyes, I try to convince my brain to let the rhythm of the train lull me toward peace. Before I can get even ten seconds of rest, images of the stranger's face and smile jolt me awake. I think about the trail of fire his touch scorched on my skin when he sheltered me from danger, and how his low and commanding timbre still sent a shiver down my spine even when he treated me like a member of his staff. And then I recall the way he looked at me as if I were the only thing in the world worth seeing.

As the train slows and the lights of Carlisle appear, my thoughts return to the present. A peculiar sensation settles over me as I gather my belongings and make my way to the doors. Carlisle is safer than Los Angeles, but you still won't find me loitering near a station at this time of night.

The weird sensation grows when the train glides to a stop. The car is nearly empty, so fellow commuters aren't to blame for my body's odd responses. My emotions feel swept up in the chaotic storm the stranger's attention whirled around me when he commenced chasing me.

Just as I'm about to step onto the platform, the rain starts up again. It splatters the dry concrete with big fat droplets that will drench me in under a minute.

After pulling up the collar of my shirt and saying a silent

prayer not to get sick, I venture into the downpour. Shockingly, my clothes remain bone dry. Not a drop of water lands on me or my clothes.

I understand why when I look up. As a bodyguard would shield a princess, the stranger I left in the dust in Palermo holds an umbrella above my head, uncaring that the downpour is ruining his pricey suit and hundred-dollar haircut.

For a moment, I just stare at him, stunned.

How did he beat me here? It's not possible. The train is the fastest thing on this island. It operates at a top speed of 190 miles per hour. No car could have made it in time.

Yet here he is, standing so close that his expensive cologne adds to the pulse between my legs.

A mix of excitement, disbelief, and fear rains over me. Are his interests so potent that he chased me all the way from Palermo? That isn't something a sane individual would do, but I'd be lying if I said it didn't excite me.

If only I could erase the memory of where I found him as easily as his interest captivates me.

He was at a clinic commonly visited by couples, which prompts many questions. Is Valeria his girlfriend? His wife? Or worse, is she about to be the mother of his children?

The questions burn in the back of my throat, but before they're voiced, the dark-haired stranger guides me across the platform. With one hand on the small of my back and the other commanding the umbrella, he moves with such animalistic grace that several passengers pause to admire him.

My pulse spikes as I debate whether I should fight or follow. His basic touch makes what should be a simple deliberation seem impossible. I'm not even sure which way is up. All I know is that the further the train slips behind us, the more the questions I need to ask disappear with it.

When he stops mere feet from the SUV he was leaning against in Palermo, I finally find my backbone. "What are you doing here?"

"Driving you home," he answers nonchalantly, his tone both authoritative and kind.

I attempt to assure him that I'm fine, but the truth is, I'm not. The rain is coming down harder now, and my phone is well and truly dead. If I don't accept his offer, I could be stuck at the station for hours.

The knowledge has absolutely no effect on my hesitation. I'm torn between caution and curiosity.

He must notice my hesitation. His slow, knowing grin weakens my knees. "Come on, Valentina. I'm offering to drive you home. What's the worst that could happen?"

I almost insist that I can manage on my own, but something about him makes me throw caution to the wind. For all I know, he could just want to make sure I get home safely.

Furthermore, the last text I got from my aunt was that my mother had gone to bed, so the only time I'm stealing tonight is from my sleep.

"All right." I try to sound casual. I shouldn't have bothered. My voice is drenched in ambiguity. "But only because my phone's dead and I don't fancy walking home in this weather."

With a triumphant grin, as if he sees straight through my lie, he takes my bag from me and places it in the back seat of the SUV. When he holds out his hand palm side up, I cock a brow and stare at him in suspicion.

"You said your battery is dead. I can charge it for you during the commute."

"Oh..." I give him my phone without thinking, but instead of plugging it into the charging port in his SUV, he slips it into his pocket, then opens the passenger-side door for me.

I swallow the frustration and fear tangling in my throat, then climb in. I tell myself that it's okay to be led when you don't have a choice. The platform is empty, and the parking lot is just as desolate. The only noise is the thud of my pulse and the whispers of the questions I've yet to ask.

"Before anything else," he says after jogging around his vehicle and sliding behind the wheel. "Have you eaten tonight?"

The memory of where I spotted him today has a lie sitting on the tip of my tongue, but my stomach betrays me with a loud, insistent grumble.

The stranger's deep, rich chuckle makes my lips involuntarily twitch. He has a beautiful laugh. It's as appealing as his panty-wetting face. "I'll take that as a no."

My breath hitches when his knuckles brush my chest. He's not making an unwanted advance. He's reaching for my belt.

"There." He fastens the buckle with a quiet click before his thumb traces the stitched line in my belt. "Now there's less chance of you outrunning me again."

I resist the urge to tap a loose fist against my chest and murmur, "Thank you."

Maybe the sedation hasn't worn off and I'm dreaming? This can't be real. Surely. Men like him never notice women like me. He's so attractive that people's heads turn without meaning to. His face belongs in glossy magazines or behind the velvet ropes of movie premieres, not close enough to me that the weight of his attentive stare becomes a second layer of skin.

He arches a brow and smirks when he notices me staring. "See something you like?"

Though I've been caught out, I don't look away. I could miss my only chance to showcase my flirtatiousness if I give up now. "Maybe."

I more than like what I see, but there's no chance of telling him that while still unaware of his relationship status.

He grabs at his chest, feigning injury. "Maybe? *Ouch.*"

When I playfully stick out my tongue at him, he laughs again, and the tingling in between my legs intensifies.

The further we travel, the more my nerves settle. The SUV's heated interior dries my wet shoes, and the steady whirr of the engine gives me the perfect excuse for the buzz thickening my veins.

A short while later, we arrive at a family-owned eatery hidden on a side street. Steam has fogged the windows, and the scent wafting outside smells of fresh garlic and homemade pasta.

After parking the SUV, the stranger approaches my door, opens it, then helps me out. A jolt of electricity races up my arm with the slightest touch, yet I pretend not to notice.

Inside, the restaurant is cozy and bustling, and locals crowd its tables. The still-unnamed man greets the owner by name before exchanging a few words with him. I overhear portions of their conversation but nothing that identifies the handsome stranger. It's the small talk you have with someone you know but wouldn't classify as a close acquaintance.

After the owner notes the extended period since the stranger's last visit and inquires about his father, a deep groove mars his forehead as he replies that his father is well. Since his curt reply ends their conversation, we're shown to a corner booth tucked away from the noise and the glare of the overhead lights.

He orders for both of us with a commanding edge that declares he knows exactly what he wants, and he won't stop until he gets it.

I don't protest. I'm too preoccupied trying to figure out his identity to care if he upgrades our meals to include sliced chicken breast.

When fragrant pasta, bread, and red wine arrive only minutes later, I realize how hungry I am. I dig in. Rich, comforting flavors envelop me, and the wine warms me from the inside out. We eat in silence until the tension becomes unbearable.

"Are you going to tell me your name, or should I continue calling you 'the handsome stranger'?"

His brows disappear into his rigorous hairline as a devilish grin carves onto his mouth. It takes a moment for the truth to dawn, and when it hits, it hits hard.

I just told him I think he's handsome.

His smile is lazy, and it makes my heart flutter. "Giovanni..." His following words are as delayed as his first. "Giovanni Caruso."

A shiver skates across my arms when I realize I've heard his name before. The Caruso family is legendary in Sicily. They're powerful, untouchable, and rumored to have their hands in everything from importing to politics.

I won't mention the things better left unspoken.

My attempt to mask my shock is fraudulent. The playful glint that's been firing in Giovanni's eyes all night vanishes, replaced with a serious gaze. "Does that scare you?"

Lying crosses my mind, but I decide against it. "A little," I admit. "But I'm unsure why it should."

He leans back in his chair and eyes me intently. "You're honest. I like that."

"I don't see the point in pretending to be something I'm not."

Dark hair falls across his eye when he nods as if I've passed some sort of test. "Good. Because I don't either."

Once more, silence falls between us. It isn't uncomfortable. More an unspoken understanding and mutual respect. I can't judge him for what he does for his family. That would make me a walking contradiction. Especially today.

After finishing my meal, I sit back and enjoy the wine. The buzz it hits me with makes me a little giddy but not close to tipsy. For once, my belly is full, so the alcohol's potency will lessen before it enters my bloodstream.

If only a full stomach could prevent my mouth from running away on me.

"Who was the woman you were with earlier?"

Giovanni coughs through the pasta suddenly trapped in his throat before he briskly swallows. "Woman?"

My defenses immediately bristle.

I detest men who can't be honest.

When I hightail it to the exit, Giovanni shouts my name. I'm out the door and racing down the alleyway beside the restaurant before he leaves his seat.

"Valentina..." He's so close I feel his breath on my ear.

I don't understand how he arrived so fast. I'm not sprinting—who can in wet shoes?—but my speed is similar to the one I used earlier when I evaded him.

I nearly break my heels from the force of my steps as I desperately try to get away.

"Valentina..."

This time, he grabs hold of my wrist and yanks me back. His tug boosts the strength of my swing when I slap him hard across the face. A crack ripples the air faster than I thought possible.

I expect Giovanni to respond with as much violence. Most people would. But Giovanni only stills for a second before the most seductive grin I've ever seen spreads across his face.

Then, in the blink of an eye, he's on me. His lips violently crash into mine as his fingers tangle with my hair. My protest is silenced as he thrusts his tongue past my lips and slowly strokes the roof of my mouth.

My knees buckle as all my worries fade. He kisses me with an angry aggressiveness that shouldn't turn me on but does. It overwhelms my efforts to maintain control and leads to a swift and embarrassing defeat.

The anxiety I felt in the restaurant is insignificant compared with how I'm feeling now. I kiss him back with the passion of someone who won't regret it later, and make no move to stop his advances as he pins me against the alley wall and pushes my underwear aside.

I'm hoping for refreshing salty air to cool the intense heat, but Giovanni's large, authoritative hand keeps us too close for any air to get in.

As his thumb holds the material of my panties, which are drenched from his kiss, to the side, his mouth strokes, caresses, and torments me.

"Do you know how long I've waited for this?" He doesn't wait for me to answer. "Since the moment I heard you cursing at your phone." His thumb slips away from my panties to caress my clit, and I can't think of a single word that he wouldn't classify as begging. "Tell me it's been the same for you. That I'm not the only one who's been wandering Carlisle at all hours, searching for a needle in a haystack."

I don't speak. I can't. The strokes of his tongue are too powerful, and I won't mention the perfect pressure of his thumb as he circles it over my clit or I'll make a fool of myself.

A shudder rolls over my body when he bites my bottom lip before he drags his nose down the throb in my throat. Tingles pulsate through my pussy when his lips graze the shell of my ear. "What's the matter? Cat got your tongue?"

"It isn't a cat," I murmur on a moan, my voice trembling with unbridled horniness.

He laughs, and its husky vibrations strip me of all sense of normality.

I want him now more than I want anything, and I can't wait a second longer.

Giovanni's growl rings in my ears when I impatiently tug on his belt. I need to move this exchange forward now before I remember my prior concerns.

My impatience isn't exclusive. Giovanni watches me with untamed lust for barely a second before the urge for skin-on-skin friction sees my back climbing the brickwork, and my legs wrapping around his waist.

"I promised myself I wouldn't claim your pussy until its juices were dripping off my chin," he says between long, hungry kisses. "But you've got me breaking all my promises tonight." My clit throbs with desire as he finishes unfastening his belt. Then the hiss of a zipper overtakes the strumming of my pulse in my ears. "So that feast will have to wait until we're at my penthouse."

I've been dying to find a guy to go down on me and know what he's doing, but when Giovanni frees his cock from his trousers, nothing but panic fills my head. He's huge. The girth and length of a Pringles can may be a slight exaggeration, but if he wants to do that trick where he stuffs his penis inside before offering his partner a chip, he might want to lube up first. It *will* be a snug fit.

"Ah... I'm not sure I have what it takes to accept *that* without preparation." My eyes bug more the longer I drink him in. His penis is sexy. It's cut and glistening with pre-cum, and an envious number of veins will give it a ribbed feel. I still don't think I can take it, though.

"I guess you're right." Giovanni's rough tone coerces my eyes back to his face.

I assume his agreeance will correspond with my feet returning to the ground, so you can picture my shock when he hoists me higher up the wall. The roughness of the brickwork scratches my back, but it isn't painful. It's the same delicious scratching sensation that the stubble on his chin causes when he mushes his face with my pussy.

He wastes no time finding my clit and teasing it with urgent, hungry strokes. I shake all over and thrash my head side to side as I attempt to stave off my climax.

He circles my clit with his tongue before slowly biting down. I yelp, but it's all a lie. The sensation roaring through me is impossible to ignore. It races heat to my cheeks and skyrockets my pulse.

While Giovanni devours me, the restaurant's noises vanish, and I focus solely on the imminent tsunami about to engulf me.

"Oh... sweet Lord," I moan when he strikes my clit with rapid-fire hits.

He takes me to the brink, soaring my body temperature higher than the sunbaked Sicilian countryside.

When he slips his tongue deep inside me, his nose grazes my clit, and I'm done. Grinding down hard on his mouth, I ride the furious storm with everything I have.

Giovanni's approving growl intensifies my orgasm. It stretches for several long minutes and utterly drains me. By the time he presses his erection against my entrance, I am too weak and tired to speak.

I don't get the chance to admire how much thicker his cock is after he went down on me. In one ardent thrust, he buries himself to the hilt. Tears burn my eyes as pain blurs with pleasure. It's euphoric being so filled, but I'd rather it seem less like I was losing my virginity all over again.

"Work with me, *dolcezza*. You've got to open up for me so I can fuck you how you deserve to be fucked."

Two fingers slip between my legs to toy with my clit as he slowly withdraws. I swivel my hips, opening myself to him more, before silently whining about how hollow I feel.

My gripe doesn't last long. Giovanni slams back in before his tip can relish the salty breeze wafting in from the coast.

Pleasure spasms through me as he drives into me as if he is a savage animal in heat, rubbing my clit with the same uncivilized savagery.

As sparks of a new climax form low in my core, he pulls me away from the brickwork so the scratchiness won't interfere with the brutal pounding he's giving me. He fucks like an animal, and I sing his praises as if dozens of patrons enjoying overpriced pasta and wine aren't mere feet from us.

"Oh God. Please. More."

Those pleas couldn't have come from me. I don't beg during sex. Well, I do. But since they're usually about hoping I'll come before my bed companion, I've never vocalized them.

"Who, *dolcezza*? Who is fucking you?"

I mutter about his arrogance before giving in as if I don't have a single brain cell. "You. You're fucking me."

"Yes." His cock pulsates inside me, making me even more daft. "Me. I'm fucking you. *Finally.*"

He grips my ass so firmly as he pumps into me over and over that I'm certain he'll leave a mark, but I'm too horny to care. This is the best sex I've ever had, and even exhausted, I'm not eager for it to end.

"This is better than anything I imagined, *dolcezza*. So. Much. Better." He enunciates his last three words with brutal jerks of his hips.

The thickening of his cock when I squeeze him with my vaginal walls, and the knowledge he's imagined this as often as I have, sets me off for the second time tonight.

I come with a roar, my orgasm crashing through me with a ferocity I've never felt before.

"Fuck, *dolcezza*," Giovanni grunts as the spasms of my pussy cause him to lose control.

He fucks me viciously and possessively. He takes all the control, and I give it to him. It's such a wild, bestial display that I fail to realize we didn't use protection until it's too late.

8

GIOVANNI

The alleyway buzzes with the aftershocks of what just occurred. I've never felt more alive and so fucking out of control. The pounding in my chest subsides with the fading throbs of my penis. I anchor Valentina with my hands on her hips as she descends from the bliss of her second orgasm.

She's breathless and her hair is a wild mess, but I pay attention to her kiss-swollen lips the most. They're plumper now. Ruddier. They're exactly what I envisioned while contemplating how divine she'd look while I finished down her throat.

And then the truth finds me like a wayward missile.

I didn't use a condom.

For a split second, I freeze. I've never gone without protection, not even when my latest hookup assured me she was on contraception. I've even gone as far as watching women swallow the morning-after pill before asking a member of my family's extensive staff to drive them home.

The realization I forgot something I'm usually so stringent about should engulf me with panic. It doesn't. Instead, a slow, satisfied smile touches my lips. This is precisely what I'm looking for, isn't it? Not the recklessness, but the possibility.

This is my chance to tie Valentina to me in a way a slammed door or a vicious tongue can't undo.

My father's dying wish is for me to settle down and secure the Caruso legacy with a wife and child. Who better to help me grant that wish than Valentina?

The plan was to wine and dine her before casually easing her into the possibility of being Valeria's replacement, but sparks this hot don't wait for permission. They burn their own path.

Still, I expect Valentina to panic. Most women require an in-depth screening for STIs before ditching protection. Instead of being filled with trepidation, Valentina leans against the brick wall and catches her breath.

Her cheeks are flushed and her mouth is ajar, but her eye contact is steady.

She doesn't appear the slightest bit worried.

I clear my throat before striving to sound casual. "I, uh... didn't use anything. Are you on birth control?"

She makes a dismissive gesture with her hand. "It's fine. I had a... *procedure* not that long ago, so I'm safe... for now."

A procedure? My mind races, suddenly worried that she means something permanent. My father's plan might unravel before it's even begun.

"Permanent?" I ask, my jaw twitching.

Dark locks slap Valentina's cheeks when she shakes her head. "No. Just for the month. I had to do it for... medical reasons. We'll have to be careful next time."

Relief floods me so fast that I almost laugh. A month is manageable. I can wait a month to knock her up with my child. Don't ask me to pledge the same when it comes to tasting her again, though. That isn't a promise I can make. It's killing me now watching the high rise of her skirt slowly covering the visual of her swollen pussy lips that are glistening with the residue of both our climaxes.

I sweep a lock of hair from her face before tracing the tiny capillaries in her cheek. She looks exhausted, and it expands both my chest and my cock to an unmanageable size.

I'm on the cusp of taking her again, in this dirty fucking alleyway, when cutlery on dishware reminds me of our location. Emilio, one of my father's eldest friends, may never forgive me if I wipe out his entire clientele. Just the thought of anyone hearing Valentina's moans of ecstasy have me wanting to do precisely that, so it's best that we take this elsewhere.

"Come on." I nudge my head to the exit. "Let's get you cleaned up."

I help her dress, my movements slow and languid. She's still floating somewhere between reality and the high we just shared, and I have no desire to rush her back to the real world anytime soon.

I button her blouse, careful with the fabric, as Valentina watches me with a bemused smile. If I can read her as well as I want to believe, she appears shocked I can be so gentle after being anything but only minutes ago.

I told you the Caruso men fuck hard.

Once we're suitably dressed, I guide Valentina back onto the street. The rain has softened to a fine mist that sizzles on my skin since my blood is still the heat of lava. Although my SUV is parked at the curb, I don't head for it. Instead, I signal to one of the security details my family has stationed throughout Carlisle that I require assistance. I was impatient earlier, and I rushed things, so I want to do it right this time.

Within seconds, a sleek black town car glides to a stop beside us. I assist Valentina into the back seat before fixing her belt, and then I announce our destination to the driver.

The ride to my penthouse is quiet. Valentina admires the twinkling city lights, compliments to the driver's reckless speed, while I study her reflection. I appreciate the curve of her jaw, the hue still dusting her cheeks, our intermingled scents, and the handful of pounds she has put on the past six weeks. They've made her body even more appealing.

The way she carries herself is magnetic. She's confident and unashamed, and it makes her even more beautiful.

I've never understood the obsession some men have with women who look like they haven't eaten a proper meal in years. Give me curves and softness any day, especially if they're attached to a woman who embraces them.

Valentina is all that and more. Her body is a celebration of Sicilian heritage. Her hips are as full and generous as her bust, and her thighs promise nights of rigorous fucking. Even if she followed all the fad diet obsessions, she'd never be super slim.

Thank fuck.

I like the way her blouse strains at the buttons and how her skirt hugs her thighs and stomach. Her curves announce that there's nothing fragile about her. She won't break if I fuck her too roughly. She's built for passion, and that's precisely why I didn't hold back in the alleyway.

I fucked her like a wild animal and loved every damn minute of our exchange.

I've bedded women who prioritized counting calories over living. None of them ever made me lose my ever-fucking mind. I don't solely want to taste Valentina again. I want our exchange to stretch into the morning so I can witness the sunlight dancing across her skin.

Valentina catches me staring, but because we've arrived at a hotel I have a majority share in, I pretend I don't need my head examined.

This is the height of my obsession.

As accustomed, heads turn when I help Valentina out of my Bentley and escort her through the lobby. Not everyone stares with worry. Some watch in admiration, but unfortunately, not all their focus is on me.

Valentina is receiving an equal amount of attention. If I weren't itching to reacquaint any part of my body with Valentina's, I'd take names.

Alas, patience doesn't seem my forte when Valentina is in my sights.

Our footsteps echo on the marble lobby floors as we move through the luxurious surroundings I intend to make Valentina accustomed to. Curiosity darts through the elevator attendant's eyes as he nods in greeting, somewhat bowing. His interest is expected. The penthouse is usually where I come for solace. I've never brought anyone of the opposite sex here before.

Even if I had, he would have never met anyone like Valentina. She isn't the arm candy constantly photographed with my brothers. She is the heir of the Caruso legacy.

My fingers tap the curve in Valentina's back in rhythm to the tick of the numbers in the car position indicator above our heads. The higher the number, the more curious Valentina becomes.

The elevator glides straight to the penthouse. I step out first and then extend my hand for Valentina. When she accepts my offer, we cross the threshold together.

The floor-to-ceiling windows offer panoramic views of Carlisle. City lights stretch in every direction, and a generous wrought iron balcony wraps around the open-plan living space. The décor is contemporary but not cold. Plush sofas in deep charcoal material hog the living room, which is separated from the kitchen by a large marble-topped island. Art that costs more than most people's cars adorns the walls, and a subtle scent of cedar and expensive whiskey filters through the air.

Valentina stops inside the living room entrance, her eyes wide as she takes it all in. I enjoy watching her absorb every detail. Her gaze remains fixed on the city skyline while her finger traces the sofa's fabric. Then her focus shifts to the fireplace mantel and the bookshelves flanking it.

It doesn't take long to deduce that she's searching for something. The tiny veins thumping in her fists suggest she's checking for my marital status or if a woman is waiting for me at home.

She won't find anything. I retreat to the penthouse when the family compound becomes too noisy and I require solitude for contemplation. Most of my time is spent at the compound, surrounded by brothers, cousins, and the endless demands of the Caruso legacy.

The penthouse contains only a well-stocked bar, a change of clothes, and now, the intoxicating scent of Valentina's arousal on my skin.

I wasn't lying when I said my agreement with Valeria was strictly professional. She is a friend and an ally, and our agreement would have strengthened our families' bond. But that's done with now. My decision is made, and she's standing before me, wide-eyed and uncertain.

That's on me. I regret being untruthful when she inquired about Valeria, though initially, I didn't know who she was referencing. It hadn't occurred to me that she'd witnessed me walking Valeria into the IVF clinic hours earlier. I sensed someone nearby, the prickling of the hairs on my nape extremely telling, but even after scanning every face, I didn't spot the cause of the peculiar sensation.

If I had, I would have chased her then and there.

Finding nothing that ties me to another woman, Valentina spins around to face me. "Can I?" She gestures her hand at the custom bar in the living room.

"Help yourself."

After removing my coat and tossing it over one of the sofas, I join her for a nightcap. When I reach for a glass, our hands brush. That slight touch sends a jolt through me, and it makes me disinterested in an aperitive.

I have one wish, and the seductive scent pluming from Valentina confirms she knows exactly what I want.

Strands of caramel hair weave around my fingers when I fist her hair and seal my mouth over hers. I kiss her hard, spelling out my intentions without words. I want her with an intensity that rivals my lungs' desire for air, and I'm disturbingly aware I won't be able to stop, even if asked.

Valentina is happy to accommodate my needs. She returns my kiss with equal enthusiasm, and then her singsong moan sends a needy zap to my balls. "I want your cock in my mouth so badly."

She shoves me back, and I land on the sofa with a thud. Then the most beautiful fucking sight in the world presents itself. Valentina is on her knees, yanking at my belt.

Leaning back, I hand over the reins. She loosens my belt before moving her hands to my dress shirt. I hiss when her impatience becomes too much. Pearl buttons scatter across the floorboards when she tears open my shirt after undoing only two measly buttons.

Her fingers sketch the contours in my stomach before her index finger traces the circular wound in my left pectoral muscle. When she peers up at me, the panic I anticipated earlier swamps her impressive eyes.

I could explain that battle scars are an occupational hazard of my job, but since I want to ease her into my life, I distract her by raising my ass off my seat and tugging down my trousers.

My boxer shorts stretch against my erection and dampen with pre-cum.

A second later, Valentina curls her hand around the bulge in my boxers. She holds my cock like her pussy did while milking it of cum, then shifts forward.

Her desire for me—and perhaps my cock—is evident on her face.

Fuck.

Just the rise and fall of her chest as she gazes at me with untapped hunger is enough to make me come, so I won't mention how I could achieve release just from looking at her beautiful face.

Fortunately for all involved, I'm all about self-control.

I can last for hours if needed.

Pre-cum pools at the tip of my cock when Valentina pulls down the waistband of my boxer shorts. My dick bobs free before steadily rising toward my belly button. Its long stretch doubles the dilation of Valentina's eyes and makes her mouth water.

"You can take it," I assure her, gripping the base. "You just need to go slow. Your face alone has my release rapidly building. I don't want to make a fool of myself."

My underhanded compliment returns some of the confidence her eyes lost when my dick sprang free from my boxers. Invisible wings flourish behind her as a cock-thickening smile stretches across her face.

After licking her lips, she lowers her head to my cock. A groan rolls through my chest when her tongue darts over the slit in my crown. She's barely touching me, but my balls are already pulling in close.

"Tell me something about yourself."

Valentina laughs, disarmed by my question. "Now? You want me to tell you something about myself now?"

With my hand fisted in her hair, arrowing her lips back toward my knob, I nod.

She licks the length of my erection and circles her lips over the crown before asking, "What do you want to know?"

"Everything."

She rolls her eyes, but she continues sucking my dick. "That's a tall order."

"I have all night." I grunt my last word. The feeling of my cock's head brushing her tonsils is too intense for a casual reaction.

My body heats and my eyes struggle to remain open when she takes me to the back of her throat over and over before she submits to my silent bidding.

"All right. I was conceived in Sicily but was born in America." Another suck, another confession. "I grew up on the outskirts of Los Angeles. My mom is Sicilian, and my father isn't in the picture."

When her chin quivers at the end of her reply, I thrust my hips upward, re-piercing my cock's head between her pillowy lips. I'm distracting her. She knows this. But since she's more grateful than annoyed for the distraction, she allows it.

It takes all my control not to shove my cock deep inside her mouth when she teasingly licks the tip, but I show restraint since her non-gagged mouth allows her to speak. "We moved back a few months ago on the promise of a better life. It hasn't gone as planned."

I listen intently while fighting not to blow my load. Her lips are fucking heaven, and it's taking all my willpower not to come. "Why Carlisle?"

Her shrug is way too fucking cute for a woman devouring the monster dick her curves and beautiful face inspired. "The health-care was supposed to be good here."

All too familiar with how her story will end, I wince but can't offer a single sympathy since she accepts me back into her mouth.

My cock flexes when her lips move to within two inches of the cropped hairs splayed across my pubic bone. No woman has ever come close to taking me so deeply before, and her eagerness takes everything off the table—except my urgency to come.

9

VALENTINA

"Valentina..." Giovanni groans when my fingertips skim the sensitive skin at the base of his manly yet maintained balls. "You need to slow down or I'll drench your throat with my cum."

My pussy becomes wetter at the thought of his salty, masculine taste swamping my tongue.

Wait, what? When have I ever been excited to swallow? Giving head is an awkward experience I usually avoid at all costs, and I've never volunteered for them to finish down my throat.

It must be Giovanni. He's outrageously attractive and has the cock to back up his confidence. It's addictive being craved so much you have a man willing to throw more than caution to the wind.

Or perhaps it's the extra hormones running rampant through my body?

Some pamphlets warned about an increase in sexual desire due to heightened estrogen levels. I assumed I'd be one of the poor statistics that had a decrease in libido, since the only form of excitement I've had in the past twelve months was being flattened against an SUV by a dark and brooding stranger.

The reminder of how Giovanni saved me has me sucking his dick with even more eagerness. I drag my lips down the shaft until I trigger my gag reflex, and then I flatten my tongue against the vein feeding his magnificent manhood.

My cheeks burn from my envious sucks, but I refuse to give in. I'm dying to taste him. It's as potent as my craving for his mouth to be reacquainted with my pussy, but I won't stop until I've made things even.

When I get the perfect combination of speed and suction, Giovanni's breaths quicken and his hands seek something to grip. One sinks into my hair, fisting it firm enough for the roots to sting, and the other grips the side of the sofa.

Knowing I have a man as confident and gorgeous as Giovanni at my mercy is thrilling. Excitement skates up my spine when the sturdiness of my sucks doubles the throbs of his cock. I draw him to the back of my throat while squeezing his balls with my spare hand.

His grunts are lyrical gold. Every one he releases turns me on more. Even if I don't come, I won't leave his penthouse unsatisfied. That's how enthralling his moans are. I'm on the cusp of climax, and I'm seemingly not the only one aware of that.

Before I can protest, Giovanni plucks me off his cock, lays me over the expensive rug cushioning my knees only seconds ago, and then buries his head between my legs.

"Hmm... I smell so good *in* you."

"Fuck... No, I..." Entire sentences are above me, and so is Giovanni. He eats me with a starvation that will never wane. A hungry, impulsive feast that doesn't solely remove the reins from my hands but also shreds them to pieces.

His name rumbles from my throat as an orgasm scorches through me. Stars blister as a revitalizing zap shudders my wary bones. My climax is draining and long but rejuvenating. I'm floating on a cloud that's sailing too high for anything bad to invade, and it makes me feel safe.

Do I deserve this level of protection? Giovanni lied to me. He made out that he didn't know who I was referencing while trying to unearth his connection with Valeria, but instead of bringing it up again, I'm allowing my libido to dictate our exchange.

That's wrong.

"Who... was... the woman?" I ask between pants, my body unco-operative with the interrogation my brain wants to undertake. I know Valeria's name, but I can't mention it since I'd have to disclose why I was at the clinic with her.

Giovanni sucks my clit into his mouth, upending my campaign. I can't speak through the sparks firing through my body. Can't move. I also can't breathe.

I've never felt so good.

But this isn't me. My father came close to killing my mother because I was proof of his extramarital activities, and I am deter-mined not to make the mistakes my mother made.

"Giovanni..."

When I rake my fingers through his hair, more to pull him off me than hold his mouth hostage to my pussy, he clamps my hands to my sides, then goes to town.

He eats with an expertness that announces his skills at giving head, and in seconds, he takes control of my body.

It's a pity for him my brain is controlled by a different entity than my body.

"Who is she?" My shout reverberates throughout the penthouse and drowns out Giovanni's noisy licks as he laps up the remnants of the orgasm I tried to stave off and failed.

I shake through the aftermath of a climax that makes me more angry than happy before I un-suction Giovanni from my pussy with a cruel tug on his dark locks.

He's furious that I'm denying him. And his sneer is the sexiest thing I've ever seen.

"Who is she?" I ask again, with less shouting this time.

I slap his hands away when he grips my thighs and drags me closer. It does me no good. Faster than I can snap my fingers, he lifts me onto his lap and notches the crown of his cock at my opening.

Although I hate to admit this, even with my anger at a pinnacle, my breasts grow heavy with desire at how easily he tosses me around.

His ease gives the impression that I'm weightless.

"Gio—"

"Valeria is a friend," he interrupts, his tone a harsh bark. "A business associate."

"A friend?"

He hums in agreement, and the vibrations of his deep timbre dart straight to my core.

Stupidly, I examine his eyes for any hints of dishonesty. I hardly know the man stealing my astuteness with a fantastic cock. I found out his name only hours ago, so how can I possibly know if he's lying just by looking at him?

Insanity. That is the *only* logical excuse.

My inner muscles clamp around his thick cock when he enters me like we're not in the process of an imperative conversation. I'm drenched front to back, but it still burns to take a man as well-endowed as him.

"Giovanni..." This call of his name is more a silent demand for comfort than answers. I'm stretched wide and painfully riding the crest of pleasure and pain.

"I've got you, *dolcezza*. All you have to do is let me in."

I nod, naively believing his statement means more than unclenching my vaginal walls.

"Good girl," he praises when I swivel my hips, loosening their grip.

He sinks in deeper, veering this wreck more toward pleasure than pain.

With one hand, he guides me on and off his cock, while the other stimulates my clit until nothing but the chase is on my mind. I'm sensitive all over, both mentally and physically, but content. *Like that makes any sense.*

As my moans turn into cries, Giovanni's speed picks up. He plunges into me, harder and deeper with every thrust. I claw cruelly at his back, certain I'll leave a mark. His brutal pounding gives me no choice but to hold on for the wild ride, but part of me—clearly the negative side—wants to leave a trace of my existence. That way, if I can't read him as well as my hazy head believes, the signs a woman looks for when they believe their man is straying will be as obvious as the sun hanging in the sky.

Giovanni doesn't seem bothered by the prospect of being marked by me. With his rhythm unaffected, he shimmers his shoulders, discarding his ruined dress shirt with an effortless shrug. Then he places my hands back on his shoulders before fucking me to oblivion.

Now the choice is completely out of my hands. If I don't sink both my nails and teeth into him, I'll scream so loud that my mother and aunt will hear. That's how well Giovanni fucks.

"Oh... God..." I murmur through the tang of blood filtering across my taste buds. I bit him firmly enough to bleed, but I'm swamped with too much ownership to care.

I want him to wear my marks and know where I touched him for days.

Imagining him discovering my dental impression days after our romp denotes a bomb low in my stomach. An orgasm shatters inside me, but it doesn't weaken Giovanni's pace in the slightest. He continues to toy with my clit while fucking me deep and hard.

He drives into me on repeat until I'm overwhelmed again. I don't conceal his brilliance this time around. I shout it for the world to hear, certain if I die from the exhaustion of too many orgasms, I want it marked on my headstone.

"Yes! God, yes!" I shout when the tension becomes unbearable for Giovanni as well. My insides clench around his fat cock as spurts of his release double the wetness between my legs.

I did that.

Me.

And the knowledge is powerful.

With his cock still sheathed inside me, Giovanni leans his back against the sofa he was seated on hours ago, pulls me into his chest, and then buries his nose in my dark locks.

That safe feeling I was experiencing earlier returns more powerful than ever, and euphoria pumps into me as I relish his closeness.

It's comforting in his arms. Right.

It feels like home, and before my foggy head can warn my heart to slow down, the steady rhythm of his heart and the gentle lulls of his chest drift me into a peaceful slumber.

10

GIOVANNI

Since I wake before the sun, the city is still wrapped in a blue-gray hush that only comes before dawn. The penthouse is quiet. The only sound is the soft, steady rhythm of Valentina's breaths. She's lying beside me, restfully sleeping.

After rolling to my side, I prop myself on one elbow and watch her sleep. Dark-brown hair spills across her pillow, and her nostrils flare slightly as she takes shallow breaths. Unlike last night, her brows are smooth and trouble-free.

Although this could be my cockiness talking, I swear a satisfied smirk is hiking one side of her lips high.

Our connection last night exceeded my wildest dreams. That brutal, frenetic spark I felt for her the second I saw her turned into something wild and dangerous. My obsession with this woman is a wildfire raging through everything I thought I knew about myself and turning it into ash.

It could burn me if I'm not careful.

Until the early hours of this morning, I took her every way imaginable, but my hands still ache to touch her. I want to feel the quickening of her heart rate in the seconds leading to her climax, and the sting of her nails as they scour my back when the intensity becomes overwhelming. I want to hear her scream my name, and I may get the opportunity sooner rather than later when she shifts slightly.

Her sleepy murmurs bring a smile to my face. Her mumbles are undecipherable, but as she nestles deeper into the sheets, looking at home, I take them as a compliment.

She's comfortable here. Protected.

I could stay like this forever, but the world has other plans.

My phone vibrates on the nightstand, shattering the peace. I ignore it, but within seconds of me silencing it, it buzzes again. Cautious not to rouse Valentina, I reach for my phone.

Matteo's name flashes on the screen, and I roll my eyes. My brothers have been texting me nonstop for the past hour, but Matteo's messages are hard to overlook. It isn't that he has a habit of making things urgent when they aren't. It's because I know he is as deviant as his messages suggest.

MATTEO:

You've got five minutes to message me back before I show up at your penthouse with my dick hanging out.

He *believes* he has the biggest cock in Caruso history.

I've yet to reach the same conclusion.

My phone buzzes again.

MATTEO:

And I'll bring Nico, Elio, and Dante with me.

I'd like to say they lack the audacity to go against me like this, but having previously faced this threat and lost, I slide out of bed.

Killing family members is against the rules, but I wouldn't be able to restrain myself if Valentina saw a single inch of my brothers' cocks.

Since our father is already broken-hearted from the death of our mother twelve months ago, I must do everything in my power to keep another mafia war off the table. Answering my brother's text is the easy way out.

After covering Valentina's luscious curves with a sheet, mindful my brothers prefer FaceTime chats over standard calls, I grab my phone and pad barefoot onto the balcony. The view never fails to remind me that Carlisle is unlike anywhere else in the world. The city sprawls along the coast, and its ancient Sicilian heritage clusters in a patchwork of traditional and modern elements. Beyond the rooftops of the terracotta buildings my family is endeavoring to save, the Tyrrhenian Sea glimmers a vast, restless blue that holds the secrets of the families who've lived here.

I reply to Matteo's "dicks out" message first. I use a simple emoji —the middle finger. His reply comes through fast. It's typical Matteo style. A string of expletives and a blurry selfie of him and Nico at the compound, looking far too awake for the hour.

Unintentionally, I find myself smiling while composing a response. As I hit send, another call comes through. It's a FaceTime request from Dante this time.

I look back at the bedroom to ensure Valentina is still asleep before accepting his request.

"Yeah?"

Dante doesn't waste time. "It's Dad."

That carefree, can-take-down-the-world-with-my-pinkie feeling I've been experiencing for the past fifteen hours slips away. "What happened?"

"For once, it's good news." He sags against the wall outside his daughter's room, and his eyes look up toward heaven. "He's out of bed. He walked to the kitchen on his own."

I wiggle my ear, positive I heard him wrong. Our father hasn't left his room in months. I'll admit, there's no incentive for him to leave. Everything he needs is brought to him. But still, I'm shocked.

Dante takes the words right out of my mouth. "Makes you wonder if the first doctor was right. Maybe he is suffering from a broken heart."

I close my eyes and fight like hell to remove the image my next question conjures before blurting it out. "What's got him so excited? Did he finally accept one of those special *nurses* Matteo's been trying to add to the payroll the past six months?" The nurses might wear white uniforms and know how to use a rectal thermometer, but I'm certain they didn't spend a single second studying nursing in college.

Dante's throaty laugh barely conceals his gag. "No. Though he did have a late-night visitor last night."

"Who?" My one word snaps out of my mouth. I'm fine with our father moving on. He loved our mother for thirty-six years and gave her the world, but he's never shown an interest in finding love again. We also need to be cautious. The lengths some people will go to slate their name next to a Caruso are outrageous. Dante knows this better than anyone.

Furthermore, my brothers and I helped make the Caruso name what it is. There's no way we will step aside and let someone come in and steal it from under us right when we've crossed the finish line.

I balk when Dante answers, "Valeria."

"Valeria?" I double-check. "My Valeria?" Bile burns my throat from the unwanted possessiveness in my tone. Valeria isn't mine. I'm just lost why her visit would rejuvenate our father's will to live, so perhaps I have her confused for the other thousands of Valerias in our country.

"Yep." The P pops from his mouth. "She came by last night to update him about the procedure. She said it was a huge success."

My blood runs cold. "What?"

"The implantation." Dante speaks slowly, as if I am daft. "She said it went well and everyone at the clinic is positive she will have sticky eggs. Whatever the fuck that means."

I grip my phone firm enough to crack the screen. "I told them to cancel the procedure. The driver—"

"Apparently arrived too late, from what Nico said. It went ahead, Vanni. Yesterday afternoon, your offspring were placed inside Valeria."

I glance back at the bedroom where Valentina is sleeping. How am I supposed to tell her this? How do I explain that the one thing I tried to stop could now become front-page news?

My focus returns to the view that's nowhere near as appealing as it was minutes ago when Dante says, "Valeria told Dad herself. He's over the moon. Said between your child and mine, the Caruso legacy is secure."

"Why did she tell him?" My fury rises as rapidly as my pulse. "Even if she didn't know I'd asked for it to be canceled, it was supposed to stay between us until the test came back positive. It's in our fucking contract."

Dante's sigh rustles out of the speaker of my phone. "I have no idea, Vanni. But it's everywhere. Have you seen the news?"

A chill creeps up my spine. "What do you mean *everywhere*?"

"There's a photo of you and Valeria on the front page of the *Carlisle Chronicle*. The story states the reporter snapped it at your engagement party last month. Where the fuck was my invite?"

He laughs.

He. Fucking. Laughs.

I don't pay it any attention. I don't even hang up. I run back to the bedroom, my fists balling when I find it empty. The covers are thrown back, but the sheets are still warm. That means Valentina could still be here. I had her clothes laundered last night. Not because they were dirty, but because it guaranteed she'd remain naked for as long as possible.

My heart hammers my rib cage as I scan the living room. The concierge must have brought up breakfast. A silver tray rests on the entryway table, and to its left is the local paper, unfolded and glaring with dishonesty.

It's the final nail in my coffin.

A huge photograph of Valeria and me takes up most of the front page. We're smiling for the cameras snapping pictures of attendees of a charity gala we attended jointly years ago, and the headline splashed in bold letters states:

CARLISLE ROYALTY SET TO WED IN SPRING.

After slapping the newspaper down, I race through the penthouse, calling Valentina's name. I don't get a single response. The bathroom is empty, and her clothes are gone.

First instincts have me wanting to pop a bullet between the concierge's eyes. I ordered breakfast but requested for it not to be brought up until I called again.

His imprudence is the reason Valentina's delectable body is no longer warming my sheets.

Instead of dressing in a suit that will conceal my gun, I return to the balcony. Call it intuition—or perhaps I tend to seek out trouble—but a restless energy is pulling me toward the balcony.

When I step outside, the cool morning air brushes against my skin as I lean over the wrought iron railing. Below, the streets of Carlisle are already stirring, and the aroma of baked goods and lemons mingle with the briny tang of the Tyrrhenian Sea.

I scan the crowd for only an instant before I catch a glimpse of molten locks. Valentina is standing on the sidewalk of the building across from mine, waving down a taxi.

"Valentina..."

A flash of heartbreak darts through her eyes when she looks up. She doesn't return my greeting. She simply gives me the one-finger salute before she slips through the back passenger door of a cab and disappears into the city.

11

VALENTINA

I can't believe how easily I fell for Giovanni's tricks. I was so foolish. Am I that desperate for a fairy tale that I let myself believe I was in one? Giovanni didn't want me because he found my double-digit dress size sexy or my sass endearing. He needed someone who was unaware he's mere months from marriage.

Anger envelops me as the crumpled newspaper on the kitchen table mocks me. It's the same newspaper I casually opened while filling a mug with coffee this morning, hopeful a quick dose of caffeine would remind me of my responsibilities.

A naked-head-to-toe Giovanni standing on the balcony of his penthouse made my obligations seem inconsequential. My only wish was to wrap myself in his arms again.

Then it all came tumbling down.

The headline screamed my stupidity at me on repeat. Giovanni and Valeria looked every bit the power couple the city needs them to be, and I felt the size of an ant.

I don't recall getting dressed or how I was greeted by name when rushing out of the hotel foyer Giovanni took me to last night. I just wanted to go home and bury my head in shame.

My guilt worsened the further the taxi traveled. News of Giovanni's engagement was featured on every newspaper in the newsstands my taxi rushed past during my journey home. If that isn't bad enough, the commute stole the last of my funds and left me with only the bitter taste of regret.

I feel sick and used. And stupid. So very stupid. I'm not solely angry that I believed him. I'm furious I allowed myself to become the other woman.

It's my fault. I loved the way he looked at me and how he made me feel special. But countless orgasms and a night beyond comprehension can't displace morals.

I should have pushed harder for the truth. Then maybe I wouldn't feel like I'm walking around this city with ADULTEROUS written in thick black ink across my forehead.

During the first hour home, I was worried Giovanni would track me down. He's relentless, and I learned firsthand last night that he doesn't take no for an answer.

He raced a high-speed train to catch me, and the remembrance had me terrified he'd do it again. I was so worried he'd show up at my door and cloud my head with so much lust again that I'd find it impossible to push him away. Then I remembered that although I'd left my purse in his car, I couldn't afford to update my details when we moved to Sicily, so my license still has my US address on it.

Thank goodness for small mercies, like my phone slipping out of Giovanni's pocket during our foray on his living room floor. It's financially impossible for me to get a new one. All my salary goes toward my mother's medication. I can't spare a single cent.

Even though I'd prefer to hide my shameful face for a little longer, I can't. My shift at the pub starts in an hour. I'm getting dressed in my uniform with hands that won't quit shaking when my phone trills. The sound startles me, and I jump.

When the caller ID flashes across the screen, the dinner I scarfed down with my mom and aunt sinks to my stomach like a rock. The IVF clinic I attended yesterday is calling.

I consider letting it ring out, preferring to pretend yesterday never occurred, but I can't. I need this.

No. Correction. My *mother* needs this.

"Hello?"

"Valentina Raimondi?" The voice on the other end isn't as devastated since she's close to clocking out for the weekend. "This is Guilia from the Palermo IVF Clinic. I'm calling with the results of yesterday's procedure."

For how often she swallows, anyone would swear her life was precariously dangling on the wire, and not my mother's. I could kill her for the delay.

I gasp in disbelief when she says, "It was a success."

I can't breathe or move. All I can do is cry. Overwhelmed with relief, I grip the dresser to keep from collapsing.

"Thank you," I whisper as fresh tears sting my eyes. "Thank you so much."

My relief is short-lived. "There's just one minor issue." Guilia's tone shifts from friendly to anxious. "We've had trouble processing your payment. The bank details you provided aren't working."

I laugh like my anguish over the previous twenty-four hours has left town. "I lost my purse yesterday, so I had to put a freeze on my account." After lowering my eyes to the floor, I endeavor to lie my way out of being stamped as a homewrecker. "I was issued new account details today."

"Okay. Great. If you could bring them with you to the clinic, we will process your payment immediately."

I hesitate. Returning to the clinic and risking another encounter with Giovanni fills me with dread. I can't trust myself around him when I'm this vulnerable. But I really need the money. My mother's life hinges on this.

"What time?" I ask, forcing the words out.

"Now would be great."

"Now?" I check my watch. I'll never make it to Palermo before the clinic closes. The train takes an hour, and it's nearly six. Not to mention I'd have to stay in the city overnight since the train I'd catch would be the last train to Carlisle for the evening. Some lines run well into the evening, but Carlisle bucks the trend with advancements that would bring it into the twenty-first century.

When I explain my concerns to Guilia, she replies, "That's fine. We're happy to wait for you to arrive before locking up." When I remain quiet, still hesitant, and if I'm honest, a little perplexed, she adds, "Unless you want to wait to process your payment until next month?"

"Next month?"

I gasp in a quick breath when she hums in agreement. "We only process payments on the fifteenth of each month. If we miss today's cycle, it will have to wait until next month."

"I can come today. That won't be a problem." My words are crystal clear since my mind is made up. I'm sure I can find a quiet corner of a shelter in Palermo to rest my head.

"Great." I can't tell if her sigh is in relief or panic. "We will see you soon."

When she disconnects our call, I stare at my phone, hands shaking, before dialing the landline number of the pub. Calling in sick isn't something I do—ever—so I'm half expecting the owner to sound worried, maybe even a little suspicious. Instead, when I tell Alessandro I'm not feeling well, there's a pause, a faint sigh, and then he says, "Yeah, all right."

With that done, I walk into the living room to break the news to my mom and aunt. Mom is sitting in her new favorite chair, wrapped in a blanket, and her eyes are close to closing as she fakes interest in the show Aunt Maria is watching.

"Mom?" I whisper, not wanting to scare her.

She opens her eyes fully and smiles at me. "*Tesoro*... You look lovely. Glowing, even. Doesn't she, Maria?"

I brush off their praise like I did their disapproval this morning when no amount of scalding could remove the heat from my cheeks from more orgasms under my belt than I've achieved my entire life.

"I got a call." I almost go the honesty route, but I'm too choked up to do it. God, I wish I could tell her everything, but I'm unsure how to initiate a conversation like that. Furthermore, everything is still so fragile right now. It feels seconds from snapping. "Alessandro needs me to come in early. The pub is overrun with soccer fanatics. Something about possible World Cup contention."

"That would be Palermo FC," my aunt chimes in. "They're in with a real shot this year."

Her tone is friendly, but the suspicious glare she shoots me makes me worry she's about to call me out as a liar. "I'll have to sleep on the cot in the office tonight. I'm closing and don't want to walk home at three a.m."

Mom squeezes my hand in support. "I doubt it will be any worse than the cot you've been using here." When I groan, agreeing with her, she smiles for real. "Don't worry about me. Your aunt is here, so go do what needs to be done."

I hug her before pulling away and mustering a smile. "I'll text you when I get there."

"At the pub?" She laughs, hiding the suspicion growing in her eyes. "It's only three blocks down." As fast as her curiosity grew, worry replaces it. "But best to be safe. These streets aren't as safe as they once were."

Before retreating to my room to pack a bag with essentials, I return my eyes to my aunt's and wordlessly ask if I can speak with her in private.

"Oh... I think the tomatoes in the pasta were a little too ripe. I have horrible heartburn." Aunt Maria asks my mom if she'd like anything from the kitchen while she fetches heartburn medication. When my mom shakes her head, I follow my aunt into the kitchen. "Before you say anything," she jumps in, freezing my words, "are you okay?"

Incapable of expressing with words how much I appreciate her concern, I hug her. "I'm fine. I promise."

She hugs me back. "Then what is this about, *tesoro*? You look like you just found out your mother's condition is terminal." She hits me with a stern glare. "It isn't. We still have plenty of options."

I nod, agreeing with her. The payment I'm about to receive could be instrumental in my mother's recovery.

I just wish the knowledge would ease the delivery of my next set of words. I hate asking for anything, but I don't have a choice.

"Could I borrow a couple of dollars?" Not wanting my aunt to think I'm mooching off her more than I already am, I quickly add, "I'll pay you back the instant the bank opens tomorrow. I lost my purse, and I had to get a new account, so I have—"

"It's fine, *tesoro*." She moves for her purse to collect a handful of notes and coins. "I know you wouldn't ask unless it was urgent." She presses the last of her funds into my hand before her eyes meet mine. "Just promise me you will be careful."

She doesn't announce she knows I'm skipping work. She doesn't need to. The worry in her eyes paints the picture.

"I will. I promise."

After packing my toothbrush, spare panties, and a hairbrush, I leave the apartment.

It's different witnessing the city at this time of night. It is already buzzing with life, but in a playful, poetic way instead of the dark columns of a back-alley pub.

I keep my head down, avoiding the eyes of my neighbors and the curious glances of strangers as I proceed to the station. The last thing I want is for Alessandro to find out I'm not sick. I can't risk getting fired. I need my job.

The train to Palermo is crowded, and the air smells of salt-slicked skin and too many bodies packed into too small a space. Carlisle's coastline is one of the best in Sicily, and people often flock here for day trips when they want to escape the hustle and bustle of the city.

As I seek a seat in the packed carriage, the photo of Giovanni and Valeria haunts me at every turn. Locals and tourists are equally invested in what reporters are broadcasting as the wedding of the century.

I wish I could tear today's newspaper out of the hand of a man with a seedy mustache, but since the seat next to him is the only one empty, I excuse my interruption before slipping past him and sitting next to the window.

As the train speeds toward Palermo, I block out the noise and try to center myself. Nothing works. I replay every second of my time with Giovanni. His expression when he entered me bare and the flare that sparked through his hooded gaze when he tasted my arousal feature the most. But I also recall the warmth of his eyes when he raked them over my body, and his command when he led our exchanges with authority.

I hate him, but I hate myself more.

I could have not allowed lust to speak on my behalf. I could have said no. I didn't because I didn't want anything to disrupt what I'm confident will always rate as the best night of my life.

By the time I arrive in Palermo, I'm mentally exhausted. I beeline to the clinic. Though my confidence lags, my steps are quick and sure. I don't bother with the side entrance this time. My embarrassment has already reached its pinnacle, so what's the point in hiding?

I walk straight up to the front doors of the clinic with my heart pounding so loudly I'm sure anyone passing by can hear it. The glass entry door slices open with a hiss, and I step inside and brace for the usual bustle of patients and staff.

The waiting room is empty. There are no receptionists or nurses. There isn't even the faint whirr of the coffee machine that taunted me for hours on end when I was required to fast.

The silence is eerie, amplified by the prickling of awkwardness already coating my skin.

I hover by the desk for a few minutes, certain someone will eventually come out. When no one does, I clear my throat.

"Hello?"

My greeting bounces back to me, my request for help unanswered.

I wait a little longer. When the emptiness of the space homes in on me, I pace down the corridor toward the procedural rooms. My shoes squeak on the gleaming surface, and each shriek makes me feel more and more like an intruder.

When I walk by closed doors, memories of my last visit steamroll back in. The nerves, the paper gown, and the sterile scent I thought I'd never scrub from my skin bombard me.

Partway down, I hear voices. They're muffled at first. Barely a low rumble. But the closer I get, the more one voice stands out. I'd know it anywhere.

Giovanni.

I freeze, and my breath catches halfway to my lungs. Turning around and retreating to Carlisle is tempting, but my feet root in place as my mind is caught between dread and something I refuse to name.

When the voice grows louder, against my better judgment, I press myself against the wall and listen intently. I shouldn't care what has Giovanni so worked up he has to shout, but I do.

My concern is as insistent as my wish to see my mother grow old and has my feet refusing to budge for anything.

Even him.

12

GIOVANNI

I'm not a patient man, and today, my patience is stretched so thin it will snap at the slightest provocation. The head doctor's office is suffocating. It's too clean and lifeless not to deliver bad news with a fake smile and legally binding paperwork you signed without reading it.

I'm only here because someone couldn't follow a simple instruction. I told them to cancel Valeria's appointment, yet here I am, wasting time I could use teaching Valentina that I never back down when challenged.

I have a lead—finally. Valentina's license was for a US address, but there was a card tucked in the bottom of her purse for a local pub. From what I gathered from the owner when I visited to ensure both he and his patrons know Valentina is off-limits for anyone, her shift begins in an hour.

I'm so close to winning this game of chase that I can taste it. I merely have to conquer this last obstacle first.

Dr. Di Petro's droning monotone brings my attention back to the present. He hasn't shut up for nearly half an hour. It's mostly gobbledygook medical jargon that means nothing to me.

I hurry him along by tapping my foot and glancing arrogantly at my watch. Nothing works, so I glare at him, silently announcing he has five minutes to get to the point or I'll bring my gun to the party.

I have stalking to do. That doesn't wait for anyone.

The good doctor would already be dead if he weren't a close friend of my father's. That's how infuriated I become when someone doesn't follow my direct order. I won't just take down the fool responsible for the mishap. Anyone associated with him will also endure the brunt of my wrath.

"Stop wasting my time and state your business. I don't have all day." I lean forward and glare at the doctor sternly enough for the tremor of his hands to be visible from across his desk. "We won't know if the embryo transfer was successful for another five to ten days, so why the fuck did you call us in early? If it's to apologize again for not heeding my request to cancel the procedure, it's too late. The harm has already been done."

Valeria, seated beside me, scoffs as if disgusted. The doctor doesn't pay her any attention. His focus is solely on me. "*Signor* Caruso, there was a mix-up on the day of the procedure."

"And?"

His face pales. "The sperm you donated months ago, to be placed into Valeria's eggs... there was a mistake. They were placed into someone else."

I don't understand what he's saying. I'm not stupid. His confession is just tainted with too many murky undertones to be comprehensible.

Then, slowly, the meaning of his words sinks in.

My child—the blood and legacy of my family—is out there in someone else. Not Valeria as per our contract and the woman my family expects. Someone else.

The mind swirls as my vision narrows. "You're telling me"—my voice is dangerously calm but loud—"that a Caruso could be born outside the family? That my child, the fucking heir to my fortune, is in the stomach of a stranger?"

The doctor nods as his eyes widen with fear. "We're so sorry, *Signor* Caruso. It was an administrative error. We're doing everything we can to rectify—"

"Rectify?" I cut him off, my temperature rising. "How do you rectify something like this? This isn't a missed appointment or a lost file. This is my family. My fucking blood. This is the Caruso name. Do you have any idea what you've done?"

Valeria scoots to the edge of her chair, her face ashen. She's crying and clearly devastated. "I can't believe this. You promised—"

I barely hear the remainder of her words as fury and disbelief rage war inside me. The Caruso legacy is everything. It's what my father built and my brothers and I have fought to protect. It's the reason for every sacrifice I've made over the past thirty-four years. And now, because of some idiot's mistake, it could all unravel.

I clench my fists while fighting the urge to put one through the wall. My jaw aches from how ruefully I grind my teeth. "Who?" I demand. "Who has my child?"

"Our child," Valeria corrects. "They used my eggs too, Giovanni. This is as much my child as it is yours."

The doctor shakes his head. "We can't disclose that information. Patient confidentiality—"

My laugh is harsh and bitter. "Patient confidentiality? You think I care about your rules? You've made a mistake that could change the course of my family's history, and you're hiding behind paperwork? A signature won't protect you from what you've done!"

Instantly, I regret leaving my gun with my driver. Valeria knows I am a hothead, and when my short temper is combined with the frustration of my direct order being ignored, I become a raging lunatic.

The doctor would be dead at my feet if she hadn't convinced me to go into this meeting with an open mind.

I understand her objective. She still wants to go through with our agreement. She even pledged to turn a blind eye to any "indiscretions" I might have throughout our marriage.

I told her I was no longer interested. That if this round of IVF was successful, both she and the baby would be taken care of for the rest of their lives, and our child would inherit his or her share of a billion-dollar fortune. But if it failed, our contract would be voided.

Now I don't know which way is up.

Valeria is sobbing now, and her hands cover her face. A pang of guilt strikes my chest, but it's hardly felt by the flames of my anger licking my insides. I'm itching to tear this place apart and to make someone pay, but I can't until I have answers. If there is a Caruso descendant in the making, I deserve full disclosure on the person bringing him or her into the world.

Valeria's composure breaks as she confronts the head doctor. "I'll sue you for this." Her eyes blaze with unbridled fury. "You ruined everything! I'll make sure everyone in the clinic never works again!"

Foolishly, the doctor stands his ground with the protocol I'll abolish the instant I burn this hellhole to the ground. "You signed a waiver, Ms. Raimondo. You knew the risks and agreed to them."

Raimondo? Valeria's surname is Giuffrida.

With Valeria's anger boiling over, she shoves away the paperwork he flapped in her face, her expression contorted with despair. "It's her, isn't it? The one with the similar name." Her eyes dart wildly over the paperwork scattered across his desk. "I joked that they might get us mixed up. I didn't think it would actually happen."

"Who are you talking about? What woman?"

Dr. Di Petro's lips twitch, but before he can speak, Valeria strikes him hard across the face. Her slap is firm enough that I must intervene. I seize her wrist to prevent further harm, mindful that the man she's attacking is our only source of information. More than a hand mark will mar his face once I'm done with him, but I need him coherent enough to speak at the beginning of our exchange.

"She has my baby, doesn't she?" Valeria shouts as I carry her toward the exit, tears streaming down her face. "That *reject* is carrying my child, isn't she? Tell me the truth!"

When I throw open the door to deposit Valeria into the waiting room so I can conduct "business" man-to-man, I unearth the reason the hairs on my nape are standing to attention. Torturing men for information doesn't give me any satisfaction. I do it as a means to survive. This woman, however, makes me doubt all that I know.

Valentina is standing in the hallway. Her eyes are wide, and her face is pale. For a second, I'm too stunned to speak. What is she doing here at this hour? My appointment this evening shows that this clinic operates outside business hours to conceal their mistakes from new and potential patients. They wouldn't let a random person stalk their halls at this hour.

When I see the glimmers on Valentina's cheeks, fury surges through my chest. She's been crying. Tears blotch her cheeks, and her posture is rigid, as if her confidence was sideswiped by a truck.

"What happened? Did someone hurt you?"

My anger hardly diminishes when she shakes her head. Her dismissal is weak, and she is aware of that fact as much as I am.

"Then what happened? Why are you crying?"

Her wet eyes shifting between the doctor and the paperwork Valeria dumped on his desk swirls something inside me. It isn't the carnage and brutality I'm accustomed to. It's hope.

What the fuck?

Gradually, the situation becomes clear. The timing of our reunion, her confession that she had a procedure done that would keep her safe from pregnancy for a month, and the name the doctor used when trying to calm down Valeria. It all makes sense.

I stare at Valentina as my thoughts race away on me.

Could it be?

Is it possible?

Valeria's distraught accusation answers my unvoiced questions. "It's her." The rattle of her sob reminds me that she's still in my arms. "She's the woman carrying *our* child."

I stumble backward, shocked. My child, a direct descendant of the Caruso legacy, is growing inside the woman I am obsessed with.

I couldn't have planned this better if I had tried.

13

———

VALENTINA

The clinic's air turns suffocating when my dazed head translates Valeria's wildly inaccurate accusation. "She's the woman carrying *our* child."

I'm overcome with shock. Then denial sets in. Her words can't be for me. I'm not pregnant. I attended the clinic to sell my eggs, hoping I'd scrape together enough money to extend my mother's life beyond the two to three months the medical professionals had given her, not to become the center of someone else's tragedy.

I glance behind me, confident the once-desolate waiting room now houses another body.

Only the ghosts of karma remain.

When I return my focus front and center, the doctor gestures for me to enter the office next to the one I'm frozen in front of, clutching the bag I hurriedly packed as if it is a shield.

"We can talk in there." His gaze bounces between Giovanni and Valeria, anticipating they'll get the message and let him pass.

Giovanni doesn't budge an inch. He plants himself beside me, folds his arms over his chest, and sets his jaw. His narrowed gaze expresses the words he doesn't need to speak.

He isn't going anywhere… and neither am I.

Valeria's eyes are red-rimmed, yet she remains as obstinate as Giovanni. "If she's carrying *my* child, I have every right to be here."

I stare at her, bewildered. "I have no idea what you are talking about. I'm not pregnant. I didn't come here for IVF. I…" My words trail off as shame swamps me. I honestly don't know what makes me want to crawl under a pillow and die more. Selling my eggs for profit or being confronted by Giovanni's big fat lie again in less than twenty-four hours.

I face the doctor with a look that asks him to corroborate my statement. He hesitates, peers at me in sympathy, then murmurs, "I understand this is overwhelming, Ms. Raimondi, but if you will give me the chance to explain, perhaps you won't be so bewildered."

"The chance to explain what?" I abandon all pretense of doctor–patient confidentiality when he looks at Giovanni and Valeria with weary resignation. "Say what you need to say. I've got nothing to hide." *Except my shameful face.*

It's astonishing that out of all the people in the world, two of the most glamorous people will learn about my desperation.

Valeria is crying but still possesses an air of sophistication. And don't get me started on Giovanni or I'll expose his adulterous ways with more than my fists. I've never wanted to kiss the arrogance off someone's face as intently as I do right now.

Why does he look so cocky? It makes no sense.

Giovanni's eyes never leave mine, and Valeria's stare is heavy with distress when the doctor clears his throat before he begins to speak. "There was a mix-up. A junior associate confused your file with another patient's. Instead of retrieving your eggs for donation, he prepared you for an embryo transfer." The world spins following his next words. "The embryos created from Mr. Caruso's sperm and Ms. Raimondo's eggs were implanted in you."

Despite not being able to see my reflection, I'm aware my face lacks color. My soul vanished along with the blood in my cheeks many minutes ago.

"No," I whisper. "This can't be right. I didn't agree to this. This isn't what I signed up for. I was to donate eggs, not have them put inside me."

The doctor's professional demeanor collapses with regret. "I know, and I'm so sorry. The associate misread the schedule. He saw your name and mistook it for Ms. Raimondo's. The similarity in names and the pressure must have become too much. He didn't double-check, and as such, he followed the protocol for an embryo transfer instead of an egg retrieval."

Valeria rocks on her heels as her entire body shakes. "So it's true. My eggs and Giovanni's sperm are inside her?"

When the doctor nods, face abundant with regret, I stumble into his office and sit on the first chair I see, my legs too weak to support me.

The remorse in Dr. Di Petro's eyes is for Valeria, but the sympathy in his words is for me. "The error was only discovered when we reviewed the post-procedure paperwork and realized the samples didn't match the intended recipients. By then, the transfer had already taken place. It was too late to change anything."

I can't move, speak, or comprehend. It feels like someone yanked the floor out from beneath me and then sat back to watch me fall.

After what seems like a lifetime but is barely seconds, I finally speak. "There's a possibility the transfer will fail, right? I might not be pregnant?"

"There's a possibility," the doctor concurs, permitting me to breathe. "But you're young, Valentina, and extremely fertile. The odds are in favor of conception."

The gravity of the situation slowly emerges from the mud when I discuss it out loud. "I could be pregnant..."—I lock eyes with Giovanni, who is still as cool as a cucumber—"with *your* child?" A thin layer of sweat covers my skin when I turn my focus to Valeria. "And yours?"

Again, the doctor nods as his eyes plead for understanding. "We could run some tests now to confirm, but it's too early for certainty." He crouches down like eye contact will mend the mistakes his team made. "I can't apologize enough. This isn't the usual standard of care we provide our patients. I know it won't make it any better, but I suspended the associate this morning, pending investigation."

It's difficult for me to catch my breath. My thoughts are a tangle of panic and outrage. "How could this happen? I just wanted to help my mom. I needed money for her. That's all. This wasn't meant to happen. Do you not have checks and safeguards in place to ensure stuff like this doesn't occur?"

"We do. There are multiple checks. Names and dates of birth are standard. But the associate—"

"Fucked up." Giovanni jumps into the conversation, finally, as I brush a solemn tear from my cheek. "And I'm interested in discovering how he did that."

Before the doctor can speak, Valeria's confession stills the room. "It's my fault. I used my grandmother's maiden name for the paperwork. I didn't want people to think our... *arrangement* was staged."

"Even though that is precisely what this was. An *arrangement*."

She acts as if Giovanni never spoke. Tears well in her eyes as she lowers them to my stomach. A healthy appetite has made it a little plump, but it's far from looking pregnant. "But now it's all a mess."

The doctor tries to mediate, but his words are just noise. My head is spinning, and I'm angry. So fucking angry. Not solely at the clinic. I also blame myself for the desperation that led me here.

It's also frightening being pushed into a role you've never truly considered.

Well, I have considered having children, but not like this. I always thought they'd come after the bells and whistles of a whirlwind relationship. A predicament like this never entered the equation.

"If the test comes back positive, I can have an abortion." That was hard to say, but what other choice do I have?

Giovanni's stern timbre drills through my panic. "No. That's *not* happening." His seemingly laidback composure is terrifying. He should be furious, but for some reason, he's not. He's in control, as if he's already decided my fate for me.

The certainty in his eyes makes me want to run, and the urge doubles when Valeria's sob reaches my ears. "Please, don't. My egg supply is already low. This cycle could be my last chance to be a mother. Please, Valentina, don't kill my child." Her pain is raw, and it slices through me with the brutality of a knife. I know all too well the pain of clinging to hope with bleeding fingers, but I can't be her savior. I can barely save myself.

I'm torn in two, conflicted between compassion and self-preservation. My heart hurts for Valeria, but my head screams at me to run. I need time to think without this additional burden breathing down my neck. I hate that I'm not strong enough to face this with grace, but the tank has been empty for months. There's nothing left to give.

My body reacts before my heart's pleas can be heard. I bolt for the exit, eager to escape this nightmare. As I reach the door, a sharp jab pricks my neck. In less than a heartbeat, my vision goes hazy, and the world spins around me.

I assume Giovanni isn't happy about my plan to flee him again, but a voice I've heard more in ecstasy than in an everyday setting proves me wrong. "What the fuck did you do?"

"That is *my* child," replies Valeria as I fall forward too fast to be safe. "I refuse to let someone like her take him or her away from me."

I'm caught by a powerful set of arms a second before Giovanni's earthy and expensive cologne fills my senses. A comforting illusion of safety swamps me as everything fades to black. I shouldn't want Giovanni's comfort or protection, but I do. Badly.

14

GIOVANNI

Fleeting lights from Carlisle's cityscape streak Valentina's beautiful face when they pass the tinted windows of my town car. She's sprawled on the seat opposite mine, her head lolling with the car's gentle sways. Her parted lips suggest her sleep is unaffected by the sedative that stole memories of the procedure that will bind her to me for eternity.

Valeria hasn't assembled the puzzle pieces as effectively as I have. She's still of the belief that Valentina has something she owns.

I've yet to reach the same conclusion.

Dr. Di Petro said that instead of retrieving Valentina's eggs, they implanted Valeria's embryos inside her. *Instead.* Not after the procedure she'd gone to the clinic to have. Not in addition to. He implied that the egg retrieval procedure had been *completely* overlooked.

This not only boosts the chances of conception but also places Valentina alongside Valeria as the potential mother of my child. It isn't solely from the number of embryos inserted, which was only two since Valeria refused to carry multiples, fueling my campaign, but also that we failed to use protection.

Last night, I took Valentina bare—more than once.

I've never been more grateful for the lapse in judgment.

Although I'm not an expert on women's psyches, the pamphlets I perused during Valeria's repeated visits to the clinic taught me that women are more fertile during the stimulation of eggs. Valeria also offered that as her excuse when she snuck into my bed earlier this month. She hoped a meaningless hookup would mean avoiding an invasive procedure.

While she'll never admit this, she also desired our partnership to seem legitimate and would do whatever was necessary to make that attainable.

I once again opposed her plans. I'd met Valentina by then, and no amount of alcohol could have me mistaking Valeria's waif-thin frame for Valentina's sultry curves. I also didn't want it to. Perfection can't be copied, and no man would sign up for a cheap imitation.

As hope thickens both my veins and my cock, I watch Valentina's chest rise and fall. Her slow, steady breaths are a comfort amidst my fury over her unconsciousness. While the world outside is a chaotic blur of revenge plots and death notes, in here, time feels suspended.

Calm always precedes a storm.

Valeria clears her throat, unsubtly reminding me that she's beside me. Her posture is rigid, and her hands wring the silk handkerchief I refused to use to ensure Valentina didn't "get away."

I don't mind if she runs.

The chase will mark the commencement of our foreplay, and I'm more than ready to have Valentina back underneath me.

Valeria's tension is palpable. It's the kind of anger that makes my jaw ache from tensing it too frequently, and it worsens when her sniveling words infiltrate my ears. "How do you know her?"

When I arch a brow, silently warning that I don't answer to anyone, she lowers her tone. Too bad it does nothing to diminish the whistle of audacity in her words.

"You're looking at her like you know her. Like she isn't some random woman who came in and snatched our child out from beneath us."

"What happened was a mistake." Not even her pounding pulse would have her missing my scathing tone. "Valentina didn't do anything wrong."

Valeria scoffs. "She did this on purpose, Giovanni. I know she did." I'm about to point out that her insults to Valentina are also insults to me, but she keeps talking before I can. "You fucked her, didn't you? She's the girl your brothers have been talking about all month. The damsel in distress you swooped in and saved."

"If I did?" My tone is a warning that I'm at the end of my rope.

She pays it no attention. "Then you fell into her trap like Dante did Camille's mother, and for what?" A bitter, jealousy-filled laugh reverberates around the cab of the car. "She isn't even your type."

Even though her eyes are red from crying, and more than mascara clumps her lashes together, I still struggle not to respond to her ill-formed misconceptions with violence. For one, this is *nothing* like what Dante went through. Not even close. And two, Valentina is more than my type.

She is the *only* option.

Valeria locks gazes with me, and her eyes plead for me to understand. "When we were filling out our paperwork, she mentioned how similar our names were. She joked about how it would be easy for the clinic to get us mixed up. She seemed hopeful. Like she wanted it to happen."

With a scoff, I shake my head. "Why would she do that? What benefit could she get from a mix-up like this?"

"She agreed to sell her eggs for money, Giovanni. You've clearly overestimated her self-worth."

Valeria twists her lips, and her leg bounces with anger and something else. Fear, maybe? It's expected. I haven't stopped shooting daggers at her since she juiced up Valentina's veins with a sedative.

"After the doctor mentioned my low egg count, he went over surrogacy options and their financial implications. She'll get five times what she would have with a simple donation, and that with a standard, everyday couple." Her huff announces she doesn't class herself as anything close to standard. "She knows the power she now holds, and if she's smart, she'll exploit it for all it's worth."

My initial impulse is to dismiss her claims outright and attribute them to her desperation to assign fault. The way she looks at me, however, eyes glistening and pleading, prevents me from doing so.

For several miles, I attempt to talk some sense into her.

Why would Valentina orchestrate something like this?

What could she possibly gain?

Valeria remains persistent. She paints Valentina as a cunning opportunist who saw an opening and took it without a second thought.

"She saw you outside the clinic, walking me in. I'm confident she did."

Since I'm unable to deny her claim, I remain quiet. Her theories are nonsense. Valentina is different. But I can't control the memories that surface. For years, women have tried to worm their way into my family's good graces. They lie, manipulate, and scheme for a taste of the Caruso legacy.

Dante's baby mama is the most recent and painful example. Her brief intermission in the Caruso household left a trail of chaos in its wake.

Furthermore, I've seen what desperation can do. It can twist even the most innocent intentions into something ugly. But Valentina? She doesn't seem like that.

As rows of lemon groves whiz past my window, I go over every moment we've shared, searching for signs I might have missed. She looked at me with an open rawness that was also defiant, and she was clueless of my identity until I revealed my name.

If she'd known my influence aligned with Valeria's perspective, what was the reason for her repeated escapes?

Because she knows you like the chase.

Loathing my inner monologue, I ball my hands into fists. Trusting my instincts is as natural as breathing, but is an attraction powerful enough to thicken my cock even while I'm being played for a fool impairing my judgment?

In all honesty, it doesn't matter. Just the memory of Valentina's lips on mine and the way her body fit against me, as if designed for me, has me willing to hand over every dime I have, so who cares if Valeria's claims are true?

You can't be played when you sign up to participate.

Don't get me wrong, I want Valentina to be innocent. I'd rather she be, but obsession is a dangerous thing. It can make a man rush to his death without thinking twice.

I'm more than obsessed with this woman. I am consumed. Fanatical. My cravings for her are near pathological.

I want her enough that I'm willing to play with fire and risk being singed to ash.

"She'll wake up soon," Valeria says, drawing my attention back to her. "And then you'll realize that I'm telling the truth."

As the car turns onto the long drive leading to the family compound, I tighten and loosen my jaw. The gates swing open, and the Caruso mansion looms ahead, illuminating the safe haven built for the residents of Carlisle.

Our home isn't solely the biggest house in Carlisle. It is also the best. Marble columns flank the entrance, and the gardens stretch out in manicured perfection. Fountains and statues that hint at old money are scattered throughout the compound, while the imposing wrought iron gates silently acknowledge our power.

This place is more than a home. It's a fortress. A statement. Every stone used to build its thirty-six bedrooms is a testament to the strength of the Caruso name. My brothers and I all live here, together, under one roof. Some say it's old-fashioned, but to us, it's tradition.

It is what keeps our bond unbreakable.

The compound's layout offers ample space for privacy but is tight-knit enough that loyalty to the family is never in question. Here, we eat together, argue together, and plot together. Our unity is our greatest weapon, and I'm eager to use it to sail through my latest dilemma.

Inside walls steeped in history, portraits of our ancestors line the halls. While the dining room accommodates fifty guests, the library, game room, and private bar are where the real business happens.

Port and cigars have been part of many agreements struck here.

It's no secret that outsiders desire what we have. Even those already wealthy will do anything to be a part of our success. They swarm like sharks, seeking invitations or an offer of partnership. Some even dangle their daughters in front of us like prized fish. They want the Caruso name on their side, and the security and prestige that come with being one of us.

That's why we keep the gates sealed shut. They open for us, but for others, they signify that not everything can be bought, no matter how deep your pockets. I've seen men and women of great means debase themselves for a seat at our table. Some succeed, but most fail.

Here, only the strongest survive, and Valentina is about to be put through the most brutal test.

15

VALENTINA

I emerge from the sedation like I'm clawing my way out of a deep, dark well. My limbs are heavy, and my thoughts are sluggish. I'm unaware of my location and how I got here. The world is muffled, as if I'm wrapped in cotton wool, but gradually, sounds and scents filter through the blackness.

I don't feel sick, and there's no pain. Just bone-deep exhaustion that makes my eyelids the weight of concrete. I force myself to breathe while attuning my senses. The seat under me is buttery soft, a clear sign of the leather you find in luxury cars, and the ticking of cooling metal soon overtakes the gentle purr of a high-powered engine.

Giovanni's cologne is the first scent that hits me. It's distinctly him, but instead of tripling the output of my heart, it triggers sirens in my head. His powerful scent reminds me of whose world I've entered, and that I'm not a player on this team.

My name isn't even on the signup sheet.

Against the screaming protests of my head, I crack my eyelids open.

Though they barely open, the world comes into view. We're parked in an estate so grand it could be a palace. The endless grounds feature vast lawns, marble statues, and impeccably trimmed hedges. Beyond the gates, the lights of Carlisle twinkle in the distance. No other houses or signs of life are close by. It's seemingly just Giovanni, Valeria, and me.

I snap my eyes shut again and feign sleep when a conversation drifts through the haze.

Valeria speaks with a clear, professional tone, and it grates on my nerves. This is as personal as it gets. "I'll have the attic room made up for her. It's private, and she'll have everything she needs, but it will keep her away from prying eyes." I picture her raking her nails over Giovanni's chest when scratching fills her brief pause. "We should keep news of her surrogacy on the down-low until we know if the transfer was successful."

Surrogacy? The term is a brutal slap to the face. It twists my stomach with an equal amount of anger and humiliation.

Is that all I am to them? A vessel? A means to parenthood?

The thought of being called their surrogate for the next nine months makes my skin crawl. I'm not a part of their family, nor am I a willing participant in their prearranged agreement.

I'm the woman who got caught in the crossfire of their scheme.

Shame creeps across my face. I'm nothing but a problem to be managed. A dirty secret they want to hide in an attic room like a shameful mistake.

The sting of admitting it is intense and deeply gutting. It maims my chest and makes it hard to breathe. I loathe how I am being treated, but more than anything, I can't stomach the idea of carrying their baby only to hand it over at the end.

Anger replaces my shame when I imagine the months ahead. How will I look at myself in the mirror, knowing I'm growing someone else's child? How will I survive them taking what I've carried and nurtured for nine months like my sacrifice meant nothing?

The thoughts are unbearable.

Mercifully, a car door opening before gravel underfoot jolts me back to reality.

It's a struggle, but I control my breathing so I can maintain my lie that I'm asleep.

Giovanni's cologne is still dominant, so Valeria must have exited the car. Though I'd rather not possess this skill, I can feel the tension radiating off him. Beneath his anger and frustration, a darker, unidentifiable feeling seethes within him. I can't pinpoint it, but it's extremely suffocating.

It's a fight not to sigh in relief when Giovanni intervenes with Valeria's plan to make me the villain of her story. "Valentina will stay on the main floor. Put her in the room next to mine."

The air crackles with tension during a brief pause, and I hear Valeria's back molars grinding together. "That isn't necessary. The attic is—"

"I said, put her in the room next to mine. I want her close."

"The staff—"

"I don't care about the staff," Giovanni snaps, his voice a roar. "She isn't to be hidden away like a dirty fucking secret. She is to stay on the main floor. End of discussion."

Silence falls, thick and resolute, as a peculiar blend of relief and humiliation melds through me. I'm glad I won't be imprisoned like a monstrous creature, yet I feel degraded that my destiny was determined without my consent.

I'm not a piece of furniture they can move and rehome at their convenience.

The reality of the situation settles over me like a heavy blanket. Every decision about my life is being made by someone else. Even the smallest things—where I'll sleep, who I'll see—are out of my hands.

Forget that. I'm my own person, and they have no right to steer the course of my destiny.

I stabilize my breathing, then slide my hand toward the door keeping me upright. The handle feels cool in my palm as I test if the door is locked. A soft click signals that it is unlocked.

I inhale deeply to prepare my lungs for the exertion they're about to undertake, but before I can make a break for it, Giovanni's warning has me torn on whether I should run away from him or to him. "You can run, Valentina. But remember, when I catch you, I get to fuck you."

I freeze as my heart hammers in my chest—*and several inches lower.* There's no point pretending now, so instead, I push against the restraints. I'm not a prisoner, and I refuse to allow my lust-crazed head to treat me like one.

Adrenaline surges through me when I fling open my door, slip out of my seat, and then break into a sprint. I gasp for air in short, broken breaths as I weave through the endless lemon groves bordering the Caruso estate. The trees are heavy with fruit, as if overdue to be harvested, and their waxy leaves glisten under the moonlight.

Grass tickles my ankles as I race across the uneven and squishy ground, and my lungs scream for a quick breather, but I can't slow down. Behind me, I hear loud, breathless pants. They could be from guards who protect properties like this one, but I'm reasonably sure they belong to Giovanni. The thudding of my pulse tells me this, not to mention the dampness between my legs.

When I merge deeper into the shadows of the trees, hopeful they'll conceal me from the moonlit sky, branches whip at my arms and legs. I push through the pain, desperate for freedom.

When the light from a flashlight slices through the darkness, I flatten my back against a large trunk and finally answer the demands of my screaming lungs.

I've barely caught my breath when my panic recedes. The guard is armed, but seemingly unaware of my attempt to escape. He doesn't reward me a second glance.

Still, I duck low before slipping past him unnoticed.

The perfume of fresh lemons crushed underfoot streams into my nose when I recommence my sprint two rows later.

The further I run, the more my calves burn, but I refuse to let fear win.

Or is it excitement?

As I reach a clearing, Giovanni calls my name. The heavy, deliberate steps that accompany his chant indicate that he's close to catching me.

I should be terrified, but I'm not. Giovanni is a force of nature. He's dangerous and unpredictable, but as his stomps drown out my thudding heart, my fear transforms into something else.

A strange exhilaration rises from being chased, and it fills me with feral disregard.

As I emerge from the orchard, the moonlight halos my locks, announcing my location.

Giovanni reaches me in less than a nanosecond. One of his arms wraps around my waist to haul me against his chest, while the other cushions our fall when he tackles me to the ground.

Even though none of the sweat covering me is from fear, I fight him with all I have. I kick and twist, yet he pins me to the rain-soaked earth as if I weigh nothing.

A wave builds in my womb when he blows his hot breath against my ear. "What did I say, Valentina? When I catch you, I get to fuck you."

"Leave me alone!" I shout in the direction I last saw the guard, praying he will hear my screams and prevent an imminent assault. "Get off me!"

All my protests are fake. I ache for Giovanni, and although I hate myself for it, there's no use denying the truth.

Giovanni's thumb grazes the throbbing vein in my throat, wordlessly calling me out as a liar, before he lowers it to the top button of my shirt. My nipples harden at the slightest brush of his palm against my breast, and I grit my teeth.

I'm not meant to enjoy being treated like a commodity.

After popping two buttons, he raises his dilated eyes from my erratically panting chest to my face. "Why did your appointment at the clinic take so long yesterday, *dolcezza*?"

Huh?

Why is he interrogating me? I did nothing wrong.

When I say that to him, his smirk makes my insides squeeze, and then he undoes another two buttons. "Valeria claims your actions were intentional. According to her, you saw us at the clinic, and it prompted you to exert yourself into our arrangement. Is that true?"

"No!" My fight picks back up, and I whack into him. "Of course it isn't true. Why would I do that? What benefit would I get from doing something so heinous?"

My throat burns with uncertainty when he murmurs, "Two hundred and fifty thousand dollars."

"What?"

He dances his eyes between mine for several heart-thrashing seconds before he repeats, "Two hundred and fifty thousand dollars. That's how much Valeria is willing to pay for you to carry her child."

My anger is already at its boiling point, and the reminder of how I'm being portrayed adds gasoline to the fire. I'm not a money-hungry gold digger willing to do anything for some coin. My only wish is to help fund my mother's cancer treatment.

I'll keep that information to myself for now, though.

Revenge forever trumps someone else's reprieve when you're angry.

"And you, Giovanni? How much are you willing to pay?"

He balks, and that's when I make my move. I slam my knee into his groin, push him off me, and then clamber back onto my feet. "You can keep your damn money. I don't want it."

Mud splashes my face as he grabs my ankle and yanks my legs out from under me. I land breasts-first on the ground a second before Giovanni flips me over, and then he looms over me like the slosh beneath us didn't saturate my shirt and skirt.

I push at his chest and claw at his arms. "Get off me, Giovanni. I'm serious this time!"

This could be my anger talking, but I swear his balls are gargling in his throat when he replies, "You're serious?"

"Yes!"

"You want me to get off you?"

"Yes!"

He rocks his hips forward, immediately making me a liar.

"Tell me again you want me to get off."

I look him dead set in the eyes while growling, "Get. Off. Me."

This time, he digs his shoes into the soggy earth to leverage his rock.

The instant the head of his throbbing fat cock rolls over my clit, my brain turns to mush and nothing but the chase of climax is on my mind.

Two more grinds and I'll be done.

Stupid hormones.

What? Blaming others is easier than taking responsibility. Why do you think Valeria is so determined to make me the villain?

Giovanni uses my attraction to his advantage before he recommences his interrogation. "Valeria—"

"Is looking for a scapegoat. She wants someone to blame." I dig my elbows into the ground and thrust out my chest before deepening my tone. "Unless the accusation centers on her fiancé's inability to keep his dick in his pants, I'm not her fall guy."

He tweaks my nipple, setting my blood on fire. "I saw the way your pulse spiked during our meeting with Dr. Di Petro. You know my situation with Valeria is an arrangement."

"Doesn't make it any better."

Another tweak, with his thumb and index finger this time, and another shiver of excitement. "What you don't know is that I tried to cancel it."

"You're a liar."

"I'm not lying." My fight loses steam when he adds, "I swear on my mother's grave that I thought the procedure had been canceled when I took you to my penthouse."

For several lengthy seconds, I hunt for any cracks in his armor.

When I fail to find a single iota of a hairline crack, the silence stretches, punctuated only by the distant murmur of a guard and the faint chirp of crickets.

"My father is dying." Giovanni's hushed words fall around us like boulders. "He's been sick for months. Some days, he barely gets out of bed. So when he said all he wanted was to see the future of the Caruso dynasty before he went, I made arrangements." His eyes are on me, hot, heavy, and full of regret. "I didn't know you then. If I had—"

I Band-Aid the pain tearing through him by kissing him. I understand wanting to give someone you love a reason to hope, and the desperation that comes with watching them slip away, knowing there's nothing you can do to avoid it. Wholeheartedly.

It makes you careless. Impulsive enough to drug someone and kidnap them? I honestly don't know. It's undeniable how far I'll go for my mother, so it's reasonable to assume Giovanni would do the same for his father.

In seconds, I realize I am in way over my head.

Giovanni kisses me without reservation. It's a claiming embrace that brings back my earlier worries. He could do whatever he wants to me, and I'd let him.

I inch back, hoping some fresh air will restore my smarts.

An unsanctioned mouth doesn't help. With my mouth removed from the picture, Giovanni's focus shifts to my breasts. He squeezes one in his big manly hand while the other rolls my hardened nipple between his thumb and index finger.

Pleasure blazes through me as my hips involuntarily arch upward. I rub myself along the leg wedged between my thighs, moaning when the crease in his trousers grinds past my clit.

"Oh... God," I breathe into the humid night sky when he pulls down the cup of my bra and traps my nipple into his mouth. I dig my fingers into the squishy ground when he tongues the hardened nub like he does my clit before he draws it deep into his mouth.

"Who, *dolcezza?*"

Giovanni groans low in his throat when I thread my fingers through his hair and force his mouth back onto my breast. Our race through the grounds of his palatial mansion knotted his hair, making my tug violent.

Heat forms in my core when he kisses a trail down my flabby midsection. He tongues my belly button before pressing his lips to the bow at the top of my panties.

I watch him in anticipation when he gestures for me to lift my hips so he can remove my skirt and panties. I'm dying for him to taste me again, but what he does next is even better than that.

He drags his nose down the seam of my soaked pussy, growling when the briefest skim of his nose across my clit almost sets me off.

"Mmm," he moans, doubling the sparks rocketing through the lower half of my stomach. "I smell good *in* you."

I don't get the chance to comprehend what he means or take

offense before he spears his tongue between the lines of my pussy. Lights blister as a fiery heat singes my veins.

Moaning, I bury my hand in his hair, pinning his mouth with my pussy, before riding the erotic surge cresting through me.

Giovanni knows how to give head. In seconds, the signs of climax re-cluster in my core. I sink into the plush grass, eyes glazing over, and writhe when he hits my clit with back-to-back rapid-fire licks.

When he takes my clit into his mouth, I ride the tsunami for all it's worth. I shudder and shake as a charge of electricity spasms in my womb.

"Gio…" His entire name is too much for me to get out. Sparks are darting, and it's taking all my willpower not to scream his brilliance into the evening air.

I'm spread-eagled and practically naked in a field. Now is not the time for a guard to rush in and save me.

I've scarcely come down from the clouds when Giovanni pushes two fingers inside me. He's hovering over me, powerful and in control, and it's the sexiest thing I've ever seen.

Only one thing could top it.

"Take your shirt off."

His eyes shoot to me, heavy with outrage. I hardly know Giovanni, but I am confident he's used to giving the orders. He's never taken them.

"Please…" I murmur, not above begging. I'm dying to feel the heat of his skin under my hand, and to drink in his rippling abs and tattooed pecs—desperate enough to plead.

"How can I deny when you ask like that?"

With his fingers still pumping in and out of me, Giovanni pulls his shirt over his head by the collar with his spare hand, unconcerned that he pops several buttons on the pricey garment.

"Now your undershirt."

There's no hostility in his tone when he replies with a smirk, "Has anyone ever told you that you're quite bossy, Ms. Raimondi?"

In the blink of an eye, he freezes. It's a fight not to whimper. Even though I've already climaxed, my wonderful night with Giovanni only twenty-four hours ago taught me that I'm more than a one-and-done girl. Multiples are *very* much anticipated.

"Valeria was the one who joked about them getting your files confused, wasn't she?" Even though he's asking a question, I don't reply. Realization flickers in his eyes. He knows the truth. He just needed to crawl out of the rubble the clinic threw on us before he could see it. "She lied," he murmurs to himself. "She lied to *me*."

I nod, the relief bittersweet. The damage has already been done. I've been drugged, accused, and dragged into a nightmare I never asked for. But even as Giovanni's anger shifts away from me, I can't shake the unease that settles deep in my bones.

Even if I'm exonerated, will I ever truly be free? And do I want to be?

GIOVANNI

Every instinct in me screams to confront Valeria right now, to demand the truth and make her pay for the lie that nearly tore me apart. The urge is as primal as a storm after a humid day.

Her face when she realizes I know the truth and that her game is over will be worth the delay. But this... this urge is more potent.

Valentina writhing beneath me, her face flushed with ecstasy and her scent permeating above the smell of recently squashed lemons, trumps everything. My obsession with her is a living thing. It's fierce and unrelenting, bordering on madness.

Even if she had accepted the bribe I offered to test her loyalty, I couldn't walk away if I tried.

So, for now, Valeria must wait. She lost this battle. There are no misgivings about that, but for the next hour, she can cling to the shred of hope that my intuition isn't right. That Valentina won't be the mother of my children.

I know differently, so there's no need to panic.

I merely need to relish.

A quiet growl rumbles in my rib cage when I only need to trek my thumb over Valentina's clit for the briefest second for her expression to shift from anarchy to pleasure. Her clutch on the grass firms when I press my thumb on the nervy bud before I lower my mouth back to her pussy. My tongue goes straight for her clit, and every ounce of blood in me rushes to my dick.

She tastes heavenly, so without concern for the dozen guards who protect our compound, I feast on her pussy as if starved of taste.

My brothers have chased women through these orchards more times than I can count. Matteo and Nico will never admit it, but I'm reasonably sure they've chased the same woman at the same time.

I used to laugh while telling them I had better things to do than play hide-and-seek in the dark.

I was a fool.

Chasing Valentina tonight... *Dio.* I've never felt more alive. The rush. The anticipation. I finally get it, and I can't wait to do it again.

With Valentina.

It will only *ever* be with Valentina.

I lick and suck her clit while my fingers move in and out of her. She throws her head back and moans as I eat her like the delicious dessert she is.

"So fucking wet." My words pulsate against her clit. "I love how you taste." I drag in a long breath through my nose before releasing it with a growl. "And how you smell."

Her moan when I suck her clit into my mouth before swirling it with my tongue sends a sizzling sensation down my spine before it clusters in my balls. My body is alive with pleasure, and Valentina hasn't even touched me yet. That's how much I enjoy pleasing her.

Her pleasure is mine.

"So. Fucking. Tasty," I murmur between licks.

My cock throbs with need when I stuff my tongue deep inside her, curling it around my fingers. Her arousal coats my palm. I'll smell her for days after our romp because there's no fucking chance in hell I'll scrub her scent from any region of my body.

As my tongue returns to her clit, my fingers still pumping in her with surprising gentleness, I run my spare hand up her stomach and marvel at the softness. I love how silky her skin feels under my hand, and the squishy comfort a healthy appetite instigates.

"I love your tits and your stomach and how your thighs can withstand hours of fucking."

When I pinch her nipple, I admire the red hue that spreads across her breasts before I suck in her scent. My obsession grows tenfold with each inhale. Her taste and smells sink so deep I feel them in my balls.

"I need you to come again, *dolcezza*. Because I'm dying to be inside you, to feel you quivering beneath me as you beg for my cum."

Molten heat spreads through me when a throaty garble leaves Valentina's mouth half a second before her back arches and her eyes roll to the back of her head.

I grip her fantastic ass and pull her pussy firmer against my mouth, not wanting to miss a drop.

As she shakes through a brutal orgasm, I grind myself against the ground. I'm so hard it hurts, and my dick is leaking pre-cum.

"One more," I demand when she slowly emerges from the clouds of climax, her expression exhausted.

Sweaty locks cling to her cheeks when she shakes her head. I don't pay any attention to her silent pledge for lenience. She's got another orgasm or two in her, and I'm more than willing to spend hours proving that to her.

It'll be my pleasure.

I nuzzle her pussy, soaking up her scent, before I test how close she is to taking me again by switching from two fingers to three.

Pain fetters her face for half a second before it's replaced with need.

As she meets the thrusts of my fingers pump for pump, lust burns through her impressive eyes.

"Good girl," I praise, loving her trust while endeavoring to give her the same.

It's exhausting forever being on alert, constantly wondering about people's objectives and motives. Sadly, sex rarely escapes the chaos. But right here, right now, I don't feel like I'm putting on a show. I'm not searching her eyes for any signs of deceit or strategies. I'm watching in fascination, mesmerized by the change in intensity and rawness when she's about to come.

Like now. Her pupils dilate before the muscles in her eyes lose tension and naturally roll back.

Fuck. Her face in ecstasy is enough to make any man come.

My cock throbs with so much need it looks angry when I pull it out of its tight constraints, too impatient to wait a moment longer.

The tension is stifling, and I can hardly breathe.

Valentina and I exchange a look when I curl her legs around my waist and guide my cock toward the entrance of her pussy. It isn't filled with suspicion or anger. It's derived from nothing but mutual obsession.

A growl rumbles deep in my chest when I enter her bare for the fifth time in less than twenty-four hours.

Valentina's lips part when I sink in deep, and then bliss filters across her face.

"Christ..." Satisfaction runs hot through my blood from the sheer awe on her beautiful face. She's never been taken like this before. So deep and full.

I wait for her to acclimate to the intrusion before I dig my feet into the ground and use their grip to my advantage to pump into her again and again.

In minutes, Valetina's eyes darken to match the sky above our heads, and a pink hue spreads across her cheeks. She's close to coming again and squeezing my dick of its cum, but I pretend not to notice since we're no longer alone.

17

———

VALENTINA

As sparks of an orgasm ignite, my lips tingle and my heart thunders in my chest. I'm trapped in a vortex where nothing exists but Giovanni's hands in my hair and the soft, hungry press of his mouth on mine as he screws me senseless.

Then an unsettled and deliberate cough slices through the night.

I freeze in horror as Giovanni's body tenses against mine. He whirls, instantly on guard, and his cheeks burn with fury.

"Who the hell—?" Giovanni's voice is a possessive Sicilian thunder, but his words fall short when his squinted gaze lands on the person approaching us.

Awareness dawns on his face when a man with polished dress shoes and an immaculately tailored suit clears the shadows of the lemon grove.

Even though he covers his eyes with one hand and turns his body away from us with exaggerated modesty, I still want to disappear. I press my back against the rain-sodden ground and silently pray to melt into the blades of manicured grass.

Sensing my unease, Giovanni's stance shifts. With his body

alone, he protectively shields me from further embarrassment while telling our interrupter to leave.

"I'd rather stay," the man says, amusement curling through his words.

Clearly, he has a death wish. Giovanni's anger is evident, yet it doesn't diminish the impressive size of his penis. It's still pulsating inside me, and it steals my embarrassment as easily as it does my morals.

"We need to talk."

"Now?" Giovanni's reply conveys an edge of authority. It isn't the same commanding tone he used while speaking with Dr. Di Petro. He addresses this man as if he is just as high up the food chain. As if he is his equal. I learn why when he adds, "I know it's been a while for you, Brother, but I'm kind of in the middle of something."

The brother's deep laughter drowns out the husky chuckles of three other men concealed in the darkness. "Yes, Vanni, now. It's important."

Giovanni's growl brings to mind the compromising position we were caught in, but the only thing that deflates my excitement when he slowly withdraws is disappointment.

The determination on his face when he entered me signaled that our exchange would be an all-night affair. Now, he dresses me as hurriedly as he'd removed his cock from his pants.

Once my clothes are on and straight, Giovanni's hands gentle despite the tension still hardening his features, he assists me to my feet.

Upon hearing the shuffle of my unsteady feet, the stranger drops his hand and twists to face us. In seconds, I notice multiple Caruso resemblances. Giovanni's brother shares his determined jaw, dark hair, and relaxed self-assurance. And don't get me started on his natural arrogance. He's not at all bothered that he interrupted us. If anything, he looks pleased.

"Is this what you're doing with your nights now, Vanni? Playing hide-and-seek in the orchard?" While shaking his head, he laughs, his eyes sparkling with playfulness. "You always said you were too busy for games. Looks like you finally found a reason to play."

Giovanni scowls and his jaw is rigid. "Not now, Dante."

Although Giovanni's tone is a distinct warning, Dante's grin only intensifies. He's clearly enjoying himself. "Don't worry, I won't tell the others you've gone soft. Or maybe I will. Depends on how much you're willing to pay to keep me quiet."

"And me," pipes up a voice from behind, before another two comparable requests follow it.

I can't help the strangled laugh that escapes me. I'm a mess of nerves, but I am also amused. I've never had siblings to bicker with. Being an only child is the only part of my childhood I wish I could change.

Giovanni shoots me a look, but there's a softness in his eyes, too. He's grateful my laughter demolished the barrier between us.

His relief doesn't linger long. Dante's expression morphs when he looks at me, and humor fades from his face. A subtle gleam in his eyes reveals he has more walls to knock down than Giovanni.

He studies me as if he's searching for proof that I'm an opportunist. His caution is understandable. Not only are the Caruso brothers drool-worthy gorgeous but they're also obviously wealthy. Dante's watch could cover my property tax arrears and several decades in advance.

As I start to tell Dante that greed will never motivate me, he hooks his thumb toward the main house. "Come on. The old man's out of bed. You'll want to see this."

With Giovanni's hand warm and steady on my back, I walk through the orchard this time instead of running. The sight of three men snickering as we turn toward the main house sends a shiver of embarrassment up my spine. The Caruso brothers, though different, share distinguishable genetic qualities.

Out of all the people to catch us, why did it have to be Giovanni's family?

The mansion looks straight out of a fictional fairy tale. It's alive with light and laughter. Giovanni's father is in the courtyard, surrounded by a handful of well-wishers. Even though his body is frail and weak, he is full of energy as he converses with his guests.

He looks *nothing* like the dying man I imagined.

I avert my eyes from a man I'd guess to be mid to late fifties when Giovanni brushes his lips against my sweaty temple. "I'll be back in a minute." He breathes in deeply, as if obsessed with our intermingled scents. "There are drinks by the entryway, and waitstaff will serve hors d'oeuvres shortly. Make yourself at home. My casa is your casa, Valentina, and you're welcome to anything your heart desires."

His wish to make me comfortable in his domain has me desperate to reacquaint our lips. I hold back the urge—barely. His brothers are waiting for him near the large outdoor space, and Dante's foot is tapping with impatience.

Giovanni waits for me to nod before he joins his brothers for an impromptu Caruso family meeting. Things seem tense between them, but nothing can detract my focus from the patriarch of the Caruso dynasty.

Giovanni's father's lively interaction with his guests makes me hope my mother will one day be as animated. He seems happy and content, as if nothing can bring him down.

I'm not the only one noticing his spiritedness.

Even with all his brothers speaking to him at once, Giovanni's eyes rarely drift from me. On the odd occasion they do, it is to take in his father.

Several long minutes later, the patriarch's gaze settles on me. His watch is curious and direct. "And who's this fine young lady?" His accent is thick, and contradictory to his age, it brims with natural flirtatiousness.

Now I know who Giovanni inherited his charm from.

"Hi. I'm Valentina R—"

Out of nowhere, Valeria appears at his side. Her smile is bright when directed at Giovanni's father, but the instant it lands on me, it turns brittle. "This is the surrogate I was telling you about, Papa." Her tone is light-hearted, but her eyes are cold.

Giovanni's father raises a solid brow. "Surrogate?"

Valeria loops her arm through his and steers him away from me before launching into an explanation of surrogacy, as if that is all I am to his son. A vessel of conception. "A surrogate is a woman who carries a baby for someone else. It's all very modern..."

Humiliation flushes my face as the odds of a stomach ulcer intensify.

Giovanni knows I didn't deliberately set out to deceive him, but that's only the beginning of the issues we still need to work through.

It wouldn't be an issue if I didn't immediately lose focus the instant he dragged his thumb over my nipple.

Too angry to remain around over two dozen people, I seek the closest exit.

Giovanni isn't the sole recipient of my anger. I'm more mad at myself than him.

I barely get two steps away when Giovanni foils my attempt to get some air by snatching up my arm. Violently, I yank away from him, and the pop my arm makes draws a crowd of curious onlookers.

"Not now, Valentina." Giovanni's voice is as cold as ice. "I can't chase you right now."

My anger is already at a pinnacle, but it escalates into uncharted territory when he turns to face a nearby maid and orders her to take me to my room.

Her head barely reaches my chin, and she's so tiny a breeze could carry her away. She's no competition for me, and I'll make sure she knows that the moment we're alone.

"Make sure she gets there safely."

This time, Giovanni's barked command isn't for a five-foot-five maid with cutesy curls. It's for one of the men lurking in the shadows earlier. The biggest and baddest looking of the four interrupters we faced only twenty minutes ago.

His beard is the same cropped style as Dante's, but he has sleeves of tattoos, and a menacing glint lightens his murky baby blues.

I glance at Giovanni, hopeful eye contact will force him to see sense through the madness. All I hit is a brick wall. He works his jaw side to side while loosening the cuffs on his jacket as if he's preparing for battle. His anger is no longer simmering beneath the surface like mine. It's about to boil over.

Still, I step forward as desperation rises from my stomach to my throat. "Can I please talk to—"

He doesn't register my words. He's already pursuing Valeria and his father, who are retreating inside.

After how intimate we were only minutes ago, his rejection stings worse than a thousand bees, and it lodges a hard lump in my throat.

I startle when the maid gently touches my arm. She wordlessly apologizes before gesturing to the entrance Giovanni just stormed through. "This way, *signorina*."

I shake my head. I can't breathe, so how can I be expected to walk? The walls close in on me as secrets and over-the-top expectations make the room feel claustrophobic.

I need air so badly I'm willing to undertake a second marathon.

"Really?" a voice shouts from behind as I reach the foot of the grand staircase that leads to the gardens. It's dry, unmistakably brutish, and belongs to the man Giovanni placed in charge of my watch.

I run as fast as the wind, but Giovanni's brother is faster. I don't even reach the edge of the manicured lawn before a hand clamps around my wrist and I'm yanked back.

"Let go!" I shout, twisting hard.

With my mind on the fritz, I slap him across the face without considering the consequences of my actions. I wince when the contact sets my palm on fire. Giovanni's brother only growls. It vibrates through my bones but does absolutely nothing to my insides, proving I'm ruled by my libido only when it comes to Giovanni.

The dark-haired brute steals any further protest by hauling me off my feet and tossing me onto his shoulder. I kick and squirm, but his grip is ironclad. I don't gain an inch.

"You know this is illegal, right? You can't hold someone against their will. It's against the law."

He snorts. "Says you. You know, you're lucky you slapped me and not one of the guards. They would have called Giovanni. Trust me, you don't want that."

"Why? Because he might have something to say about his baboon brother manhandling me?"

His laugh is the loudest I've heard to date. "If you think this is me manhandling you, *sweetheart,* you're not close to getting an invitation into Matteo's bed."

"Who?"

He slaps my backside, popping my eyes from their sockets. "Matteo. Pleasure to meet you, Valentina." As he enters the Caruso mansion with me dangling off his shoulder, he continues. "You've caused quite the ruckus in the Caruso realm. Haven't heard so much speculation since Dante's baby mama showed up at his door, carrying his child in her arms instead of in her gut."

I'm lost for a reply, so I stick with insults. "Has anyone ever told you only narcissists speak about themselves in third person?"

His miffed *Ha!* rumbles through my core. "Sounds about right."

With my shock too high to continue with our spar, Matteo follows the maid through a maze of hallways and grand living rooms with marble floors and gilded mirrors in silence.

Even with all the blood in my body rushing to my head, I catch glimpses of opulent chandeliers, velvet sofas, and distant sounds of laughter.

Huh?

Humiliation burns my face when the reason for the boisterous chuckles enters my head, but beneath it is a reminder that I'm not invisible here.

It just seems the Caruso brothers have yet to learn that.

Matteo finally stops outside a heavy wooden door. He sets me down, not ungently but not gently, either, before he fixes my feet in place with a stern look. I'd give more of a fight if I weren't exhausted. Multiple orgasms are draining, so I won't mention the toll of an emotionally draining day.

When the maid slots a key into the lock, Matteo's wolf whistle is as arrogant as his words. "The presidential suite. You must give good head."

I shoot him a dirty look while rubbing my wrists as if I'm injured. I'm not. I just want him to sweat.

Matteo acts nonchalant, but I see the way his eyes dilate when the thought of me being hurt pops into his head.

After opening the door wide enough for his gigantic shoulders to fit through, Matteo gestures for me to enter first. I'm hesitant, but Giovanni exhausted the last of my energy in the orchard.

Furthermore, it's late. Carlisle is safer than Los Angeles, but I still don't want to wander its streets at this time of night.

I'll take the evening to regather my bearings. Then, first thing tomorrow, I'm out of here.

I'm such a liar. The desire to confront Giovanni isn't the only reason I'm digging in my heels. I've always been curious to see how the other half live.

Upon entering my room, I'm momentarily taken aback by its sheer extravagance. The room is vast, easily twice the size of my apartment back in Los Angeles. Dark, polished walnut panels cover the walls, and their surfaces reflect the soft golden light from a crystal chandelier.

The ceiling is high and adorned with intricate swirls and medallions that catch the rainbow hues of the chandelier, and a heavy mahogany desk dominates the space. Its surface is so glossy I can see my reflection in it.

Behind it, mahogany bookshelves stretch from the floor to the ceiling. They're filled with leather-bound books and the occasional marble book bust. The rug beneath my feet is so thick and plush, it muffles my footsteps.

A pair of wingback chairs is arranged before a fireplace that looks like it's never seen a speck of dust. On the mantel, a gilded clock ticks quietly, and vases overflowing with fresh lilies flank it. The windows are tall and draped with velvet curtains the color of midnight.

It's a beautiful room, but in a cold, intimidating way. This room was designed to impress, not to be cozy. The biggest telltale? There's no bed or anything remotely domestic. It's more the private office of a king than a place for someone to rest.

I turn to face Matteo, who's milling by the door. "Is this the right room? I was told I'd be next to Giovanni, but I don't see a bed."

A sly smile plays at his lips. "This is the only room next to Giovanni's."

"Then where's the bed?"

He nods toward a discreet door set in the paneling. "It's in there."

I march to the doors and throw them open. My heart launches into my throat when I take in the oversized bed in another male-dominated space.

"Our rooms are interconnecting."

I'm summarizing, but Matteo doesn't know that. "Uh-huh."

"And there's only one bed."

He makes another agreeing gesture, and the implication behind it makes my blood boil.

I'm to share Giovanni's space but only be known to his father as his surrogate.

Anger surfaces when my heart reaches the same conclusion as my head.

I'm nothing but a gimmick to this family.

With her hands folded neatly in front of herself, the maid appears. "Would you like anything, *signorina*? Tea? A blanket?"

I shake my head before forcing a polite smile. "No, thank you." I don't need anything because I won't be here long. The instant I'm alone, I'll be in the quickest transport home. I'd rather risk the streets of Carlisle at night than be treated like an object.

Matteo seems more adapt at reading minds than knowing when someone needs space. "It's for your privacy as well as Giovanni's. The family doesn't need to know every detail of his personal life."

I fold my arms over my chest to hide the shake of my hands. "Privacy or secrecy?"

He doesn't answer me. He just glances at the interconnecting door again. "If you need anything, ask."

He loiters for a moment, then finally leaves.

As soon as the door clicks shut, I test the handle. It's locked, so I try the windows next.

Each one is sealed shut as if they anticipated I'd attempt an escape. What other reason would they have to lock the windows?

Even desperate, I wouldn't risk death by scaling down from this height.

As I stand amid the opulence, I feel more trapped than ever. The grandeur is suffocating, and the secrecy shrouding it makes my skin crawl.

I need to get out of here.

I just have to survive tonight first.

18

———

GIOVANNI

The loud slam of the door behind me bounces off the walls of my family's estate. My blood is still sizzling from my confrontation with Valeria. It lasted too long and tested every ounce of my patience. I stood my ground, though. I told her unequivocally that she either pulls into line or removes herself from the lineup entirely. I'm tired of her deception and manipulation. Compromise is no longer an option. What she damaged cannot be fixed, and frankly, I don't want to fix it.

Her sniveling defense replays in my mind as I stride through the halls with my fists clenched at my sides. I loathe that no amount of wishful thinking will allow me to resolve this dilemma with my gun. But more than anything, I hate that she tried to use my brother's loyalties against me.

She wove her story so tightly around Valentina that even Dante started to doubt her.

I smelled the controversy on his skin when he reminded me how the "Surprise! You're a father!" ruse knocked him on his ass. But this is different. Valentina isn't Anna. She wouldn't play me like that.

I get he wants to caution me about not making the same mistake, but it's too late for that. I'm already in too deep. I'm obsessed with Valentina—snowed under by a force too great for mankind to budge. It's savage. The hunger I have for her won't let me rest, and the need grew tenfold after having her beneath me.

Leaving Valentina to settle into my room alone was the last thing I wanted to do. It felt like I was abandoning her to the wolves. But I couldn't risk Valeria getting to my father first and feeding him the same lies she told my brothers.

She's painting Valentina as the villain, and until I told my brother with utmost certainty that I won't tolerate a bad word spoken about Valentina, everyone had believed her lies.

Stories root fast in this family, and it's virtually impossible to dig them out once they're planted, but I gave it my best shot. I've spent hours adjusting Valentina's ledger from bad to good, and for months, I'll have no clue if it's paid off.

When I reach my suite, I find the door locked. My initial annoyance fades when I realize Valentina most likely locked it for privacy. After slipping a key out of my pocket, I quietly unlock the door and enter my room. The space is dimly lit, and the scent of Valentina's perfume tinges the air.

My heart strums my ribs when I find Valentina curled up in a wingback chair near the fireplace. Her knees are tucked under her chin, and her cheek is resting on her open hand.

This could be my cockiness speaking, but it's as if she didn't want to sleep in my bed without me.

The thought turns my cock to stone.

I cross the room in three lengthy strides. When I lift her gently, careful not to wake her, she murmurs my name but doesn't wake.

I carry her to the bed, bombarded with previously unventured emotions. I'm relieved that she's here, in my space, and not lost to

Valeria's schemes. But I also feel guilty for letting family politics take precedence over her comfort.

Additionally, there's that fierce, possessive longing that borders on obsessive.

I want her close, always, and for her to know she's *mine*.

After laying her down, I remove her shoes and tuck her in, unconcerned that she hasn't showered. I love that she still smells like me. It's a selfish comfort that reminds me our connection is unique and unbreakable.

As I brush a stray lock of hair from Valentina's cheek, she sighs and sinks further into the pillow. Without shame, I watch her so closely that I can count the thuds of her pulse in her neck. I'm captivated by how peaceful she looks in my realm. It's as if she knows I'll keep her safe. This feeling isn't new to me, but it's usually reserved for my brothers and our father.

I've spent years building walls so I can keep everyone at arm's length, but with Valentina, those defenses crumble. I'll be the man she can rely on and the one who never lets her down, because I'd rather take an axe to my cock than disappoint her.

After a prolonged stalk, I lock the entry doors of my room and office with the master key, then enter the bathroom. I'm reluctant to wash Valentina's scent off my skin, but if I don't ease the throbbing in my balls, I'll take her in her sleep.

Since I'm meant to be showing her a new side of me, not displaying the tendencies of a rapist with no morals, a quick self-release in the shower will have to do.

I strip fast before letting the hot water take care of some of the tension in my shoulders. It does little to ease the ache in my cock, so before I've even loaded my hand up with suds, I curl it around my shaft and give it a handful of tugs.

As I stroke my cock in rhythm to my frantic pulse, I picture Valentina's dark locks sprawled against the earthy green ground, and her face glowing with ecstasy. I stroke myself harder as I remember how her pussy was on display for everyone to see, yet I experienced no worry about her being exposed.

The guards aren't brave enough to look in the Carusos's direction in general, but when we enter the orchards, they turn a blind eye to everything. Drugs. Guns. The woman who's taken me back to my youth, where it's essential to come three times a day to function anywhere close to normal.

With my eyes closed, I do everything not to come on the fucking spot.

That's what Valentina's sultry curves and beautiful face do to me. I could come just recalling the charge that zapped through me when she spun my way for the first time.

I stroke my cock faster.

It feels good, though it has nothing on how it felt when Valentina wrapped her lips around the crown and sucked down, or the way her pussy pulsated both in pain and euphoria when I pushed in a little impatiently.

Sweat breaks across my forehead as I recall the sucks of her pussy when I rode her bare. They're similar to the greedy sucks of her mouth when she gave me the best blow job of my life.

My skin is on fire now, and my lungs saw in and out, desperate for air. I stroke my cock cruelly while flaring my nostrils, hopeful to catch a portion of Valentina's seductive scent in the air.

I need only the quickest whiff and this show will be over before it's truly started.

When I flatten my hand to the tiles above my head, needing something to stabilize my sways, my cock rages. I can smell Valentina's arousal on my hand. It's sweet and a little musky, a perfectly enticing palette for an obsessed man.

After lifting my hand to my nose, I work my cock faster. I pump it in and out of my fist on repeat, squeezing the base with every stroke.

My release builds when I picture Valentina on her knees and peering up at me as I stuff my cock deep inside her mouth.

Dipping my knees, I rock my hips back and forth. My grunts are unlike anything I've ever heard when the tension bundled in my balls spills over my fist.

My cock jerks as streams of cum erupt from the crown. It coats the tiled wall in front of me and drips off my engorged knob.

My release is rapid and powerful but unsatisfying.

It isn't enough.

Confident I know why, I rinse my cum down the drain, step out of the shower, and then sling a towel around my waist. When I return to the bedroom, my eyes lock on my target with military precision. Then a knock sounds at the door.

I grit my teeth before cursing karma to hell. It knew my intentions were bad and stepped in before I could make a mistake.

Considering the hour, I expect trouble, so I dress in a pair of jeans and a shirt before answering the door. Dante is on the other side, dangling Valentina's backpack off his index finger. Somehow, he looks older than he did this morning.

Still pissed he trusted the word of a woman like Valeria over my intuition, which has contributed greatly to our family's mammoth wealth, I snatch Valentina's bag out of his grasp.

While baring teeth, I attempt to slam the door in his face. Dante shoves his foot in the way, foiling my wordless request for him to fuck off.

I almost tell him with my fists until he confesses, "I shouldn't have taken what happened to me out on anyone else." He lifts his head, but his eyes don't quite meet mine. "I let Valeria twist things, and I doubted you. *Both* of you."

When he attempts to peer past my shoulder, I block his view with my body.

He doesn't get to apologize to Valentina until I say so.

"Sorry doesn't fix anything. It doesn't undo the way you looked at her in the orchard and how you treated her as if she were lesser than you."

He looks me in the eye, his gaze steady for once. "No, it doesn't. But I'm trying, Vanni. That has to count for something." I scoff, but he acts as if I didn't react at all. "I know what it's like to have your life turned upside down by a lie—"

"Then you should have known better than anyone not to jump to conclusions." *Especially when those conclusions have you so concerned you interrupt the best sex I've ever had.*

Dante nods without hesitation as remorse sparks in his lowered gaze. "I know. You're right. I'll talk to the others and set the record straight."

As I return his stare, I look for signs of the man who once had my back no matter what. He's there. He's just swamped with too many secrets to fully break free. The past couple of months have been hard on him, and I've not been as supportive as I should have been the past six weeks, because I've had other matters on my mind.

By matters, I mean locating Valentina.

The remembrance sees me offering rare leniency. "See that you do."

I curse under my breath when those four simple words have him believing he's off the hook. With a grin I've not seen him wear in weeks, he steps into my room, wraps his arms around my shoulders, and draws me into his chest as if I'm his younger brother.

"Get the fuck off me," I growl into his ear when he takes a long sniff of my hair.

I smell like cum, and normally I wouldn't care, but because Valentina's juices are part of the scent, I do today.

I itch to beat into him for more than a perverted mind when he heads down the hallway while saying, "Charge her phone. Her battery's flatter than Valeria's tits the first time she pranced around you in a bikini."

He says his suggestion as if it's a peace offering, but I know what it really means.

He's a snooping piece of shit.

Valentina stored her phone in a secret compartment in her backpack. He wouldn't know that unless he riffled through her belongings like I did when Dr. Di Petro checked her vitals after Valeria drugged her.

"Just looking out for you like you always do us, Vanni," Dante says from the safety of the stairwell.

He's smarter than he looks.

I may have pushed him over the landing if he were still in front of me.

After slamming my door shut, giving it extra oomph for leverage, I plug Valentina's phone into a charger on the bedside table. A photo featuring Valentina and a woman, presumably her mother, brightens the screen. She looks a lot like Valentina, but twenty years older.

She's beautiful, but her kind eyes expose her exhaustion. The dark rings circling her eyes remind me of what Valentina said at the clinic. She was there because she wanted to help her mother.

And that's when it hits. I can't rest yet. Injustices still need to be corrected.

Plans flood my head as I put on my socks and shoes. While most revolve around Valentina, a few are for my own benefit. I won't let someone like Valeria Giuffrida write my story, and I also won't let her depict Valentina as the antagonist in it.

When I step into the hallway outside my room, the resolve in my chest burns brightly. Tonight, I'll set things straight, and I won't even need my gun. Yet.

19

VALENTINA

The heavy feel of an expensive comforter on my legs jolts me awake. I am briefly disoriented by the paneled walls and expansive space. Then, slowly, the other penny drops.

I'm in Giovanni's room.

Traces of his aftershave mist the air, and let's not forget his aura that depletes even the largest space of oxygen. I remember now, but one question remains. Why am I waking in his bed? I drifted off in the armchair with my arms folded and my brows narrowed. I was determined not to get comfortable in his space, but now I'm under the covers, snuggling in as if accustomed to high-thread-count sheets.

I sit up too quickly, and my heart launches into my throat. It sinks several feet when I scan the room. Giovanni isn't here. I don't think he came back last night. The bedding on his side is untouched and cold.

The negativity I've been unsuccessfully dodging the past six months conjures up many theories. None of them are good.

What was so urgent that he needed to stay out all night? And worse... who was he with?

When only one name ripples in the crisp morning air, my back molars smash together. I shouldn't care if Giovanni spent the night with Valeria, but I do. The thought of him out all night with her turns my veins to ash.

Why bring me to his room, then vanish for hours on end? It doesn't make any sense.

Eager to wash his aftershave from my skin and perhaps drain my screams with a gallon of water, I slip out of bed. Partway to the bathroom, I notice my backpack on a dresser by the windows. I frown. That wasn't there last night. I searched for it, convinced Giovanni's staff would have delivered my belongings to my room. Yet here it is, within view, as if it were put there for me to notice.

I'm about to grab it when a familiar ping breaks through the blood rushing in my ears. I crank my head back to the bed so fast my neck muscles protest. They won't be the only things requiring assessment when I get out of here. I'll need to get my hearing checked as well. That's how loudly my heart rages when I spot my phone on the bedside table.

It's lit up with the alarm I set to remind myself to give my mom her tablets, and it prickles my skin with guilt. I set reminders to prevent my aunt from adding more responsibilities to her already overflowing task list.

After crossing the room in three quick breaths, I unlock my phone and tap out a message to my aunt.

ME:

Can you please give Mom her meds?

When I press send, nothing happens. I don't have enough signal to send a text.

As I walk around the room, I raise my phone to the ceiling, trying to get a signal.

Frustration bubbles inside me when I don't get a single bar. I need to get word to my aunt, but I'm trapped in a dead zone.

I shoot my eyes to the main door, anxious enough to consider ramming the wood until someone comes to check if I'm alive, and that's when I see it. A key is in the lock, glinting in the morning light.

Suddenly, the room transforms into a sanctuary instead of a cage, yet my jealousy remains undeterred. I slip the battery out of my phone, snatch up my backpack, and then tug on my shoes like armed guards are sluggish during daylight hours.

Stealthily, I approach the door and press my ear to it. The only noise is the faint tick of an antique clock somewhere down the hall.

Carefully, I turn the key, flinching at its faint click, then slowly open the door. The hallway is dark because thick curtains obscure the morning sun. Hugging the wall, I move quickly past closed doors that announce most of the household is still asleep.

I halt at the bottom of the grand staircase upon hearing the distant clatter of crockery. A maid's voice trills through the swinging doors near a large dining table, followed by a butler's low reply. I don't catch all their words, but what I hear gets my feet moving. They're preparing breakfast, which will be served in ten minutes.

Holding my breath, I dart across the marble floor of the dining room. Cool air slaps my cheeks as I slip through a side door. I arrive at the lemon grove before I know it, and for some stupid reason, the citrusy tinge in the air is more comforting than confronting.

After reaching the clearing I wrestled with Giovanni in last night, I quickly gather my bearings. I could keep running, but the dimming glimmer of Carlisle's lights last night when I stared out the window, plotting my freedom, confirmed a walk to town isn't feasible.

My ears perk up when the distinct grind of an engine starting breaks through the quiet. I hide behind lemon trees as I advance toward the sound. A truck is being loaded at the end of the orchard. The back is filled with crates of lemons.

A stocky man wearing a cap is speaking with a worker who is loading the shipment. "The dock, yeah?"

"Yeah," the worker answers. "Boss's orders." After signing the delivery slip on the clipboard, he hands it to the driver. "Make sure you give this to the exporter."

My curiosity piques. Can you still make money exporting lemons? I thought that trade went extinct when World War II ended. Lemons were highly sought-after during the war era because of their high vitamin C content, which was crucial for preventing and treating scurvy.

If my eighth-grade history teacher could hear me now, he'd be proud. I halt gloating about the information I obtained from school when the driver slams the truck's loading doors closed. Mercifully, he doesn't lock them before he heads to the cab, still grumbling.

When the workers head for the warehouse after waving the driver off, I race for the truck.

I've only just slipped into the cargo area when the driver flattens his foot to the gas pedal. I brace myself between two crates when his reckless speed reminds me of the truck that nearly mowed me down weeks ago.

My choice of transport is less than ideal, but its destination is perfect. My aunt works at the docks, and since she's on her feet all day, she chose an apartment only a thirty-minute walk away.

As the truck winds down a twisty road, I press my forehead to the cold metal of the crate and try to control the panic flaring in my chest. Although I'm free, I feel more disappointed than relieved. The last seventy-eight hours were hair-raising, but they felt more fulfilling than the previous three years combined. There's something addictive about living life in the fast lane.

Several miles later, the truck jolts to a stop. The air in the dock's main distribution warehouse is stale and tinged with danger. Footsteps surrounding the cab of the truck signal it isn't safe to slip out yet, so I sink deeper between the two crates.

Shortly after, the truck's rear doors bang open and sunlight streams in. I squint to protect my eyes before peering through the gap between the crates. While complaining about the mechanical lift being broken, the driver thrusts the clipboard with the delivery slip at a man on his right, then gestures for him to enter the truck.

The stranger isn't what I expected when picturing a lemon exporter. If he's a citrus lover, I'll eat my hat. He looks as dangerous as Giovanni—if not more so. His accent is a blend of Russian and American, though it is his appearance that truly catches my attention. Sleeves of tattoos snake up his muscular arms and neck, and his face is devilishly handsome.

If I had to guess his age, I'd say he's in his early thirties.

He doesn't greet the driver with a smile, nor does he accept the clipboard. Instead, he roots him in place with a steely look that matches the iciness of his eyes.

"You're late." His voice is low and commanding. "I don't like people being late. It wastes time I could have spent with my head buried between my wife's legs." The driver mumbles something about traffic, but the exporter isn't having it. "I value my time with my *ahren* more than your excuses, so let's cut to the chase."

Ahren? What's an ahren?

I stay perfectly still when he tells the driver the consequences he'll face if he's ever late again, before he enters the truck to give the crates a cursory glance.

He isn't here for the lemons. I'm sure of it. He barely glances at the fruit. It is as if they're a cover for something far more sinister.

As his gaze sweeps over the crates at the back, his eyes land on me. My heart stops. I'm confident he saw me wedged awkwardly between crates of his merchandise, but he doesn't utter a word. Instead, he retrieves his phone from his pocket and thumbs the screen.

With my heart in my throat, I watch him read something off his phone. A lazy smirk curls on his lips only a second before he twists to face the driver.

I'm certain he'll tell him he has a stowaway, so you can imagine my surprise when he says, "I don't care if you have to push these crates onto the ship yourself. I want them offloaded and in transport within the hour. Understood?"

The loose skin on the driver's neck wobbles when he nods in agreement.

"But before that, I need a local's perspective on the best restaurant for my *ahren* to experience a true Sicilian feast..." The exporter's words trail off when he walks toward the office of the docks with the driver following him like a lost puppy.

A mix of relief and confusion fills me.

Why didn't he say anything?

Is he letting me go, or is there something else at play?

I'm truly lost.

Although I want to look deeper into his decision, with the driver preoccupied with playing tourist guide, now could be my only chance to escape.

After exiting the truck, I join the throng of workers covered with the grime of a long shift. The nightshift workers are clocking out for the day. My escape couldn't have been better orchestrated.

As I approach the exit, I cast a final glance at the exporter. Although he acts as if he doesn't notice me, his upturned lips betray him.

He's trouble. I can feel it. But I'm not sticking around to find out what kind.

My legs feel as heavy as bricks, and they make the walk from the docks to my aunt's place seem unusually long. They're not weighed down because I'm unfit. This is the result of how I use my muscles during back-to-back orgasms.

Sweat beads on my nape when I finally reach my aunt's front door, but the exertion of climbing five levels isn't the cause. It's from reliving every second in the lemon grove last night. It was blissfully serene.

The door creaks shut behind me when I let myself in, but the silence in the living room makes butterflies take flight in my stomach. I dump my bag by the door and call out for Mom and my aunt. A knot twists low in my stomach when I don't get an answer. I don't expect a reply from my aunt. I didn't see her at the docks, but I was too busy blending in to search for her. She's normally at work at this time of the day. But Mom? I anticipated a reply from her.

Dread runs down my spine when I enter the bedroom and find Mom's bed vacant. She wouldn't have gone out. She can't. Most days, she can barely make it from the bed to the living room unaided.

I check the kitchen, the bathroom, and even the miniature balcony. The apartment's tiny footprint allows for a quick search, but each empty room intensifies my fear.

My mother is nowhere to be seen.

I dig my phone out of my pocket, place the battery back in, and then check for any missed calls. The screen is blank. I give myself thirty seconds to panic before I force myself to think logically.

If Mom isn't here, where else would she be?

The unwanted answer slowly sneaks up on me. Maybe something bad happened, and my aunt had to take my mom to the hospital. That's probably why I didn't see her at the docks. Again, I wasn't looking, but my theory is the only one that makes sense.

I bolt for the exit as the panic curled around my throat chokes me.

As the door swings open, a shadow falls across the threshold, and I freeze. Giovanni's impressive frame, bristling with anger, obstructs the only way out.

20

———

VALENTINA

The narrowed slit of Giovanni's eyes can't hide how stormy they are, and his jaw is set so rigidly I'm surprised it hasn't cracked. He stands in the doorway, blocking my path, unmoving and unspeaking. He's angry, there's no doubting that, but a gentle softness also emanates from him. I might be mistaken, but it resembles relief.

His eyes remain on me as he takes out his phone and calls someone. "I've got her," he states curtly. "Tell Matteo to send thanks to Nikolai. Our crew eventually would have spotted her walking home, but it was nice to have a heads-up of her last known location."

Without saying goodbye, he disconnects his call, then steps inside. The door shuts behind him with a finality that makes my heart thud. Even though his composure screams for me to submit, I refuse to back down. My mother is God knows where, and unearthing her location trumps everything.

Lifting my chin, I align my eyes with Giovanni's. I'm about to demand he step aside when he blindsides me by proving he can read me like no one else has.

"Your mother is fine." His pressed lips don't match the sympathy in his tone. "Well, as fine as her condition allows." My spirit lifts considerably when he states, "And she'll only improve now that I've enrolled her in the program Dr. Russo suggested."

"What?" That's it. That is all I can get out.

Giovanni's angry mask briefly falters when he smirks at my bewilderment. "She's being transported for treatment as we speak."

His words echo in my head, crowding out everything else. The anxieties that have been gnawing at me for months loosen their clutch, freeing me to breathe in unriddled air, yet I still feel uneased.

"It's too much."

Giovanni doesn't agree with me.

While shaking his head, he steps closer.

I hold my hand in front of myself, wordlessly begging him to stay where he is.

He pays my request no attention, so I use words. "If this is about the IVF bungle—"

"It's not."

I continue as if he didn't speak. "You don't owe me anything. You're as much a victim of their error as Valeria and I are."

He stops a mere foot from me. "It's not about that." The sheer actuality in his tone pricks tears in my eyes. "That has nothing to do with this," he says, jerking his hand between us. "I helped your mother because I wanted to." His anger surges. "And because access to life-saving healthcare should be available for everyone, not just the wealthy fucks who probably have a cure for cancer but are too greedy to release it."

He's speaking words I've wanted to hear for years, but sometimes the truth is a bitter pill to swallow. "I can't afford to pay you back. I'll try, but—"

"You owe me nothing."

"Giovanni..."

"You owe me *nothing*," he repeats, sterner this time.

Relief crashes over me in slow, trembling waves. I can't believe after all this time, Mom is finally getting the medical treatment she desperately needs. Fresh tears fill my eyes as I imagine her in a clean hospital bed, moaning about the nursing staff fussing over her. She hates feeling like a burden, but if it brings back the color in her cheeks and makes her voice a little stronger, I'm all for it.

I'm grateful for the relief, but I know it will be short-lived. I'm not off the hook just yet. Giovanni's shoulders are still high and taut, and the tension emitting off him is palpable.

He's angry, and my actions this morning are the *sole* cause of his fury.

He fixes me with that stare again as his tone shifts from brutish to wounded. "You ran..."

Before I can offer him a stream of excuses, he slices his hand through the air, cutting me off. He doesn't want excuses. He wants restitution for my mistake. And he wants it now. The lust detonating in his eyes announces this, as does the growing bulge below his belt.

"What happens when you run from me, *dolcezza*?"

He's asking a question, but I keep quiet. I can't speak. It's impossible to do anything but stare. Giovanni is a brutally beautiful man. Every inch of him radiates confidence and power, but my attraction to him stems from more than that. Even in an empty room, his movements and the energy he projects are palpable.

And the fact he helped my mother without truly knowing her has me drawn to him like a magnet.

He's unaware that her smile rescued me from the dark when it became too much, or that it made my boo-boos seem nowhere near as dire. He has no clue my mother is my world, yet he still helped her.

When Giovanni hovers close, a part of me wants to avoid confrontation, but I stand my ground. He's too enigmatic to crave a woman who bows out at the first sign of trouble. He wants someone brave enough to stand by his side, not two steps behind him.

"What happens when you run from me, *dolcezza*?" Sparks zap across my face when he grips my chin and lifts it to align our eyes. "When I catch you, I get to—"

"Fuck me," I interrupt, too turned on by the chemistry hissing between us to act nonchalant.

I don't need to lower my eyes to his mouth to confirm his smirk is smug.

I can feel it in my bones.

His agreeing hum clusters in my clit. I'm wet. Already. And unashamed.

How could something so right ever feel wrong?

Instead of seeking answers to questions I haven't asked yet, I propel onto my feet and seal my mouth over Giovanni's.

I kiss him until my lips are swollen and red as if I'm wearing lipstick.

Then I kiss him some more.

Lust bubbles in my blood when his hot breath ghosts over my ear. "How wet are you? Do you think you can take me now?"

I nod without thought before tilting my head so he can shower my neck with sloppy kisses. He licks, sucks, and marks me with his mouth before he drags his tongue along the column of my neck.

"Prove it. Wrap your legs around my waist and make a mess on the front of my pants."

With one hand on my ass, he hoists me up his body. Shudders tremor along my spine when the head of his fat cock rubs at the opening of my pussy.

Giovanni doesn't waste a moment before showing me he is a god both in and out of his clothes. Again and again, he rubs his erection along the lines of my pussy, and his swollen head finds my clit with every perfect grind.

Seconds later, I bury my face in his neck when tingles blister through me without warning. They coat my skin with goose bumps and make me breathless.

I'm still striving to recover when Giovanni steps us back until my ass lands on the dining room table. Although my thigh muscles tense when he stands between them, my morals won't stoop this low.

I attempt to veer him away from the table my aunt and now my mom eat at every night, but his firm hold on my hip pins me in place.

"We... can't... do... *that*... here..." Big breaths separate my words. Giovanni is only toying with my breasts while peppering my skin with tiny, purposeful kisses, but the sparks his attention creates could be devastating during a drought. "My... aunt... eats... here."

He nods slowly, as if he understands, but instead of plucking me off the wobbly wooden legs, he pushes on my shoulder until my back flattens on the tabletop.

"Giovanni..." I swallow to lessen the husky delivery of my words before trying again. "My mom eats here."

His voice is like liquid ecstasy, and it sears straight through me. "And now I'm going to eat here, too."

In one quick maneuver, he tugs off my panties, stuffs them into his pocket, and then suspends his mouth above my clit. I buck against him when he sucks the nervy bud into his mouth. I'd like to pretend I'm rearing up because I don't want to desecrate my aunt's furniture with my arousal, but that would be a lie. I'm endeavoring to stave off an orgasm that's so ferocious I can feel its spasms in my toes.

"Gio..."

I moan louder when two blunt fingers pierce the entrance of my pussy. He pushes them in tortuously slow, curling my toes and forcing me to mark my lower lip with my teeth. His fingers are so thick that even after being taken by him a handful of times, it's a stretch to accommodate them inside me.

The combination of his fingers and mouth instigates an immediate detonation. I come with a roar as fireworks shoot in the sky.

Giovanni's greedy licks vanish my concerns about my aunt's table. He laps up every drop of my climax before he shifts his focus back to my clit as if he craves more of my taste.

My fingers rake his scalp as his name falls from my lips over and over again. I can't stop coming. Orgasms roll through my body on repeat, each one more blinding than the last.

Whoever taught this man how to eat pussy was a genius, and I can't even be jealous. He's a god, and he's using all his best skills on me, so you won't get a single complaint from me. Yet.

Giovanni licks, tongues, and sucks at my clit and pussy until I can't take it anymore. I need him inside me. Now!

When I say that to Giovanni, his teeth close around my clit, and he tugs it gently before he stealthily rises to his feet.

We were too impatient to undress again. I don't mind. His stained-at-the-crotch pants, sweat-dotted face, and seductively undone-at-the-third-button dress shirt are a good look for him. He looks like sin and seduction rolled into one delicious package.

He's so outrageously handsome that he makes me forget my own name. His jaw is sharp and dusted with stubble that looks both effortless and intentional. His hair is dark and thick and always tousled from him running his hand through it multiple times a day, and his stacked abs are a testament to his discipline and strength.

Like I could get any more captivated, his insides are as compelling as his outer appearance.

They announce that he's dangerous in every sense of the word, and that he has both the muscle and the smarts to trap a hunter in his own trap.

You'd think the knowledge would be scary, but my body acts the opposite. It doesn't receive the orders sent by my brain, nor does it care how fast he entraps me in his world. It wants to be claimed by him. *Owned.* It wants him in any way it can get him.

Giovanni knows this. He's as cocky as he is confident, exposing this afternoon's foray will be an hours-long event.

With my ass dangling off the edge of the table, and my legs wrapped loosely around Giovanni's waist, he teasingly pushes the tip of his cock inside me.

I suck at him, begging him to stay, when he commences retreating before he's even given me three inches.

"Tell me again, *dolcezza*." He rewards me with another teasing push. "What happens when you run from me?"

I'm already on the verge of begging, so I don't hold back the words sitting on the tip of my tongue. "You fuck me."

"No." His one word is a growl, and it scorches my skin. "I have to catch you before I can fuck you." He stuffs his cock in further this time, doubling the sweat coating my skin. "Is that why you ran? Because you want me to chase you?"

I shake my head, too overwhelmed by how good he feels—even with only taking part of him—to portray calm.

Giovanni thrusts in halfway, then withdraws to the tip. "Then why?"

"I..." I stop, unsure I can have this conversation while vulnerable. Jealousy is an ugly disease, and I let it control my emotions once already today. It won't happen again.

"You?" Giovanni pushes, never one to back down. When he spots the determination building in my eyes, he lowers his hand to my clit and circles it at the same dangerously slow speed he enters me. "Why, *dolcezza*? Why did you run?"

"Because you..." I raise my hips when those two words reward me with another two inches, trying to take more.

Giovanni slaps down my hips before he pulls out entirely.

"No!" I shout, devastated. I want him. Need him. I feel empty without him, both in my pussy and my chest.

I can't tell him that, though. I hardly know him, so how can I expect him to believe I'm already developing feelings for him without making it seem like I only want him for his money?

"Tell me why, *dolcezza*!"

"Because you... because you..." I stumble while trying to think of a lie. Nothing but the truth formulates. "Because you didn't come home last night! That's why I ran. You told them to put me in your room, but then you stayed out all night!"

He slams home with one thrust, and the table legs groan in protest of our combined weights. I lean into his tight, muscular body as it drives into me on repeat. He fucks like a wild animal, his hips pistoning as fast as bursts of air puff from his nose.

He pounds into me. Over and over. Taking everything and giving me just as much.

My vision blurs as an orgasm more powerful than any I've felt before gathers inside me.

Giovanni seems pleased by my response. Euphoric.

Anyone would swear I handed him the keys to the castle.

And then it dawns. I told him he didn't come home.

Home. The place where someone lives permanently, particularly with a family member or spouse.

Like a coward, I attempt to backtrack on my confession. "I... I... I..." Giovanni's brutal pounding won't let me. He screws me senseless, readjusting my position every time the sweat on my neck dampens a smidge.

He never stops. He pushes me over the edge with a beautifully brutal intensity that proves what my head doesn't want to acknowledge.

He owns me.

GIOVANNI

Right now, Valentina doesn't resemble the nickname I chose for her. How could she when my cock is driving into her, making her pussy lips red and swollen, and our intermingled sweat is rolling down her chest and gathering in her belly button? She is a Sicilian goddess. Her dark hair starkly contrasts against the faded varnish of her aunt's wooden table, and although her breasts are still concealed by her shirt, they jerk up her chest with every rock of my hips.

Cum gathers at the base of my dick, but I can't stop myself from touching her. I roll her clit with my thumb while my free hand rights the injustice of her fantastic tits being locked away.

I tug at her blouse without remorse, unconcerned when I pop several buttons. The way Valentina has been living—week to week, paycheck to paycheck—is over now.

She'll want for nothing now that she's mine. I'll give her the world.

I just need to get over my worry that eventually she'll run and I'll never find her.

When Matteo called to advise that Valentina wasn't in her room when he went to collect her for breakfast, panic clawed at my chest. His voice was strained with urgency, as if he wasn't yet convinced the bratva no longer trafficked women.

My faith is higher.

Don't misinterpret what I'm saying. Nikolai Popov is as snowed under for his wife as I am for Valentina. It still would have been a hefty decision to make, though. The sex trafficking trade is a billion-dollar industry. Nikolai's competitors mistook his stance for weakness. When he proved otherwise with both brawn and brains, the tides shifted. Old alliances fractured and new coalitions formed—hence our multimillion-dollar first-distribution contract this morning.

Nikolai would rather trade with a foreign country than hand money to men who still believe in his father's archaic practices.

Matteo's words an hour ago swirl in my head and make me unhinged. *She's gone, Vanni.*

I drive into Valentina harder. Faster. I fuck her as if I'm seeking restitution from her body for the scars she imprinted on my heart when I contemplated her being forced to leave instead of leaving of her own free will.

I'd left the door open on purpose and placed her backpack on the dresser in plain view. Her phone was charging on the bedside table, for fuck's sake. I wanted her to see my room as a place of solace, not a cell. But all I could think about was how easily she vanished, and how I failed to keep her close.

"Gio... Fuck..."

The pads of Valentina's feet dig into my ass as she endeavors to slow me down. It's all a ploy. Her hot, slick heat dampens more the deeper I impale her. She's loving my arrogance.

Her juices are coating my balls and face, but it still isn't enough.

I want more of her.

Need more.

"Say it." I lower the rock of my hips. Not a lot. Just enough that she can speak through the lust clutching her throat.

Valentina doesn't jump to my command. She grabs me by the throat and the balls. "Who... were... you... with?"

Her voice has the same husky edge mine had when I had to fight myself not to interrogate her mother for her daughter's known haunts. Since I'd left the room hours earlier and removed surveillance from the compound many years ago, no one knew exactly how long Valentina had been missing.

For all I knew, she could have been on the other side of the country.

But then I remembered how she'd stared up at her mother in the photo on her phone.

She'd come back for that, just like I now know she'll come back for me.

Where there's no jealousy, there's no love.

I keep my hand on Valentina's meaty hip while I remove my cock and swipe the glistening head across her clit. Her pupils dilate more as the most fascinating sound in the world seeps from her lips. My woman is on the brink of madness purely at the thought of my scent coating her inside *and* out.

"Tell me what I want to hear, *dolcezza*. Then I'll eat your pretty little pussy every fucking day for eternity like it isn't soaked with my cum."

Her groan makes a liar out of her before she even speaks. "I don't know what you want to hear."

"Liar."

I return to my earlier tease, inch by inch.

Passion flares on Valentina's cheeks, and the wish for me to slam my cock in deep is all over her beautiful face. "I wanted you to chase me—"

I backhand her clit, slapping the lie from her mouth. "Tell the truth."

"It is the truth."

I can't stop myself from slamming in deep when she aligns her gaze with mine. Not an ounce of deceit clouds her honey-colored eyes.

I reward her honesty with a handful of pumps. I slide in and out of her, coating every fucking inch of my shaft with evidence of her arousal, before I restart my campaign.

"Tell me."

"No." Her reply is more a sob than a coherent plea, and it sees me immediately withdrawing. I don't even leave the tip in this time. I fully remove my cock. "Please, Giovanni. I need you."

"Because...?"

When Valentina remains quiet, I bury my cock inside her, still my hips, then work her clit like I haven't overworked it in the past hour.

Valentina is a feisty little minx but a shit multitasker. Her brain won't know which puzzle to solve first. I give it ten seconds before it fritzes and she coughs up the goods.

Ten.

Acting as if her clit is the detonator to the bomb low in her gut, which appears seconds from exploding, I thumb it and press down.

Nine.

I swivel the nervy bud while maintaining eye contact.

Eight.

With the same hand that's toying her clit, I curl my fingers around the base of my cock.

Seven.

I use the evidence of her multiple orgasms to lubricate my fingertips.

Six.

With our eyes aligned, I flutter my index and middle fingers across her puckered rear.

Five.

I push the tip of my index finger into her ass. Not far. Just to the second joint.

Four... I think?

The gasp Valentina released when my finger breached her ass scattered my thoughts. Her response confirms no one has ever touched her here. Her ass is virginal, and my cock flexes like it's hit the jackpot.

Fortunately, that's all it takes for Valentina's resolve to crumble. As her shoulders meet and her muscles shake, the words I'm seeking slip from her kiss-swollen lips.

"I'm yours."

22

VALENTINA

Walking into my mother's new hospital room, I'm honestly stunned. It's bigger than our entire house in the US, with large windows that overlook the coast and spill sunlight across the floor. The bed isn't one of those narrow, squishy single beds Mom is used to. It's a proper double, with crisp sheets and space to stretch out.

Mom looks as surprised as I feel. "*Tesoro*, can you believe it?" She glides her hand across the breathtaking view not even a bedridden patient could miss. It shows the coastline in all its glory and reminds me of the luxuriousness of Giovanni's penthouse. "I keep asking the nurse if they've made a mistake. This can't be my room."

She strays her eyes to me before gesturing for me to come closer. She's missed my presence as much as I have hers the past twenty-four hours. I nuzzle in when she pulls me into her chest and hugs me tightly. I've missed her smell and her smile, and thanks to Giovanni's generosity, I'm no longer dreading that their absence will become permanent before I'm ready.

This treatment doesn't guarantee a cure, but it will give her the best chance of going into remission.

When the strength of my mother's caress tenses my weary bones, my heart aches with an equal amount of gratitude and guilt. I wish I could refuse Giovanni's generosity. Pride is a hard thing to get over. It constantly whispers that it's imperative to stand on your own two feet and that accepting help is a sign of weakness. But the reality is too stark to ignore. We can't afford the treatment my mother desperately needs. My wages are too low to compete with the endless stream of bills constantly landing in my inbox, much less thousands in medical expenses.

I probably wouldn't be so opposed to help if I weren't worried Giovanni will think I'm using our fire-sparking connection to take advantage of him. That's not what I'm doing. It isn't his job to solve my problems.

I tried to talk him into a payment plan when we discussed my mother's medical bills while showering together in my aunt's poky bathroom. Giovanni wouldn't hear a word of it. He said gifts weren't given with invoices.

I still plan to pay him back. It'll probably take seven centuries, but I won't stop working until I've repaid every cent he spent for this treatment.

After feigning innocence about the new scent coating every inch of my skin, my mother inches back. Her eyes glisten with happiness and appear pain-free. "Are you sure our insurance covers this, *tesoro*? I didn't think I could use our US health insurance here."

Giovanni jumps into the conversation before a single excuse formulates in my lust-hazed head. "Your dual citizenship altered the rules. The Sicilian government is always happy to get money out of a foreign company."

My mother's giggle is true and genuine.

She already likes Giovanni. I can tell she does.

A pink hue creeps up her neck as she returns her eyes to me. "Are you going to offer an introduction, *tesoro*? Or shall I keep referring to this young man as your Dark Knight?"

"Dark Knight is fine with me."

I whack Giovanni in the stomach before plopping my backside onto a portion of my mother's bed. It's not a squeeze since she takes up barely any space.

"Mamma, this is..." My throat constricts. I knew this moment would inevitably come, but with my brain on the fritz for countless orgasms, it isn't firing on all cylinders. I can't call Giovanni my boyfriend. Surely not. We met weeks ago, but the "we" part of our relationship is as fresh as a newborn baby. "He's—"

Giovanni doesn't let me drown in hesitation. He steps forward with his hand extended as if he owns the space.

I snort. *He probably does.*

"Giovanni Caruso." His voice is steady and full of pride. "The man obsessed with your daughter."

His confession jolts through me like electricity, and my breath catches. He said it just like that. No hesitation. No shame. It sounded so truthful it could be mistaken for gospel.

My stomach flips. Don't ask me if it is a good flip or a bad flip, as I wouldn't be able to tell you.

Mom's brow lifts, but there's no judgment in her eyes. Recognition is the only spark I see.

"Caruso?" She swirls his surname around her mouth as if tasting its familiarity. "As in Vittoria Caruso?"

Giovanni's demeanor shifts. Only slightly, but it's enough for me to feel the burden of it.

"Yes," he answers, nodding. "Vittoria is my mother."

Endearment softens Mom's expression as her eyes flicker with a memory. "How is she? It's been years since I saw her." Her eyes glaze over with fresh tears as she corrects herself. "Decades."

A moment of silence stretches between us before Giovanni says, "My mother passed a little over a year ago."

Mom twists her hand in her blanket. "Oh... Giovanni, I'm so sorry." Her brows furrow with genuine affection. "She was a good woman."

"She was," Giovanni agrees.

Mom smiles as her eyes glisten with curiosity. "And your father? How is he?"

Giovanni runs his hand along his jaw, tracing the tremor there, before he answers. "He's been unwell lately." His eyes shift to me, and their hoodedness makes it impossible not to squirm. "But he's improved in leaps and bounds over the past thirty-six hours. He's like a new man." Then, in a gentler tone, almost like a vow, he adds, "If you knew my mother, I'm confident he'd love to meet you."

If Mom's lips didn't part, I would have missed what she replied. That's how softly she speaks. "We've already met." Her gaze darts away as if tugged by a memory she isn't ready to share before her tiny frame shivers. "The air-conditioning is a little cold. Could I get a blanket?"

"I'll grab one."

I leap up from the bed and charge for the door, but Giovanni beats me to it.

"I'll get it," he says, already in the corridor that reeks of medical equipment.

His shoulders are bunched, and he looks like he needs a minute to get his head straight, so instead of protesting that I generally use these requests for a quick breather, I nod.

The instant the door clicks shut with Giovanni on the other side, my mother pats the empty space beside her with her frail hand.

"Hop back in," she whispers, her eyes bright with urgency. "And tell me *everything*."

Everything? I wouldn't even know where to start.

Many hours later, I stand and stretch. My legs are now stiff from sitting so long instead of being curled around Giovanni's shoulders when he took me to the brink in my aunt's cramped shower. Although I usually stay until Mom is asleep, I switch tactics today. Giovanni hasn't left Mom's room since he returned with a blanket, and as much as my mother is putting on a brave face, I can tell she is exhausted. Her eyelids are heavy and her complexion is pale, but I'll admit, there's a softness in her smile that makes my chest ache with joy instead of fear.

Leaning down, I kiss her cheek. Her skin is cool and smells freshly cleaned. "I'll see you tomorrow," I say, already mapping out the route in my head. This hospital is further east than Ospedale San Giorgio's, so it will take longer to get here, but I need to switch buses only twice instead of the usual three.

Mom's decisive headshake shocks me. "No, you won't."

I blink, thrown off guard by her suggestion. "What do you mean?"

"I'll be doing nothing but resting and sleeping for the next few days." Her mischievous eyes dance between Giovanni and me. "Perhaps you should try to do the same."

Even though I love her playfulness, her suggestion lands harshly in my gut. "I don't want to leave you alone."

Her IV line sways with the wave of her frail hand. "Your aunt will visit every evening. And..." She retrieves a fancy phone from her bedside table. It isn't outdated like mine. It's the latest-model iPhone, which gleams under the harsh fluorescent lights as brightly as my cheeks when I realize only one person in this room can afford such extravagance. "This hospital's services include internet connectivity. We can keep in touch using FaceTime. I already downloaded the app."

My stomach flip-flops. Once again, don't ask me if it's in despair or excitement. I hate lying.

"See?" Mom twists the phone screen to me. "You're at the top of the list, ready to be bombarded every evening at six."

"*Every* evening?" I can't believe I'm already folding. I usually fight until I'm out of breath.

Exhaustion truly is a brutal beast.

"*Every* evening," she confirms, nodding.

"Okay." I force my voice to stay steady even as emotions constrict my throat. "Every evening at six." I collect my stuff before turning to face Mom. "Please keep me informed. If anything happens before or after our call, contact me immediately."

"I promise," she says, squeezing my hand.

Even though I feel like I'm surrendering, I say, "I'll see you on the weekend. Love you."

She mimics my declaration of love before watching us walk to the door.

As we enter the corridor, she murmurs, "Have fun, you two."

I glance back at her and shoot daggers. There's no heat in my scorn. It's so weak it doubles the size of her smile. Her goofy grin is the same one she wore when she and Giovanni played Scopa. Unfamiliar with the rules, I chose to sit out and watch them play.

Their banter between games was more entertaining than being a participant. They laughed for hours, and on multiple occasions, I forgot today was Giovanni's first time meeting my mother. It's as if he's always belonged in our family.

As we move down the hall, the quiet thud of our feet breaks the hushed emptiness of patients sleeping. "You're really good at that."

Giovanni's confused face is adorable. He embodies a badass mafia boss when he's barking orders, and an alpha male while rocketing my head to the stars, but when he's confused, he appears more like a billionaire who gifts all his profits to charity.

"Being a son," I offer, my tone soft.

His mother has passed, so a conversation like this could be a sore point for him. I'd never be ready if my mother passed.

Lines crease in the corners of his eyes when he smiles faintly. "It isn't hard."

We step out into the refreshing night air, stealing my chance to ask if he means it's easy because of my mother or because of me. I'd say it is a combination of both. My mother is easy to love. She was the epitome of the neighbor mother for the less fortunate children in school. But a part of me hopes it was also for me.

While signaling as if he's hailing a taxi, Giovanni asks, "What address am I giving the driver?"

"Huh?"

His smirk would have you convinced my daft face is cute. I'm not meaning to seem foolish. I truly didn't think I had a choice. That's what last night's kidnap was about, wasn't it?

When I express my feelings to Giovanni, he works his jaw side to side before giving it a rough scrub.

"You have a choice," he says matter-of-factly. "Always."

Silently and professionally, a driver exits a sleek black car that has pulled to the curb. Giovanni opens the door for me before the driver can round the hood, like he doesn't trust anyone else to do it. The driver waits for us to be seated before he slots back behind the wheel and seeks instructions from Giovanni through the rearview mirror.

When Giovanni remains quiet, I realize he's left the floor to me.

"Um..." I nearly suggest my aunt's place, but the memories of last night crash into me. Since I don't want to lie in bed alone, staring at the ceiling, wishing he were there, I seek an alternative solution. "Where are you sleeping tonight?"

In less than a nanosecond, Giovanni replies, "Wherever you are."

Now I'm really confused. Why would he choose to sleep in a rundown building when he has both a palace and a penthouse at his disposal? He's either a foolish man or a lovesick chump...

My words trail off when the truth strikes like lightning.

He introduced himself to my mother as the man obsessed with his daughter.

My mother's favorite saying is: *If obsession isn't love, I've never loved.*

Does that mean what I think it does? Is Giovanni Caruso falling in love with me?

With my head in too much of a state to think logically, I brainstorm out loud. "My aunt only has a single bed, and with my mom at the hospital, I shouldn't really take it from her." My excuse would sound more convincing if I could get the image of my head resting on Giovanni's pecs out of my mind. "Then there's the villa... but it's—"

The arrogant tilt of Giovanni's head cuts me off. His angled chin barely conceals the cocky grin pulling at his lips, and although it should be too early to admit this, his smiles are extremely telling.

"What did you do?" I ask, already knowing that his brash grins are a telltale sign that he's done something drastic.

Pride flares through his eyes. He's pleased I can read him as easily as he can read me. "Do you truly think I'd let your aunt return to her home after what we did there?" He bops my nose, distracting my attention from how we christened every surface of her quaint apartment. "Cute."

He instructs the driver to take us back to my aunt's building before explaining to me that my aunt is currently enjoying the luxury of a five-star penthouse suite. She has a butler, twenty-four-hour room service, and a live-in maid. He left nothing off the ledger, and it unhinges my jaw.

"What?" I squeak out in shock. "You did that?"

Dark hair falls into his eye when he dips his chin.

"When?" My escape took two hours at most. How could he have achieved everything I've been striving to do for years in a matter of hours?

I hate myself with every fiber of my being when he mutters, "Last night..." He internally fights with himself before blurting out, "And most of this morning."

He wasn't with Valeria last night. He was with me. Figuratively. This isn't a paranormal romance.

Giovanni returns my jaw to its rightful spot before he continues convincing me this is a dream. "The penthouse is your aunt's for as long as she wants it. By what I was informed earlier, she's settling in nicely."

I stare at him, words failing me. First he paid for Mom's medical expenses, and now this?

My heart squeezes, overwhelmed by the sheer weight of his generosity. "It's too much. I can't ask you—"

"You didn't ask me to do anything, *dolcezza*," he interrupts gently. "So nothing I've done is your debt to repay."

I swallow hard, my throat dry. He's doing too much too quickly, but every objection I endeavor to throw out clings to my tonsils. You can't see the way he's looking at me. His stare tells me he doesn't want anything in return for his generosity.

Except perhaps me.

Instead of getting carried away in the euphoria of my dreams finally being answered, I speak from the heart for the first time in years. "Take us back to the Caruso Estate."

Wordlessly, the driver seeks instruction from Giovanni.

He jerks up his chin before telling the driver to never second-guess my command again if he wishes to remain breathing.

"Please tell me this SUV has a privacy partition," I whisper.

Giovanni's dark eyes dart to mine, and something unspoken passes between us when he nods. Then desire takes over.

23

GIOVANNI

Valentina is still asleep when I meet with the head physician of my father's medical team. I know this because the surveillance feed tells me so. A wireless system I had installed days ago streams every angle of the Caruso compound straight to my phone. Some people would call my desire to protect her obsessive. I call it a necessity. In my world, control isn't optional. It's the only way to survive.

After signaling to the doctor that I need a minute, I zoom in on the image of Valentina in my bed. Her hair spills across the pillow like ink, and her breathing is slow and even. Just like she did seven nights ago when I brought her back here—*willingly that time*—she looks like she belongs here. She suits my space, and God help me, I like seeing her in it.

My obsession over the past week hasn't waned even a fraction. If anything, it's gotten worse. Every hour I spend with Valentina feeds something I can't control. I'm at her side constantly. We enjoy breakfast in the sunlit atrium, have lunch on the terrace, and eat dinner under the soft glow of the chandeliers in the dining room.

When I'm not with her, I'm watching her. *Stalking her.* The surveillance system streams her every move twenty-four-seven. I tell myself it's for her safety—and it is—but it's also for me. I need to see her and know what she's doing as much as I need to know she's still here.

That she's still mine.

Waking up and finding her gone will be worse than a blade to the throat.

I drink in Valentina's perfect profile for a few more seconds, then lock the screen and slide my phone into my pocket.

"How is he?" I ask the doctor without a greeting.

As always, his reply is clinically detached. "Still stable. Vitals are on par, and he's alert."

A sense of relief transcends over me. "So he's improving?"

His long pause offers no comfort. "I need to be honest with you. Sometimes in cases like this, what looks like improvement can be misleading."

I ball my hands so fast my knuckles pop. "Misleading how?"

"It can be what we call a terminal surge," the doctor explains. "A final burst of energy before the body begins to shut down. It's common in patients with advanced cardiac failure."

His words slam into me better than any fist has, but denial is a game I've been playing for decades. "No," I say flatly, shaking my head. "That isn't what this is."

"I hope you're right." The doctor's voice is surprisingly firm for how hard his thighs are shaking. "But you should prepare yourself. His heart is fragile. The stress of losing your mother and the heart attack that followed her loss accelerated its decline."

Prepare myself? As if that's possible. It's not his time yet. It can't be. Everything *he* planned is finally aligning, so he needs to stick around to see it occur.

When I stare at the door of my father's room, my chest tightens enough to ache. "He's strong. He's *always* been strong."

"I know," the doctor agrees, squeezing my shoulder. "But even the strongest hearts have limits."

When he enters my father's room to take his vitals, the scent of recently cleaned hospital equipment and old books wafts out. My father insisted on keeping the shelves even though they're lined with leather-bound books he rarely reads.

After checking the security feed and noticing Valentina is still asleep, I balance my shoulder on the doorjamb and monitor the doctor's checks. My father looks smaller than the giant I remember from my childhood, and the sight stirs the anarchy living inside me.

It doesn't swirl for long. The doctor's stethoscope doesn't get within an inch of my father's chest before my father snatches the doctor's wrist firmly enough to break it.

"*Signor* Caruso, it is Dr. Marino. I just want to—"

"Interrupt a man while he's sleeping."

When my father's grip firms, causing Dr. Marino's hand to go white, I enter the sterile-scented space. The floor creaks under my weight, and my father's eyes dart to me.

"He's doing his job, Papa."

He huffs as if miffed before he drops Dr. Marino's wrist. "I told you I don't need a doctor."

I gesture for the doctor to leave before he loses the ability to breathe, and join my father at his bedside. Treating my father as an invalid is a quick way to the grave. Doesn't mean I won't tease him, though. I'm his eldest son. That automatically makes me his favorite. "You also said you weren't having a heart attack when you were."

"Vanni..." His brows lower down his face as he scolds me in a dialect that's hardly used anymore. The Old Castilian language is only known by the greats.

"Such a grump." I pull a chair close to his bed. "Is this what happens when you wake early? You become a grouch?"

"This is what happens when your eldest son keeps everyone awake at all hours of the night, entertaining a female guest." He sits up, his movements stable for a man on his deathbed. "Who knew Valeria had it in her? She—"

"Isn't the woman sharing my bed."

He watches me with astute eyes. Shockingly, his gaze holds no judgment.

For several long seconds, we sit in silence, with only the hum of the machines once responsible for keeping him alive filling the space.

Then he tilts his head and studies me with those shrewd eyes that miss nothing. "You look... different."

"Different?"

"Like a man with something on his mind."

I hesitate, then exhale slowly. "I met someone."

"And?"

I wait a beat before murmuring, "She's... different."

His eye roll is as immature as my laughter that bounces around his room.

"She reminds me a lot of Mamma."

That secures his attention. "Do we know who this girl is, Giovanni? Her roots? I won't try to dissuade you from her, but please make sure her intentions are good. The family looks up to you. Your brothers mirror your actions. We can't have an outsider coming in and cracking the foundations we fought so hard to build."

I nod in understanding. I might not like it, but I understand his worry. "They're good people, Papa. You know her mother." He waits with bated breath for me to fill in the gaps. "Concetta Gambino. She recognized our name when I introduced myself. The fact she didn't seem wary announces you've met previously."

I twist my lips, still unsettled by how calm Valentina's mother was when I pulled off the cloak I'd been wearing all morning the day of our official introduction. I couldn't exactly walk into her home, tell her I'd participated in the kidnap of her only child, and expect her to trust me.

Only Matteo is cocky enough to pull off something like that.

"She smiled with fondness when the familiarity of our name fell around her." I bark out a husky laugh. "Most people run in fear."

My father grins faintly, amused. "Concetta Gambino..." He draws in a prolonged breath through his nose like I do every time Valentina's arousal slicks my palm. "She can smile." The amusement in his eyes deepens. "She's the only woman to have ever turned down a Caruso."

I stare at him, my pulse spiking. "What?"

"She turned me down," he says simply, as if discussing the weather. "I asked her to marry me, and she said thanks but no thanks. That this life wasn't for her." He waves his hand around his elegant yet manly room.

Panic grips my throat. The math isn't mathing, but my knowledge about the tricks some women will do to attach themselves to a Caruso isn't solely from personal experience. It's also from the many stories my mother shared over the years. Our father was a catch, and she often said her sheets wouldn't even be cold before there'd be a line of women at our door, ready to seduce our father.

Her assumptions weren't far from the truth.

Women came in droves, but our father turned them away.

"You were only with Mom, right? No one else in your thirty-six-year marriage?"

His expression hardens until it showcases the man who built an empire from nothing. "Don't insult me, boy," he says coldly. "I loved your mother. I'd never step out on her like that. Why do you think my heart is failing now that she's gone?"

I swallow hard as shame replaces the worry burning through me. "I didn't mean—"

"Yes, you did," he interrupts, his reply sharp enough to cut. "I never strayed, Giovanni. Not once."

I nod quickly, the certainty in his reply too honest to discount.

Another stretch of silence falls between us before my father eventually breaks it. "Tell me about her."

"Concetta?"

He smacks me up the back of the head, rattling my brain against my skull. "The woman who has you walking around with love hearts bouncing from your eyes."

"Valentina. She's... ah..." A sigh finalizes my reply. I'm a fucking soft cock admitting this after only a week, but I'm snowed under. Gone. I won't *ever* move past this, so if Valentina takes after her mother and turns down a Caruso, I'll have to get inventive.

None of my plans will involve her leaving the country while carrying another man's baby.

"Those are the exact words I spoke to your grandfather when he asked me about your mother." My smile reaches only half its ability, but it's still the biggest he's given in months. "Does she know about Valeria?" Before I can speak, a light bulb switches on in his head. "Valentina was at the gathering last week. Valeria said she was your surrogate."

My jaw clenches. I want to tell him Valeria is a liar, but until the baby is born, no one will know the truth. Although I hope the test comes back positive and we discover that the child is mine and Valentina's, there's a niggle that's screaming this was too easy.

The game is meant to be harder than this.

The utmost certainty in my father's tone could cut diamonds. "You're worried."

"Fucking terrified," I admit. "If it's not Valentina's—"

"There's a possibility the child is Valentina's?" My father shouts his words loud enough to wake the house.

My nod sends him sprawling back, and in this very moment, I realize Valeria didn't tell him everything. She told him only what would favor her.

That ends now.

I tell my father everything. The chase, the capture, the hiccup at the IVF clinic. I leave no stone unturned.

He processes the deluge with the shrewdness that comes from years of experience before asking, "The clinic?"

"Ashes."

I burned it to the ground seconds after securing an unconscious Valentina in my SUV.

Papa hums in approval. "The staff?"

I look at him—*really* look at him. Dr. Di Petro was his friend, but I couldn't let a mistake like this go unpunished. Our family would be a mockery if I had.

"Very well," he says after a brief pause for contemplation. He places his hand over mine, frail but steady. "Invite Valentina and her mother to the compound."

I balk, taken aback. "For what?"

"Dinner," he replies, as if it's obvious. "I'd like to officially meet the woman who's brought out a side of you I never thought I'd see." His lips curve teasingly. "And to be reintroduced to the woman who clearly raised her right."

Since there isn't an ounce of dishonesty in his words, I nod. Concetta influences Valentina's life in a way most people will never understand. I respect it because I get it. I have a similar bond with my father. He imparted all his knowledge to me, and his guidance continues to empower me as I age.

"I'll arrange it."

He nods, pleased, and then settles back in his bed, his eyes briefly closing.

"I'll let you rest."

His reply is muffled by a yawn. "I'm not tired. I'm just resting my eyes."

He feels my smug grin more than he sees it when I press my lips to his temple. His skin isn't as clammy as it usually is, but it prompts me to remind the doctor that he didn't finish his vitals.

I'm halfway to the door when he calls my name.

I pause at the threshold, then turn around.

"Don't worry." His tone carries more than reassurance. It's also factual. "Blood doesn't make you family. Being a biological parent isn't any higher than stepping up to the plate and taking responsibility for someone who doesn't share your blood. If Valentina's heart holds one ounce of the camaraderie her mother's does, her beliefs will align with mine. I truly believe that." His words are both painful and soothing.

With my throat too dry to speak, I nod.

His eyes once again drift shut as he murmurs, "Love isn't about blood. It's about choice."

Love?

I've spent my entire life scoffing at the idea of being tied down to one person forever. I also discredited my father's claim that he knew my mother was "it" after seeing her only once. I called his notion that he "knew" foolish. A game, and a sign of weakness.

Now I understand because that's what my obsession with Valentina is leading toward. That's what she is to me. She's my weakness. My biggest challenge. But if I'm willing to put in the hard years, she could also be my everything.

What I feel for her isn't solely an obsession fueled by lust.

It's the foundation of a love story that will rival my parents'.

Love is a risk. It means Valentina could walk away, and I'd have to let her even if it kills me. Loving her isn't about owning her. It's about ensuring her happiness is prioritized before anyone else's—even my own. She must come first.

Although the thought should terrify me, no amount of caution tapers my smirk.

Valentina Raimondi is mine.

And I'll kill anyone who tries to convince her otherwise.

24

VALENTINA

Reluctant to surface from a dream I don't want to leave, I wake slowly. The sheets are soft against my skin. They feel like silk spun from clouds and scream wealth. However, my limbs are heavy and sluggish. A week of indulgent comforts has softened me. My muscles ache. Not acutely, but in that dull, throbbing way that makes you crave more.

More movement.

More exhaustion.

More him.

I toss the covers off and stretch my arms overhead until my ribs groan. My stretch is slow and deliberate, and in seconds, it coaxes life back into tired limbs and brings a smile to my face.

For the past seven mornings, I've done the same routine. Though this is the first time I've woken up without Giovanni's piercing gaze watching me as I sleep.

His possessiveness would concern me if it didn't come with a heap of benefits. The past week has been wonderful. Giovanni and I spend every waking moment together, even the hours I'm at my mother's bedside, and Mom messages every morning to assure me she's well-rested. She also calls every evening at 6 to uphold her pledge, even if we've only just left her hospital room.

Her new medical team is skilled in the downfalls of her cancer, and although it's still early days for her new treatment program, her prognosis is already showing signs of improvement. Her upbeat mood likely stems from Aunt Maria giving her all the gossip on how the one percent live rather than a Posturepedic mattress, but any progress is welcome.

Aunt Maria thought the market stallholders had the hot takes on the locals. They have *nothing* on the doorman at Carlisle's most expensive building.

With my muscles loose enough to play another game of naked Twister, I sink deep into the mattress and sigh. I can't believe it's been only seven days. It feels like weeks. Months, even. It's hard to remember a time when Giovanni wasn't a part of my life. It's as if he's always been a part of the mess, which is both strange and scary.

I have no desire to question it, though. Everything is finally falling into place, and I was taught not to look a gift horse in the mouth. Those worries can wait until we can be in each other's presence longer than ten minutes without mauling each other.

Fingers crossed that's many moons away.

Smiling, I squint through the soft morning light filtering through the sheer curtains to collect my phone from the bedside table. I've only just scanned a good-morning text from my mother when I sense a presence. It prickles my skin with awareness, though it's not the excited goose bumps I get when I sense Giovanni's presence a second before I see him. It fills me with dread.

When I snap my gaze to the corner of the room, the air is sucked from my lungs. Valeria is standing next to a dresser, trailing her manicured nails across the trinkets arranged there. They're not random pieces. They are the items Giovanni collected for me when he met with the construction crew supervisor rebuilding and remodeling my mother's building.

He didn't want them to get ruined. That's how thoughtful he is and how far he'll go to make sure I'm comfortable in his domain.

Initially, I opposed his plan to have the building remodeled. My thoughts only changed when he explained the local council would fund the rebuild. Apparently, the building citations they've issued over the past several years were illegal, thus not only giving the residents plenty of grounds to sue, but they were also entitled to a seven-figure refund.

All the residents agreed that the money go into saving one of Carlisle's oldest buildings.

She'll be a grand majesty once she's finished, and it is all thanks to the Caruso family.

The reminder keeps me calm when my guest rummages through my things uninvited.

"Valeria…" My voice is rough with sleep but assertive enough to carry my displeasure of her unexpected snoop. "What are you doing?" When I push up on my elbows, the bedding pools around my waist. "Why are you in my room?"

Her slow turn reveals an icy expression. "We need to talk."

"About?"

She picks up a small box and inspects it as if it's a piece of evidence in a murder trial. "The IVF mix-up."

I recoil as air rushes out of my lungs in a hurry. I'd completely forgotten the reason behind my reunion with Giovanni. Everything's been so perfect that the clinic's erroneous mistake slipped into the void at the back of my head.

Though I'd prefer it to stay there, now that it's back, it is impossible to ignore.

"I…" A knot of anxiety forms in my throat. "What about it?"

Valeria's smile doesn't quite reach her eyes. "Giovanni thinks you're pregnant."

My pulse spikes. *Pregnant.* It sounds foreign, like it doesn't belong to me.

"If you're not," she barks sternly, "you'll be gone faster than I can snap my fingers."

Anger flares through me, hot and volatile. "Excuse me?"

Her laugh is low and mocking. "You think he's doing all this for you? That he's here for you?" Her words spit from her mouth like venom. "Why would he go to all this trouble"—she waves her manicured hand around the opulent lifestyle I've been living for seven perfect days—"for someone like *you*?"

My throat burns with the wish to speak, but she continues, foiling my chance. "None of this is about you, *Valentina*." She says my name as if it's trash. "It's because he needs an heir. That's all you are to him. A prop to be used and disposed of once you've given him what he needs."

I nearly flinch from the callousness of her words, but I hold back. If I show weakness now, she'll eat me alive. But also, no number of nasty words can make me forget the way Giovanni looks at me, and the tenderness that reflects in his gaze when he props up my mother's pillow.

He cares for me. A lot.

"No." I aim for my reply to come out resolute, but it sounds weak, even to me.

What if she's right?

What if Giovanni did all this because of a child who might not exist?

The thought guts me. If it's the truth, none of this is real. Neither the safety nor the warmth. And most definitely not the way he makes it seem as if I belong. If it's all tied to an heir, what will happen if the test comes back negative?

I want to believe in our connection, but I've had my heart trampled on before, so I need to be careful.

Still, my backbone remains straight. "I don't believe you."

Valeria's smile is cruel and satisfied, as if I walked straight into her trap. "Then prove it." She thrusts a box at me. "Take a test."

When my gaze lowers to her hand, the contents of my stomach rush up my esophagus. Inside the box is an early-detection pregnancy test. It's sealed and glaring at me in silent accusation.

"No." Even with my insides a twisted mess, my reply is firm. I may not be as wealthy or as beautiful as Valeria, but my heart is the heaviest thing about me. I refuse to be treated as if that doesn't count. Being a good person is far more imperative than your dress size and social status. "I'll take a test, but not now and not in front of you." She scoffs, but I continue. "I feel for you, Valeria, and I understand how this affects you, but I'm not the bad guy. I am a victim... just like you."

Her eyes narrow into tiny slits. "You don't have a choice."

"I do," I snap, recalling Giovanni saying precisely that multiple times over the past seven days. "So I'll only say this once." I push the bedding aside and swing my legs off the bed. "Please leave my room."

"*Your* room?" Her throaty laugh agitates my last nerve. "Even if this were your room, do you truly believe you can order me around? You're nothing but the incubator of a Caruso heir."

It takes every bit of my will not to retaliate with violence, but I manage. Barely. "I didn't order you to do anything. I politely asked you to leave. I won't be as nice the second time around." My snarl mimics hers when I underhandedly threaten her. "Are you sure you still want to be here, arguing semantics when Giovanni returns?"

Her smile vanishes before she replaces it with something cold and vicious. "Fine, I'll go." Her hand shoots out to grab my arm. "But not until you've taken the test."

Her fingers dig into my skin so firmly I know they'll leave a mark when she attempts to drag me toward the bathroom. I say "attempt" because her svelte frame can barely budge me. Her struggles make me grateful for the extra meat on my bones.

"Take the damn test, Valentina!"

Pain lances through me when her nails pierce my skin, and I gasp while pulling free. "Let go!"

"Not until—"

The door slams open so fast it smacks into the drywall.

Valeria jerks back as fear fills her eyes. Her panic doesn't lessen a smidge when she realizes it is Dante entering my room instead of Giovanni.

Dante's presence fills the room like the gust of a dangerous storm after a humid day. It's as suffocating as it is liberating.

As his eyes bounce between Valeria and me, he grinds his teeth. "What the hell is going on?" His voice is dangerously low. "I could hear you arguing halfway down the hall."

"She—" Valeria starts, but Dante cuts her off with a look that could shatter bulletproof glass.

"Out," he orders, staring at Valeria as if she's gum under his desk. "*Now.*"

Valeria's lips curl like she believes her beauty will get her out of more than a speeding ticket. One flare of Dante's nostrils and she wises up. After dropping my arm, the sting from her nails still irritating my skin, she stalks past him without another word leaving her thin-pressed lips.

The door clicks shut behind her, and the silence that follows slackens the clutch slowly asphyxiating me, though not fully.

How could I have forgotten I might be pregnant? Giovanni is a king both inside and outside the bedroom, but one glance at his sinfully delicious face shouldn't make me a brain-dead idiot.

Dante's expression softens when he takes in the pregnancy test sitting on the bed. "Are you okay?"

I nod too quickly. The dizziness it inspires nearly makes me vomit. "Yes." I muster a smile that announces my dishonesty before my words do. "I'm fine."

Dante has honed the same skills as Giovanni. He sees straight through my lie. "Would you like me to get Vanni?"

"No." Loose tresses of hair slap my cheeks when I shake my head. "I'd prefer not to interrupt him while he's with your father."

Giovanni explained last night that the brothers take turns checking in with the doctor helming his father's medical care, and that this morning was his turn. Their meetings rarely last ten minutes, but each brother uses the time left over from the allotted hour to have quality one-on-one time with their father.

Giovanni already missed one rostered check-in because he was busy settling me in. I don't want him to miss another. He's so understanding of my sometimes overbearing relationship with my mother, so I'll give him the same flexibility with his parent.

Dante eyeballs me for a moment, then slowly turns to face the door. "If you need anything..."

"I'm good," I whisper, more convincingly this time. "Thank you."

When he leaves, my heart pounds so hard it might crack my ribs. Valeria's words won't stop playing on repeat: *Giovanni thinks you're pregnant. If you're not, you'll be gone faster than I can snap my fingers.*

My throat burns as the room suddenly feels too big and cold. As panic bears down on me, I rush into the bathroom. I need to wash off the funk clinging to my skin and remember that I've faced worse than this.

I was told nine months ago my mother had six months to live. Nothing could be worse than that. Though I'd be lying if I said this wasn't a close second.

The shower water is scalding, but I need it that way. The heat melts the tension coiled in my muscles and soothes the sting from Valeria's nails. Steam curls around me as barbs of water pelt my skin.

It helps. The highness in my shoulders slacken and the tension in my spine loosens. I breathe deeply, filling my lungs with the clean scent of soap and steam, and for a few precious minutes, I pretend the world outside doesn't exist. There are no tests or threats. And no cruel whispers that I'm nothing more than an incubator.

I feel good, but the instant I switch off the faucet, the negativity creeps back in.

What if Giovanni only wants me because he's desperate for an heir?

I'm consumed with what-ifs as I wrap myself in a towel and enter the central part of the room. My steps falter partway in. The pregnancy test sits on the mattress, glaring at me like it's a verdict waiting to be delivered. It's just plastic and paper, but right now, it feels like the most powerful thing in the world. Whatever answer it holds could change everything.

Water drips onto the wooden floorboards as I stare at a truth I'm not ready to face. Then I inch closer, as if drawn by gravity. I don't want to fold to peer pressure, but I'd like to know what's happening inside my body.

Because at the end of the day, it's my body, so it's my choice.

With my mind made up, I snatch up the test, race into the bathroom, and tear open the packet. The box hits the floor with a thud as the test strip cools the heat roaring through my palm.

After following the instructions to the wire, I place the test stick on the vanity sink and wait the required amount of time.

Minutes have never felt like days until now.

When the alarm in my head goes off, I slowly approach the

vanity. My breaths are ragged, and my heart feels like it's about to break out of my chest.

Before I can talk myself out of it, I flip over the plastic strip that holds more power than it should.

As I stare at the result, my reflection fractured in the foggy mirror, one thought screams louder than all the rest:

Everything is about to change.

25

GIOVANNI

As one of the many corridors of the Caruso compound stretches before me, I retrieve my phone from my pocket and bring up the surveillance feed for my room. It's instinct now—habit. The screen flickers before it presents an empty room. The sheets look rumpled, as if Valentina left in a hurry. Before my panic gets away from me, I notice the steam curling under the bathroom door. It licks at the wooden floorboards like smoke and switches my unease to need.

Valentina is showering.

What more incentive do I need than that to shake off my restless mood?

As my pulse kicks up, I increase my pace. I love taking Valentina hard and fast in the shower, but I also like taking care of her. I crave her shy smiles when she's lavished like a princess as equally as I do the fiery vixen who emerges when she wraps her lips around my cock.

I'm about to enter the wing where the bedrooms are when Valeria steps into my path. She gleams at me like a predator detecting the fresh blood of a virgin as her hand shoots up to my chest like she barreled me over.

"Vanni," she purrs, her smile too over the top for the hour.

When her nails graze my chest, the dangling charms hooked on them cool my skyrocketing temperature. They're similar to the charms you find on a bracelet, and they clink together when I snatch up her hand, yank it off my chest, and then drop it faster than a bomb.

She acts ignorant of my fury about being manhandled without permission. It's a performance she knows well. "The charms are meant to boost fertility." Her eyes gleam with fake sweetness, and her voice is syrupy. "Despite everything that's happened, I've been praying with a local minister for Valentina's pregnancy to be successful. You deserve an heir. It means *everything* to you."

My veins ice over as I work my jaw side to side. "No," I say flatly. "It doesn't."

Her brow lifts, exposing the surprise glittering in her eyes. "Of course it does. It's all you've ever wanted."

"Not with Valentina," I bite out. "With her, it's about more than that."

Her smile falters as confusion clouds her perfect face. There's no denying Valeria's attractiveness. She's a beautiful woman who could have more than one schmuck eating out of her palm. I'll just never be one of them. I've dated self-absorbed women before. They've never held my interest long enough to go back for seconds.

God invented kindness to be given freely, not traded. There's strength in a woman who is both kind and confident—especially when she proudly owns every inch of herself.

Just thinking about Valentina's luscious body and the confidence it yields thickens my cock. I love how her beauty feels alive under my hands when I grip it during a marathon fuck, and I'm done pretending otherwise.

"Giovanni—"

Valeria's pleading tone rots in the air behind me when I sidestep her and continue down the hall. I'm not solely racing away because the longer I converse with Valeria the less time I'll have to clean Valentina's skin with my tongue. It's to show her she has no power in this situation. No influence.

Even if she is the mother of my child, she is *not* the narrator of my story.

Sunlight spills across the floorboards when I enter my room at the speed of a rocket launching into space. Then disappointment hammers me when I spot Valentina in the corner of the space. She's already dressed. Her hair is damp, and her skin is glowing from the shower products the head maid purchased specifically for her.

My cock hardens while recalling how many times I've tasted her bodywash over the past week, but the euphoria it instigates is short-lived since her eyes won't meet mine, no matter how hard I strive for eye contact.

"I need to go." She speaks fast, like the words might vanish if she doesn't spit them out. "Work called. I finally got a shift. Because I missed so many last week, Alessandro rostered me on for a day shift. The tips will be less, but anything is better than nothing, right?"

I grit my teeth, stunned she'd lie to me. We have blockers up to stop our phones from being tapped. She can FaceTime her mother and get messages via the same app, but standard calls are impossible to receive within the compound's walls without a specially designed phone.

Her boss also told her to take all the time she needs when we popped into the pub to rearrange a handful of shifts that didn't correspond with her mother's new treatment plan. He might have been fearful of my warning glare, but that doesn't alter the facts.

Valentina is lying to me.

Lying is usually punishable by death. Valentina won't suffer the same consequences.

Doesn't make my frustration any less, though.

"You don't need to work."

"I can't pay you back if I don't work." My knuckles crack when the unease in her expression places my anger on a very steep cliff. "I also can't just sit here while you—" She bites back the remainder of her reply, but I hear it anyway. *While you do everything.*

Not wanting to push our exchange anywhere close to how I usually conduct an interrogation, I tread carefully. "What's going on, *dolcezza*?"

Her eyes glisten, and for a second, her armor cracks. "I need to make sure I can still stand on my own." Angrily, she brushes a tear off her cheek. "And that I can survive without you."

Her admission guts me. She doesn't have to consider a life without me in it. I'll carry the world on my shoulders for her if she asks.

But then I remember I can't control her.

I can only support her.

So instead of pushing, I nod. "Fine." My voice is rough and low. "We always have a driver on standby. He'll take you anywhere you want to go."

The relief that blisters across her beautiful face is painful to watch. Turmoil replaces her relief when she grabs her bag and brushes her lips against mine. She whispers, "Bye," like she's leaving forever, before she disappears into the hallway.

I reach for my jacket two seconds later. The chase won't be as exciting since Valentina's fear is genuine this time, but I'll never skip an opportunity to catch her.

Valentina is already at the car when I catch her. "I've got it, Marco."

After dipping his chin, the driver stops rounding the hood to open Valentina's door.

When I open the door for her, Valentina's lips part as if she wants to argue, but not a word spills from her plump mouth. Maybe she knows better. Or perhaps she knows even with the chase being short, it will have the same result.

She ran, and I caught her.

That will only ever end one way.

After assisting Valentina into the back seat, I slide in behind her and close the door. The scent of her rapidly building arousal fills the SUV's cab when I jab the button above our heads.

The privacy partition hums until the driver's head disappears behind tinted glass.

Privacy.

Control.

Just the two of us.

I yank at my tie when the heat blooming from Valentina becomes too stifling to ignore as she finally returns my gaze.

"I didn't run from you." Her tone is steady like she's laying down a truth that can't be bent. "You gave me permission to leave."

"Semantics."

"Giovanni..." There's no conviction in her husky delivery of my name. No power. This is *exactly* what she wanted. She wanted me to chase her. Now I merely need to work out why.

"What happened between last night and this morning that made you believe you need to ponder a world without me in it?"

She shifts her gaze to the scenery whizzing past her window. "Nothing."

Almost cruelly, I seize her wrist and yank her across the cab until her chest flattens against my shoulder and our teeth clash. I kiss her hungrily. Violently. I take, take, and take until the healthy rise and fall of her chest grazes my arm with her erect nipples and she's breathless with need.

My lips on the shell of her ear send a trail of goose bumps down her spine, not to mention the words I speak. "Take your panties off. I'll never make it through an entire shift without reaching for my gun if I ruin them so badly you have to work without them."

"Gio—"

"*Now,* Valentina."

She's torn but also horny. The rapid incline of her pulse announces this, as does the scent that plumes into the air when she slowly rises to her knees to answer my demand.

With my hands stabilizing her sways, she pulls up her skirt until it resembles a belt, then tugs down her panties, which are shadowed with wetness.

I love that my kisses drench her so much that I can take her without preparation and not feel guilty about hurting her.

Once her pussy is bare and glistening, I jerk my head to her long-sleeved shirt. "Now your shirt. Let me see those fantastic tits."

Dark locks swish against her back when she shakes her head.

I'm about to remind her that she can have the control anywhere *outside* of the bedroom, but her every want, need, and desire inside it are mine, but her backbone rises too quickly.

"No." I'm so obsessed with the confidence in her tone that I can only stare at her in awe when she adds, "The drive to town only takes fifteen minutes. I want your cock pounding inside me for every one of them."

I wordlessly confirm I'm on board with her plan by rocking my hips upward, stroking myself against her wet heat. The yearning glowing in her eyes hides the restlessness I've yet to combat. Still, I act oblivious.

I'll get the truth out of her. I just have to be buried a minimum of nine inches first.

With my cock hurriedly removed from my pants, which are now huddled around my ankles, and her knees hugging my thighs, Valentina grips the grab bar she reached for earlier before slowly lowering herself onto my cock, inch by fucking inch.

My thighs bunch when she swivels her hips, opening herself up to me. It feels amazing, but since she's a couple of inches off the nine required to push the narrative of our exchange, I clamp my hand over her mouth, then use my free hand to tug her down two more inches.

She's almost too snug, but the sparks the tight fit prompt are deliciously arrogant.

Valentina's mangled scream dots my hand with condensation when I flex my cock, ensuring she knows exactly how deep I am, and then I lower my hand to her clit. Her whimper when I roll the nervy bud with my thumb tingles through my balls. It's the desperate noise of a woman who hasn't climaxed in months, as if the endless orgasms I've given her the prior three days were merely a prelude to how combustible our exchanges can be.

"Go slow," I order when she gradually ascends, withdrawing at the same painstaking pace she used to welcome my cock inside.

She follows my command to a tee... until she reaches the wide girth of my crown. Then she slams down like the monster dick her sexy curves will forever inspire isn't girthy enough to slice her in two.

"Christ, *dolcezza*." My hands shoot for her hips as cum gathers at the base of my dick. I love when she loses control and isn't ashamed by it, but this isn't how our exchange was meant to be. I'm meant to be bending her will, not the other way around. "You feel so fucking good sucking at my cock and wordlessly pleading for its cum." Her expression reveals the luscious soreness rocketing through her core when I meet her movements, pump for pump. "That's what you want, isn't it? My cum coating the walls of your pussy and ass. You want me any way you can get me."

I palm her ass and squeeze when she nods.

"But that isn't all you want, is it, *dolcezza*? You also want me to chase you and bow at your feet."

Again and again, Valentina rises and falls on my cock, accepting a little more each time. Her pelvis grinds against my V muscle as the hue of her excitement spreads from her cheeks to her neck. She's almost too tight, but my body ignores the bite of discomfort.

"Answer me."

Our moans align when I fuck her harder and faster. I drive in deep, stuffing in every hardened inch of my cock until pain flitters in her eyes along with desire.

"If that's what you want, there's no shame in admitting that. If you want me to burn the castle, I'll burn the castle. If you want me to terrorize the world, I'll terrorize the world." I grunt when the walls of her pussy clamp around my thrusting cock. "If you want me on my knees, kissing your feet, I'll do that, too. You don't need to run to achieve any of those things, Valentina. You only need to ask."

My confession has her body going pliable under my touch and her head thrusting back.

Or was it because I said her name instead of her nickname?

As her hands brace the roof of the SUV and she thrusts her fantastic yet still-covered breasts in my face, shudder after shudder works through her wary muscles.

Her body convulses for several long seconds before the most beautiful expression I've ever seen crosses her face. She's caught in the throes of ecstasy, and I'm barely one step behind.

I just have one matter to take care of first.

Returning the confidence a soon-to-be dead man stole from her.

26

VALENTINA

ure hell. Gut-wrenching torment. That's how I'd describe the last fifteen minutes of my life. But if I'm honest, I'd also admit it was the most uplifting confidence boost I've ever had.

Giovanni's tongue is wicked, and not solely when it's lapping up the multiple arousals he forces out of me in a short period.

It should have been a stretch to make me come once, but I stopped counting at four.

I feel good, and not all the sparks are compliments to Giovanni's amazing cock and wicked mouth. Some are because I didn't succumb to his demands at the start of our exchange. I was horny, there's no doubting that, and seemingly submissive, but I could have thrown Valeria under the bus to save myself.

I didn't because I have values—unlike her.

"Thank you," I murmur under my breath when Giovanni hands me the underwear I removed earlier. I slip them up my shuddering legs as our SUV slowly merges toward the curb of the downtown district.

When the creak of the swinging sign at the front of the pub projects through the tinted windows, I wait for the familiar weight of exhaustion to settle in my bones. I appreciate having the capability to work and that not everyone is as fortunate, especially when you only have a foreign bank account, but this place is as draining to my energy as the hours I spent walking the halls of the surgical ward, waiting to hear if my mother's operation had been a success.

Alessandro is a misogynist pig. It takes everything I have not to slap him each shift, but I have to do this. If Valeria is right and Giovanni is only with me because he's desperate for an heir, I need something to fall back on when my world once again implodes.

I hate myself for distrusting Giovanni's motives, even more so after our awe-inspiring commute, but doubt kills more dreams than failure ever will.

When I crank my neck to Giovanni, not hazed enough with lust to consider stepping out while his glistening cock is still hanging out of his pants—I'm sexually satiated, not cured of jealousy—I'm met with an empty seat.

Confused, I dart my eyes between the individuals milling in close to admire a car that would have had a hefty import fee. When a pink hue creeps up the necks of a handful of women, I realize they're not envying a gleaming chunk of metal.

Giovanni is in their sights.

Because I raked my fingers through his hair, it's tousled in a sexy I-woke-up-like-this way, and his pupils, dilated with lust, appear darker than usual. He screams of wealth and sexuality, and every woman eyeing him like a tiger would a steak knows he fucks like a god. His arrogant strut announces this, much less the scent pluming from him. It's sweaty and sweet, a combination of us both.

Before I can process why I'm not gouging out the eyes of the women gawking with want, Giovanni opens the door for me. His gentlemanly act shocks the women surrounding him. I'm not at all surprised. Giovanni speaks fondly of his father, and my mother has always said to pick a man by the traits of his father.

If he's a good, honest man, you've found yourself a good, honest man.

If he's a snake in tall grass, run.

My grandfather on my father's side was the latter.

When Giovanni holds out his hand to assist me out, I roll my eyes. It's all an act. A smile is tugging at my lips, and I can feel my pulse raging through my body.

Confusion sideswipes my euphoria about his old-fashioned courtesy when he shuts the door behind me before he guides me under the pub's alcove. Assuming he's as traditional with his farewells as he is with common courtesies, I press my lips to his cheek and mouth, *Bye.*

Again, he doesn't leave. He simply smirks, and the crowd flocks closer.

Although I'm seconds away from acting like a possessive jerk, I keep my tone impassive while saying, "You don't have to stay. I can take it from here."

He sees straight through my lie. "Do you need another detour, *dolcezza?*"

Detour?

My throat burns when I glance at his watch. A lot more time has passed than I believed.

Now I know why those fifteen minutes felt like the longest fifteen minutes of my life.

It was closer to an hour.

"It isn't like we don't have time." Giovanni nudges his head to the closed sign hanging in the window. The opening hours are clear, and they scream in his face that I'm a big fat liar.

I still try to act nonchalant, though. "The staff always arrives early. We have to set up before the patrons arrive."

His brow gets lost in his hair half a second before he snatches up my wrist and drags me back toward the SUV. "Second detour it is."

Knowing I'll never survive another hour being tormented into submission, I shout, "Fine! If you want to waste your morning priming kegs for consumption, who am I to stop you?"

After freeing my wrist from his hold and dodging the thirsty women desperate to take my place, I stab the keys I normally use to lock up into the lock, fling open the door, then gesture for Giovanni to enter first.

He scoffs, disgusted. He'd never leave me defenseless to the wolves, and the women surrounding us are out for blood.

The crowd sighs as if bestiality is attractive when I dart into the pub as per the request of Giovanni's glare.

I set my bag behind the bar and spin to face him before giving him my best "boss" look. If he wants to babysit me like I'm a child and hide it under the guise of being helpful, I'll put him to work.

His dark eyes follow my hand when I jerk it to the cellar door. "The kegs are in the refrigerator down there. You need to carry them up the stairs, carefully, of course, and connect a CO_2 tank, regulator, gas line, and liquid line to a coupler. Then..." I wait, expecting some kind of backlash. When it never comes, I continue. "You need to connect it to a tap, which you will have to prime to ensure there are no leaks. Alcohol is expensive. We can't waste a single drop."

Not a hint of protest fetters Giovanni's deliriously handsome face. He simply nods before heading in the direction I nudged. "How many kegs do you need me to bring up?"

I stagger back, a little thrown by his lack of objection. "Er... two, for now. A lager and a pale ale. The kegs have labels, so just match them up. If you get stuck, shout, and I'll come help you."

Already rolling up his sleeves, he grins and winks. "Got it, boss."

I butt my hip with the bar and wait when he disappears down the cellar's creaky steps, anticipating him to reappear at any moment. The cart for the kegs is in the owner's office, and he'll need that.

Instead of a crash or a curse, minutes later, Giovanni reappears, carrying a keg on each shoulder. He sets them down near the taps, wipes the condensation from his hands, then crouches under the bar to connect the lines.

All I do is stare. I've worked with five male bar staff over the past three months. Four complained that the purpose-built stair cart should be replaced with an internal keg lift that would deliver the kegs from the cellar to the bar with the push of a button. The other one whined the entire time that he wasn't built for manual labor. He quit mid-shift.

Giovanni doesn't cite a single gripe. He gets on with it like he's worked here for years, and I'm tempted to check if he's real.

How can you look like him, fuck like him, and understand hard work like he does?

I stop wondering when he pops up a handful of minutes later. As he dusts his hand, he strays his eyes to me. "All done. Do you want me to prime the lines, or do you want to check the connections first?"

I take a giant step back. "This is your baby, Vanni, so if you've made a mistake, you'll be the only one wearing beer-soaked clothes today."

He gleams, loving that I called him Vanni, before he grabs a glass from the rack, tilts it at the desired forty-five-degree angle, then pulls a beer like a pro. He even straightens the glass slowly as it fills so it gets the ideal foam head, and he doesn't spill a drop when he sets it on the countertop next to me.

"Is that up to your standards, boss, or shall I try again?"

His molten lava voice makes me want to melt like a popsicle on a hot summer's day, but I hold my ground—scarcely.

"Try again." Hating that he mistakes my reply as being snarky, I quickly add, "It's never fun drinking alone."

By the end of my shift, I'm utterly spent. My feet are aching, but the buzz of our commute hasn't dulled a smidge. That probably has more to do with how often I've caught Giovanni's hooded gaze over the past eight hours than anything else.

He's still here, working pro bono alongside me.

I wasn't rostered for today, but the pub was the only place that popped into my head when I sought somewhere to think without reminders of Giovanni constantly entering my head. My boss was surprised to see me, but he protected my secret after he learned who had connected the kegs and stacked the shelves behind the bar.

He shook Giovanni's hand, mumbled a brief introduction as if they hadn't already met, then retreated to his office, leaving the brunt of the workload to Giovanni and me.

Giovanni didn't mind. He chatted with the regulars and replaced the empty kegs before I could ask. He even charmed Mrs. O'Malley into leaving a bigger tip than usual.

I catch him staring as I wipe down the bar, his gaze lust-filled but attentive. "You good, *dolcezza*?"

I nod, though I have no idea why I bother. Giovanni seems to have a four-dimensional paradox directly to my soul. He barely arches a brow, and I cave.

"I'm tired. For some reason, I haven't gotten much sleep the past week."

Smirking, he rests his elbows on the counter I just cleaned, then says, "Why's that?"

When I throw my dishcloth in his face, his laughter bellows around the nearly deserted space.

After dumping the cloth that smacked him upside the head, his demanding tone slashes through the haze swamping me. "It's time to go home, *dolcezza*. If you're a good girl during the drive, I might even let you sleep tonight."

I laugh at his obvious lie while pushing up the sleeves of my shirt. I need to cool my skin before I beg him to make true on his threat when he told me he won't hold back the next time I call him Vanni. He said he'll fuck me on the closest surface he finds—witnesses or not.

I snap my eyes to Giovanni when a gargled groan rolls up his chest. With his eyes glued on my arm, he stands perfectly still. Too still.

I follow the direction of his gaze, and my happy mood circles the drain.

The marks I tried to hide from him earlier stand out like a nun in a brothel. Four deep crescents from Valeria's nails glow as vividly as the anger on Giovanni's face. I could feel the sting of her ironclad grip hours later, but as my shift continued, I pushed aside the pain as one of the effects of a long day.

Pure unfiltered rage fills Giovanni's eyes as he struggles to maintain his cool. I've seen him angry before, but this is different. This level of anger is dangerous. He looks like he could tear the pub apart with his bare hands and it would disperse only a fraction of his fury.

"Giovanni..." My reply falls silent when I realize he isn't looking at me anymore. His slit eyes are locked on someone over my shoulder.

I know who it is before I even glance over my shoulder. Matteo's presence is as suffocating as Giovanni's, but since it has a playful edge, such as driving across town to witness his brother working a "regular job," it doesn't demand the attention of the entire room. You just know he's there, watching.

Giovanni wets his throat as if he's swallowing fire, and then his words come out low and lethal. "Take her home," he says to Matteo. "Now."

Matteo doesn't hesitate. He straightens up fast enough to dislodge the woman he's been sucking face with for the past two hours, nods, and heads my way.

The weight of Giovanni's fury presses against my spine even as Matteo moves closer, and it surges my desperation. "Vanni…"

I must have tossed out my line without any bait, because Giovanni doesn't even nibble at it. His focus is resolute, and he's already far from here.

I want to tell him that I'm not fragile. I have and will continue to handle this on my own, but my mouth refuses to relinquish my words. Both my head and my heart know what this is really about. It isn't control. It's protection. And right now, Giovanni's belief that he failed to protect me is burning him alive.

27

GIOVANNI

Matteo moves for Valentina before I do. One second, she's throwing out sexual innuendos like they'll pull me back from the edge. The next, Matteo's arm bands around her waist, and she's off the floor and slung over his shoulder as if she weighs nothing.

She screams Matteo's name first, then mine.

When neither slackens Matteo's strides, she shouts a heap of angry, desperate pleas. Since none of them are what I want to hear—like why the fuck she's marked—I don't pay them any attention.

The fury charging through my veins eventually drowns out Valentina's pleas. All I can see are the nail-size indents carved into her skin like some sort of fucking signature, and the bruises formed around them.

Whoever grabbed her must have been holding something sharp but small. Otherwise, how else can you explain that odd pattern? Unless...

My jaw cracks as a memory hits. Valeria's long and lacquered nails had those ridiculous fertility charms dangling off them. The pattern on the silver trinket that clinked when she raked her hand over my chest is a similar pattern to a bruise accompanying the nail indentations.

That's all the proof I need to know Valeria didn't just grab Valentina. She dug her nails in deep enough for Valentina to feel her warning for days.

The fire inside me rages out of control until it's all I can taste. I told Valentina she'd be protected in my realm and that nothing bad would ever happen to her or her family.

Valeria turned that truth into a lie, and for what? An opportunity to stake a claim to something she will *never* own.

My hands ball so fast my nails bite into my palms. I want to rip those charms off Valeria's nails one by one and make her choke on them. But more than anything, I want her to understand the consequences when you touch what's mine.

When the pub door swings shut behind Valentina and Matteo, I push off the bar. My steps are timed and deliberate, because if I'm not cautious, I'll break something and I won't stop until I level this entire fucking town.

The bartender who started his shift an hour ago looks up, drinks in my fury, and then wisely looks away. Good. I don't need comfort or meaningless words.

I need revenge.

I pull out my phone, which feels as heavy as a weapon, and then scroll to the name I swore I'd never use again. My thumb hovers for not even a second before it presses the call button.

The voice that answers is smooth and amused. "Thought our arrangement was over?"

"It is... *after* this."

A beat passes before a knowing laugh cracks out of my phone's speaker. "Who?"

"Valeria." The mere mention of her name fills me with a

venomous rage that suffocates all my objections. "I want eyes on her. Tonight."

There should be a pause or an uneasy swallow. Anything that tells me he's uncomfortable with my plan. I get nothing but an agreement. "Understood."

I end our call to avoid questions since I'm not obligated to answer to anyone but Valentina. I owe her more than answers.

I owe her blood.

The frigid night air outside feels like ice, yet it fails to extinguish the fire consuming me. Nothing will douse the flames until Valeria learns what happens when you wedge yourself between a man and his obsession.

Under the streetlight illuminating the unmanned SUV, I make a vow I'll die upholding.

Valeria marked Valentina, so now I'll mark a headstone with her name.

28

VALENTINA

I've been pacing so long a rug worth thousands now feels tatty under my feet. It's been over two hours since Matteo hauled me out of the pub like a sack of flour, and I still can't breathe right. My chest hurts, and my throat is raw from how many times I've swallowed the panic bubbling up my esophagus.

I regret not fighting harder to make sure Giovanni knew my exchange with Valeria didn't rattle me, but Matteo didn't give me a choice. One second, I was standing. The next, I was over his shoulder. I begged for the chance to tell my side, but Giovanni didn't hear a word I spoke. He was deafened by rage.

Now I'm confined in a room like a Disney princess. It should feel safe, but it doesn't.

It feels like a cage.

Hunger and unease churn my stomach, but the tray Dante sent sits untouched on Giovanni's desk. The bread and soup could settle my flipping stomach, but it's such a twisted mess I'm scared to fill it with food.

I'd hate for anyone to mistake the reason I'm sick.

Flattening my palms against the dresser, I try to level my breaths, hopeful some air will stop me from pacing. It doesn't work. My pulse drums my ribs too fast to ignore, and the walls creep closer every time I stop wearing a hole in the rug.

As I continue pacing, I replay the expression that crossed Giovanni's face when he saw Valeria's marks. Anger wasn't the only source of his fury. Something darker and more sinister had the room holding its breath like a chemical weapon had detonated in the pub.

If only Valeria hadn't worn those stupid charms. We could have avoided all this if she had been a little less vain.

Anyone would swear she wanted me to carry her marks. If that was her plan, she's more foolish than beautiful. She'd have to know how Giovanni would respond. I had an inkling, and I've only known him for weeks. Why do you think I wore a long-sleeved shirt on an extremely humid day?

Giovanni and Valeria have known each other for over two decades, so her imprudence makes no sense... *unless she wants a war.*

Further deliberation is cut short by a rattling doorknob.

My head snaps up so fast my neck aches. It's most likely Dante. He's checked on me a few times and constantly assures me everything will be fine, even though it feels anything but.

It's funny. Dante was thrown into fatherhood without preparation, but his instincts are natural. His protectiveness is as relentless as Giovanni's. Nico and Elio are the more reserved of the brothers, and Matteo has the restless energy of a crack addict. Therefore, if I have to put money on who's coming through the door, I'll only ever wager on Dante.

Faster than I can blink, the door shoots open, and then a flurry of brown tumbles into my room. My breath snags when my eyes land on the shuddering lump indenting the plush rug I wore down.

I take a step back, then another, until my back flattens against the wall.

My caller isn't Dante.

It's Giovanni.

And he isn't alone.

Valeria is a quivering bag of nerves at his feet.

Afraid I might fall, I grip the wall so hard my nails scratch the paintwork. My legs feel like Jell-O, and my breathing is frantic enough to cave my chest in.

Giovanni's face appears carved from a rock, and his dark, stormy eyes are unreadable. Heat rolls off him like a furnace, making the room stuffy and uninviting.

I shoot my hand up to cover my mouth when he fists Valeria's hair before yanking it back to align her eyes with mine. Not even the bruise circling her eye can hide the fact she's been crying. I wish that was the worst of it. Her top lip is split open, and blood is pooling under her nose.

I refuse to believe Giovanni is responsible for her injuries, but the evidence is a little hard to discount. His fury hasn't weakened the slightest since I last saw him. It's radiating out of him in invisible waves.

Giovanni's gravelly tone slices through the silence. "Apologize."

Like she isn't at his feet, peering down the barrel of a gun, Valeria's chin tilts as if she's better than this. Her smile is gone, wiped by the blood trickling over her lips, but her eyes are still mocking.

"Apologize!" Giovanni roars again, his tug on her hair cruel.

She whimpers when no number of shouts have her mistaking her roots being plucked from her scalp. Then, slowly, like this is an inconvenience, she drifts her eyes to me.

"I'm sorry." Her words are brittle, as if she forced them through a batch of vomit. They fall flat and do nothing to dispel Giovanni's anger.

"No." He drags her across the room until her rain-soaked shirt dampens my shoes. "Not like that. Apologize like you actually fucking mean it." My stomach recoils when he adds, "Like you know that this apology is the only reason you're not already under six feet of dirt."

"Vanni—"

"Apologize!"

Tears topple down Valeria's cheeks when the reality of the situation finally dawns on her. She isn't running the show around here. "I'm sorry."

"For?" Giovanni continues to push, the word shooting from his mouth like poison.

This time, Valeria falls into line. "For thinking I could mark you. That I could put my hands on you and get away with it."

Since I can't take more of this, I nod so fast that I make myself dizzy. "It's fine." My reply is thin with fragility. "I accept your apology."

I don't believe she is sincere.

I simply want this over before Giovanni does something he can't take back.

In my head, I call Valeria an idiot when she peers up at Giovanni and murmurs, "You wanted an apology. You got one. Now let me go."

Giovanni doesn't move, nor does his expression soften. His shoulders remain rigid, and his jaw locks so firmly I can see the strain. "No." The chilliness of his words causes me to shudder. "I never said I'd let you go once you apologized. What you did was inexcusable. A mistake like that is only corrected one way."

I can't breathe when he raises his gun an inch. Now, instead of being pointed at Valeria's eyes, it homes in on the wrinkle popped between her brows.

Valeria re-finds her panic. "What do you want me to do, Giovanni? Beg? I can beg."

I don't recognize the voice that comes out of Giovanni.

"I need you to grasp the implications of your actions." He speaks each word with lethal deliberation. "And how you can't take back with words what you did. You fucking marked her. You dug your nails into the woman I'm obsessed with..." He makes eye contact with me, and electricity surges through the air. His hooded gaze is dark and lethal but also burning with something that scares me more than Valeria ever could. "You hurt the woman I love."

He misses the rapid dilation of my pupils when he returns his eyes to Valeria.

Love? He loves me?

"And now you will die for your stupidity."

Aware I am her *only* lifeline, Valeria looks at me, but her silent pleas barely register as I call Giovanni's name. He doesn't look at me. He can't. His focus is locked on his target like a predator, and every fiber of his being screams violence.

Valeria's confidence is now stripped bare, but it doesn't matter. Giovanni's rage is too out of control to reel back in.

I doubt I have what it'll take to make him see reason, but I have to try. This is about more than me. It is about more than all of us.

"I'm pregnant." My confession fires from my mouth like a gunshot.

This time, my bait hooks the fish. Giovanni's eyes snap to me, and the silence that follows the deathly bob of his Adam's apple feels endless. Valeria stiffens before her lips part in victory.

I don't pay her fanning feathers any attention. This situation is too volatile for me to remove my eyes from Giovanni for even a second.

His finger is still hugging the trigger, and it's three-quarters compressed.

"You're pregnant?" I'd describe his voice as broken, though not necessarily disbelieving.

I wet my lips before murmuring, "Yes."

Giovanni stares at me like he's reading the truth on my face, and then his gaze drops to my stomach, where it lingers like my confession is the only thing anchoring him through the storm endeavoring to swallow him whole.

My steps are thunderous as I race to the dresser. With shaky hands, I pull out the test I hid a second before he burst into my room like the hour we'd spent apart was more like a decade.

When I hold it out for him, he drinks it in slowly, like it's a sacred artifact worth millions. He scans the result, and although it relights the fire in him, the flames are nowhere near as ferocious since they're watered down by the weight of what this means for his family.

His father now has the chance to meet the heir of his eldest son's legacy.

"I'm pregnant," I repeat, softer now, because I need him to understand how this changes everything. "If this child is Valeria's"—that hurt to say more than you could ever imagine—"do you want him or her to grow up hating you? Do you want your son or daughter to never forgive you because you couldn't control your anger about something their mother did to me?"

His expression morphs as the storm disintegrates before my eyes. He loosens the fist tangled in Valeria's shiny locks and lowers the highness of his shoulders.

Since we're not fully out of the woods yet, I push forward, my stance stable but also fragile. "You don't want a life like that for your child, Vanni," I say confidently. "I grew up hating my father, and I've never even met him. Don't force your child to walk the same path. Give him or her the best start possible. Spare their mother."

The furious delivery of his words skates goose bumps across my skin. "She is *not* my child's mother."

"You don't know that," I fire back, heartache in my tone. "None of us know that." I ignore the hope flaring through Valeria's eyes. "I wish I could give you a definite answer, but I can't. All I can do is stop you from making a mistake that will change the course of your child's life."

The tear that topples down my cheek reaches him more than words ever could. In under a heartbeat, he crosses the room, falls to his knees, then squashes his forehead to my stomach.

My claim of bilingualism is put to the test when he mutters words into my stomach. I don't know every word he speaks to his child. He's talking too fast. But the portions I catch make his intent known.

His child will be raised with the love of both a father and a mother.

When he lifts his eyes to me, wordlessly announcing who he wants to fulfill the role of mother, I weave my fingers through his hair, grounding him, and then glance down at Valeria.

She's still frozen on the floor with her mouth ajar.

I wait for her gaze to meet mine before giving her a look that says everything: *Go. Now.*

She appears as if she wants to argue, but the sight of Giovanni on his knees, silently pleading for me to be his rock through his latest crisis, silences her.

After standing on shaky legs, she slips out without a sound.

Five seconds later, the softness of the bedding caresses my curves, and Giovanni buries his head between my legs.

GIOVANNI

Valentina's back bends harshly when I drag my nose down the drenched folds of her pussy and my approving growl rumbles through her core. I love how her scent is changing more and more each day. It's growing in strength like our child is in her stomach.

It's been a week since she cracked my world open with two short words.

I'm pregnant.

I've replayed her confession so many times it's imprinted on my skull. It will never fade.

I also can't stop searching her body for new curves I know are still months away.

Valentina's maternal instincts are just as vehement. I don't think she realizes how often she does it, but she rests her hand on her stomach a minimum of three times a day. She's already protecting what's inside. *Our* child.

The beating of my heart is as loud as a world-famous drummer performing a rock ballad. I've spent years living in a world where nothing lasts. Now there's this. A future that's ours for the taking.

I can't wait to shout my triumph so boisterously that the stone walls of Carlisle shake, but I have a few more months left to wait.

Until Valentina reaches the safe zone, I have to keep the news in our little bubble.

I don't mind. The world hasn't earned the right to savor our bliss with us just yet.

Excluding visiting Valentina's mother each evening, we haven't left our room all week. I didn't want to, and there was no real need to leave. The maids slip in with trays of food we only consume to keep our strength up enough not to pass out, and my brothers toss treats through the door like we're wild animals they're trying to tame.

The fantasy comes to an end this morning, though. Valentina has a meeting with her mother's medical team at 10 a.m., and I have another beast to break in at 9.

My father must not know how close I came to killing Valeria. If he did, he would have requested a meeting days ago. I think he's hopeful Valentina's attention has dampened my wish for revenge enough that he can revive the storm that nearly destroyed our legacy without needing to buy a raincoat.

If the heart trekking through my veins is anything to go by, he's on the money.

I'm no longer hungry for vengeance or for a war. I'm starved for the scrumptious palette of Valentina's greedy cunt when she shivers through back-to-back orgasms.

The reminder sees me stuffing two fingers inside her wet pussy and replacing my thumb with my tongue.

All it takes is one swipe of my tongue over her nervy bud, and she fists the bedding in a white-knuckled hold. As her moans bounce around our room, her toes dig into the mattress and her expression shifts from turmoil-filled to satisfied.

I wait for the stars to finish detonating before I slap down her hips and continue my pre-breakfast workout.

My thumb and tongue work in sync to drive her to the brink while my fingers pump in and out of her in a steady, controlled rhythm.

Her lusty eyes never leave mine when she crumples under my touch only minutes later.

I love the way her eyes spark with adoration and her skin mists with sweat as she shakes through a brutal climax. I could come just from the way my name tumbles from her pouty, kiss-bruised lips, but it still isn't enough.

I can't get enough.

I'm hungry for her taste. Her smell.

Starved of anything to do with her.

I crave her more than my lungs crave air, and I eat her exactly like that.

"Vanni... *Fuck.*"

Valentina pushes on my shoulders as if she's endeavoring to get away from me when her world shatters for the second time this morning.

Her silent request for clemency is a lie.

If she truly wanted me to slow down, she wouldn't have called me Vanni.

Over the next several minutes, while watching her through lowered lids, I finger-fuck her, grip her curves, and devour her with greedy, hungry kisses.

Goose bumps follow the trail of my lips when I touch every inch of her body. I leave no stone unturned, not only loving her curves but worshipping them as well.

I work another climax out of her before the honesty in her tone can't be dismissed. "Giovanni... *please.* I'm too sensitive. I can't take much more."

As frustration gnaws at me that I still haven't learned how to deny this woman, I adjust the tilt of her hips before nuzzling the delicate flesh between her shuddering thighs.

I have no qualms answering her every whim. I simply loathe how needy her taste makes me.

If her responsibilities weren't ringing in my ears as obviously as her moans, my head would never leave the apex of her thighs.

After backhanding her clit, doubling the scent filtering in my nose, I drag my nose down the seam of her pussy for the final time this morning.

Valentina's thighs hug my ears when I say with a growl, "I smell good *in* you."

She doesn't glower like she did the first time I said that.

Her head bobs before desire sparks through her hooded gaze.

She shivers when I run my hands up her sweat-slicked back, and then I lift her until she straddles my lap. When she grinds down on my cock, I fist her hair at the nape and tilt her head back, forcing her eyes to mine.

The hunger in them grows the longer I stare.

With her hips at the right incline, I guide the crown of my cock to the opening of her pussy, giving her clit a handful of playful swipes in the process.

Once her juices coat my head, I grip the base of my shaft, then pull her down on me by her hair.

"*Ohh...*" Valentina moans.

Her tight, wet pussy feels so good I forcefully still her hips, seconds from exploding. I'm young—*and fucking obsessed*—so I'm sure I can go another round, but I like to relish each rush, suck of her pussy, and frantic quiver our exchanges inspire.

I wait until I have a morsel of control before using my grip on her hip and hair to slowly guide her up and down my cock.

Valentina's strangled moan when I freeze again makes me smile.

She's flushed with heat and sweating head to toe but clawing at me as if her addiction is as rampant as mine.

"Please, Vanni..."

I love when she begs, so instead of succumbing to her pleas, I tease her a little.

I ask her how she wants to be fucked.

"Fast and dirty like we do every time we leave your mother's hospital room? Or slow and sultry like the words you're too afraid to speak?" I pump in a handful more times, bringing the lust in her eyes to the point of exploding. "Tell me what you want, *dolcezza*, and I'll give it to you."

I've never been like this before. So open and raw. Previously, I never bothered to ask my bed companions what they desired. I didn't care.

It isn't like that with Valentina.

Everything is different. Better.

"Fast and dirty," she eventually murmurs, gasping.

Her fingers seek something to clutch when I reply, "As you wish."

We moan in sync when I take all the control, regardless of my seated position. I pull her on and off my cock while stalking every expression that crosses her face. She's so beautiful like this. So fucking gorgeous. A Sicilian goddess sent to bring me to my knees.

Her hissed "*Yesss*" rewards her with an increase in tempo.

I thrust in and out until the sound of skin slapping skin booms around my room, and it nearly drowns out Valentina's breathy moans. She's speechless from the brutal fucking I'm giving her, and too in awe to speak.

I don't stop, though. I can't. I continue to work for every moan, shiver, and whispered quiver of my name. I want her to feel where I've been today any time she moves, and for the faint thud it causes to have her clawing at my belt the second we're alone.

The thought of her helpless with need has me driving in deeper. My cock commands every bit of her pussy, and I'm too boastful to remain quiet.

"Do you feel that?" I flex my dick, sending her head thrusting back and her eyes rolling. "How perfectly you fit around me? What does that tell you, *dolcezza*? What does that announce?"

She moans, but that is the start and end of her reply.

Curling my hand around her thigh, I angle it up, opening her more for me. The bed is merely a gimmick now. It cushions my knees but leaves the entirety of Valentina's suspension to me.

When her eyes lower to me and they fire with amazement, like she's in awe of my strength, I take a mental note to remove all apparatuses we can fuck on from my room the instant we're finished fucking. If this will be her response every time I take control of her whole body, we'll never fuck on a solid surface.

Not one to back down, even with my release pulling my balls in close to my body, I continue thrusting while returning to my previous objective. "What does that tell you, *dolcezza*?"

Valentina tries to keep my focus on the insane chemistry hissing between us. She meets my thrusts grind for grind until her eyes spark with signs of an imminent orgasm.

Usually, this is where I'd force the narrative. I try something different this time around.

I take what I need.

I fuck her hard and fast. I drive her to the brink until her tits clap my brilliance with every thrust, and the words I'm seeking finally spill from her lips.

"It announces that I was made for you. That I'm yours."

My final pumps are deep and hard, and the instant they're accompanied by vicious spurts of hot cum, a climax rips through Valentina.

Her breasts flatten against my chest as she leans into me for support, the sensation overwhelming her.

Once the shimmers weaken, she rests her head in the crook of my neck and fans the sweaty skin with whimpered words. "It announces that I'm yours."

GIOVANNI

In the hallway outside my father's room, a weird sensation I don't recognize buzzes through me. I think it's nerves, but what the fuck would I know? I've never handled them before. It's a similar feeling to what I experienced when Valentina glanced up at me for the first time, but more in my gut instead of my nuts.

Valentina stands at my left. Her chin is tilted high enough to hide the tension I know she's experiencing, and her perfume blends well with the faint cedar scent on the walls of my family's home.

It validates my long-held belief that she belongs here, next to me.

My cock twitches when Valentina's hand taps my arm. Yes, that's all it takes for me to want her. She merely needs to breathe in my direction and I'm as hard as a steel rod.

"You should go in alone." Her words are barely audible. "I don't want to intrude."

When I meet her gaze, an imaginary knife twists in my chest.

Even when her aura screams beauty and sophistication, she looks scared.

I hate that she still feels like an outsider.

My casa is her casa, and I'm done tiptoeing around that.

"There's no chance of you *ever* intruding." I curl my fingers around her hand and tether her to my side. The contact steadies me more than I care to admit. "You're carrying my child. It's time to get the formalities out of the way."

I see the desire to correct me forming in her eyes, the wish to remind me that the biology of our child isn't guaranteed, but just as fast as the urge rises, it's shoved aside for understanding. I said she is carrying *my* child, which isn't a lie, so she has no reason to correct me.

Still, I can't help but reiterate what I've told her time and time again over the past week. "Even if science played its hand before we did, the child you're carrying is ours. *Nothing* will change that." By nothing, I mean no one. "I will walk away from everything I have before I'll ever allow anyone to make you believe you're only an incubator to grow a Caruso heir."

Though that settles the debate, it still takes Valentina a few seconds to nod. "Okay."

I squeeze her hand in silent support, then push open my father's bedroom door. It still smells of antibacterial wipes and old books, but something new is in the air. Something fresh but with the substance of decades of respect and knowledge.

My father sits behind a desk that was covered with dust only weeks ago. A tailored suit covers his lean frame, and he combed his hair back like a sleek crown.

He looks up as we enter, and the determination in his eyes reveals how he became a man who built an empire. He appears as fit as an ox, and the unexpected euphoria it pumps through me sees me quickening my pace.

"Giovanni," he greets, his voice smooth like a Disaronno Originale sliding down the throat after a hard day. "And Valentina." His focus shifts to Valentina, where he eyes her with a probing but not unkind glance. "Finally."

I bark out a laugh. "Finally? It's barely been a week, Papa."

He smiles sardonically before gesturing to the chairs opposite his desk. "Sit." His smile is more welcoming when he directs it to Valentina than the one he gave me. "Both of you."

When we do, the leather sighs under our weight. I brace myself for the inevitable questions about loyalty and legacy that our family meetings forever inspire, but instead, he leans back in his chair, steeples his fingers, then says something that knocks the breath from my lungs.

"Have you picked a date yet?"

Valentina chokes on the spit of her ragged gasp, and I feel the ripple of her strain.

My response isn't far from hers. I'm obsessed with Valentina. Wholly and without constraint. But marriage? That's a huge commitment.

You wouldn't believe a word I spoke if you could see my smirk.

I won't oppose my father's ruling if it further cements Valentina's placement in my life. If I weren't obsessed with ensuring every inch of her—both inside and out—smells like me, that would have been the outcome of her confession last week.

I see fear in Valentina's eyes, and her panic about the speed of our relationship, so I reach for her hand under the table and give it a gentle squeeze.

"Relax." My suggestion is unusually soothing. "He's not talking about marriage." The thudding of the veins in her neck fades... until I add, "Yet."

Cockiness thickens my cock when she doesn't object to my plan. She merely blinks before a ghostlike grin twitches across her mouth.

Good. Because I won't accept anything other than yes when I ask her to be my wife.

I gesture with my head toward my father, who's watching us like a hawk. "He wants your mother to come to dinner. He asked me to invite her last week, but with everything that happened, I've not had the chance."

Relief floods Valentina's gorgeous face as her lips part. "Dinner? That's what all this is about?" She highlights my father's makeshift office with her hand. When he nods, she sighs so loudly her chest sinks. Clearly, she thought it was something much worse. That's understandable. They don't call my father the king of the Cosa Nostra for no reason.

I'm glad our competitors can't see him now. They'd kill for a chink in the Caruso dynasty, and his frail frame would give them that.

"We should do it soon," my father says, drawing my focus back to him. "It's Concetta's birthday next week, so it's perfect timing."

Still stunned, Valentina misses his confession that he knows her mother intimately enough to remember her birthday. "Yes, it is. Perfect timing."

"Invite your aunt too," Papa demands, his tone casual but firm in a way he can't help. He is who I inherited my bossiness from. "I assume she's still in the area?"

Valentina nods as a shocked mask slips over her face. "She is. She's never left Sicily."

"Good." My father's smile is warm in a way I haven't seen in years. "Let's have a celebration. You can pick the day while visiting your mother this morning. I'll handle everything else."

"Do you think you're up for that?" I ask, jumping back into the conversation.

When he nods without pause for thought, I stare at him, floored. This isn't the man I expected when he summoned me to his side. He doesn't seem as sick as he once was, not in spirit, anyway, but he was on his deathbed only days ago.

What prompted such a drastic backflip in his prognosis? It could be the surge the doctor warned me about last week, but it seems like more than that.

He looks alive.

I scan the documents he was perusing when we arrived, and that's when I see it. A pregnancy test sits on the edge of his desk. Although a stack of papers partially hides it, I know what it is. It's the same brand as the test Valentina showed me last week. The exact brand I've been seeking for the past seven days.

I rearranged my entire fucking room searching for the proof I wasn't dreaming when Valentina told me she was pregnant, and I never found it.

Now I know why.

My jaw tics as frustration sparks an inferno low in my gut. Valeria must have taken it when my back was turned and showed it to my father. I bet she didn't tell him the possibility of the child being hers is nothing to be excited about.

Valentina is carrying our child, not Valeria's. *Ours.* Deep down in a place where science can't touch, I know this. An IVF mishap didn't give me a child with Valeria. It gave me Valentina.

That is the *only* reason I let Valeria go. I didn't do it because I doubt the bloodline of my child and didn't want to risk them growing up hating me. I did it because I couldn't stand the thought of Valentina looking at me as if I were a monster instead of the father of her offspring.

I've seen that look before, and I'll burn the world to ash before I'll ever force it onto Valentina's face.

The inferno in my stomach rages, but I douse the flames with some spit. Valeria will get what's coming to her, but not yet. Valentina is at my side, holding her hand out in offering like her suggestion for us to go easy on the PDA until my family gets used to her is now void.

After farewelling my father with a brief chin dip, I guide Valentina toward the exit. As we step into the hall, Valentina exhales like she's been holding her breath for hours.

"That was…" She trails off, unable to find the right word.

"Unexpected?" I smile, hopeful it will hide the anger brandishing my cheeks with a red hue.

Her laugh is shaky but genuine. "Yeah."

I slip my arm around her waist and pull her close as we walk. "You were perfect," I murmur against her hair. "He likes you."

She inclines her head, her eyes shining. "You think?"

"I know." Her elbow gets friendly with my ribs during my following sentence. "He can't have you, though. You're mine." The shudders of her soundless laughter shift to the shakes of fear when I add, "And one day *soon*, you'll be my wife."

31

VALENTINA

My awareness of Giovanni's closeness activates half a second before his lips brush the sensitive skin between my thighs. He grazes my clit with his teeth while slowly pushing two fingers inside me. I bite my lip, trying vainly to pretend I'm still asleep. The perfect pressure of his tongue on my clit unravels me in seconds.

I love that he's so hungry for me that he doesn't wait for me to wake before helping himself. I can't recall a single time in the past three weeks when Giovanni hasn't awoken me this way. Some days, his licks are leisured and lazy. Others, like today, they're hurried and hungry.

He wants me quivering beneath him before breakfast because we're busy the rest of the day. Today is my mother's birthday, and although I assured her last week that she didn't need to accept Mr. Caruso's invitation on any day during her birthday week, she thought the day he suggested was perfect.

We will feast like kings, and we won't have to worry about the electric bill next month because we spent all our funds on food.

It's quite clever, but I'm still suspicious. My mother didn't flinch when I announced that Mr. Caruso knew it was her birthday week. She smiled shyly as a faint pink hue creeped up her neck.

My hands slam down on the mattress when Giovanni wordlessly announces he's noticed my distraction. He eats me with so much urgency that warmth spreads low in my belly and pools between my legs before I can warn him about the violent orgasm cresting in my womb.

The violent jerks of my body as I ride the wave of euphoria assure him he has my utmost attention, but just in case, he adds another finger to the mix. This time, he inserts it in my ass.

"Don't clench." Giovanni's warm breath on my drenched pussy lips sweeps open my thighs. "Good girl."

I dig my fingers in his hair and tug hard when he returns his mouth to my sensitive pussy. As he moves his thick finger in and out of my ass, its fluency complements the residue slicked between my butt cheeks, he toys with my clit and penetrates me with his tongue.

The strength of my pre-dawn orgasm already has me gasping for air, but the way he makes something I once thought was dirty feel good has me unable to catch my breath.

He works my body with the intimacy a musician has for his preferred instrument, and within seconds, the mist of elation coats my skin.

"Slower, *dolcezza*. You're riding my finger like you can take my cock. We both know that isn't true, but if you keep making me double-guess myself, I'll do something I can't take back."

My reply is more moans than distinguishable words. "Like banning Valeria from the Caruso compound?"

Defending this woman is the equivalent of eating glass, but no matter how hard I shuffle the facts, hopeful they'll land in my favor, the truth can't be hidden. The child I'm carrying could be Valeria's.

That gives justification for however rude she wants to be.

I'd be distraught if I were in her position, so although I understand Giovanni's wish to shelter me from additional harm, I'm worried the harm he's doing to his relationship with the possible mother of his child could be worse.

"I appreciate you taking my side and standing up for me. It means more than I can say." My throat burns as the worries I can't brush off as easily as Giovanni can storm back in. "But if this doesn't work out the way you believe, it could end badly for you."

He doesn't stop devouring me, and that terrifies me more than his anger ever could. His confidence is an impenetrable fortress, but for the first time in the past few weeks, I feel like I'm standing outside in the storm.

"Giovanni..."

"It will work out," he snaps out like his word is law. "And my request for her to stay away has nothing to do with your pregnancy. It's because I refuse to give her another opportunity to hurt you."

I want to believe him—god, I do—but the cracks in my resolve keep widening.

"If that's true, you didn't need to warn her to stay away." My reply comes out with a quiver when he removes his finger from my ass, flips me over, then enters me from behind so fast my pillow does little to muffle my screams.

Grunting, he drives himself in deeper before using every inch of his fat cock to dominate me.

The growls he releases when the fingertips on the hand curled around my sweaty hip reveal the deepness of his thrusts sets me off.

I come with a cry, my entire body shaking as Giovanni continues to unravel me.

After re-angling my hips for perfect domination, he plows into me on repeat. I know what he's doing. He's filling me to the brim, aware I can't think straight while being thoroughly fucked. I'm at the mercy of my libido and him.

I wish I could put up a better fight, but who in their right mind would? Each thrust pushes me deeper into the mattress and spirals my mind. I've never felt so taken. Claimed. Nor have I felt more wanted.

"What does this tell you, *dolcezza*?" Giovanni asks as his fingers flex low on my stomach. "What does it announce?"

My lungs are too depleted of air to speak, but Giovanni doesn't realize that.

"Answer me or I'll come in your ass instead of in your cunt."

Too blinded by the lust his threat inspires not to fall into his trap, I reply, "It says that I'm yours."

The relentless churn of his hips dulls a smidge. "Then why are you doubting us?"

Us? God. The word feels like a promise and a curse all at once.

I glance back at Giovanni, gasping when my eyes drink in every spectacular inch of the masterpiece fucking me into oblivion. Tall and muscular, with chiseled features that make my insides ache. He is the picture of perfection, but it isn't solely his panty-wetting face and body that secure my utmost devotion. It's the strength of his aura and the power that radiates from him in invisible waves.

He's risking everything for me—his family, his legacy, and maybe even his soul—yet his armor is unblemished. It shows no signs of frailty.

It makes me wonder if it's strong enough to survive the pressure of a secret like ours.

"Valentina..." Giovanni growls, reminding me that he asked a question.

"I'm not doubting us."

Fingers in my hair, he pulls me back and slams in—hard. "Don't lie to me."

"I'm not." I can barely talk through the spasms erupting through me. He's fucking like he wants to kill me, and I match every grind. "I'm trying to protect you, to keep you safe. I..."

Thrust.

"Don't..."

Thrust.

"Want..."

Thrust.

"You..."

Thrust.

"To..."

Thrust.

"Get..."

Thrust.

"Hurt."

I muffle the rest of my reply with my pillow. My stance only doubles the strength of Giovanni's pumps. He screws me senseless until the words he's been seeking for the past two weeks spill from my lips. "I love you too much to stand by and watch that happen."

He groans a deep, rumbling growl that, along with the heat of his cum exploding inside me, sends me spiraling into ecstasy.

32

———

GIOVANNI

Dressed in a black suit with a midnight dress shirt underneath, I sit on the bed and watch Valentina move around the bathroom. Her hair is loose and hanging down her back in effortless waves, and her skin is glowing in the aftermath of multiple orgasms.

My glow is for a different reason. Those three words she spoke at the start of her sentence slammed into me like a bullet to the chest.

I love you.

For a second, I couldn't breathe. Then the rush came. It was hot, wild, and unstoppable.

My pulse pounded like war drums when I fought heaven and hell to coerce it out of her again. My cum was dribbling down her thighs, and she was on the verge of a coma, but I refused to give up. I pushed and pushed and pushed until every shadow she could hide behind retreated, and my dedication paid dividends.

The woman I have an immediate, borderline-possessive obsession with loves me.

Now tell me again nothing good comes from insanity.

I've waited years for this. I bled for it. And now it seems surreal.

Incapable of not touching Valentina for longer than ten minutes when we're in the same room, I join her in the bathroom, band my arm around her waist, and prop my chin on her shoulder.

She smiles at my neediness before she commences placing a final coat of mascara on her long lashes. Her strokes stammer when I whisper, "Say it again."

Her eyes—those eyes that fucking undo me—meet mine in the vanity mirror. They show her defiance, but they also reveal we don't have enough time for another marathon fuck.

Her mother is due to arrive in less than an hour.

The world tilts on its axis when Valentina answers my demand without the zaps of an orgasm coursing through her. "I love you."

Those three little words make me soft, but fuck if I can give them up. I'll shield her from the monsters I dine with and the so-called foes who hide their knives with their smiles. I'll stand between her and every blade, bullet, and lie because she's the most valued possession I own. To get to her, you'll have to get through me first.

I pull her close until her heartbeat carves itself into my bones like it did the day I first saw her. "You know you don't need all this shit, right?" I wait for her eyes to align with mine before I lower them to the makeup spread across the vanity. "Martina supplied them with your dress in case you didn't have any makeup to suit the fabric." Martina is the designer brought in to make Valentina's dress. Dad has gone all out with Concetta's birthday celebrations. It is a black-tie affair. "She assumed the heat on your cheeks when she took your measurements was artificial. We know better, don't we, *dolcezza*?"

Valentina nods slowly before she dumps the mascara into the makeup bag Martina supplied. Then she scrubs the makeup off her face.

"Much better," I murmur when her natural beauty peeks out from beneath layers of foundation and concealer.

Once she's scrubbed her face clean, she spins in my arms. Her watch is confident but also shadowed with worry.

"Vanni," she whispers my name like the spell she cast on me might break if she speaks it too loudly. "I'm not sure if you're aware, but there's an option we can take to identify the biological mother of your child before birth."

I stiffen. This is *not* where I thought she was going when she whispered my name.

With my throat too constricted for a long sentence, I keep things short. "Go on."

She walks us into the main part of our room, plonks me on the bed still rumpled from our hours of escapades, then sits next to me. She's close enough that I feel the warmth of her body, but not enough to drown out the loud thuds of my heart.

"While waiting for my appointment at the clinic, I read every pamphlet in the waiting room. One was about amniocentesis testing. It's usually done to check for genetic conditions or infections, but it can also be used for DNA testing." Her breathing is uneven now, but she pushes on. "They use a really thin needle." She traces the air with my finger as if that makes it less frightening. "It's inserted through the abdomen and into the uterus so they can draw out a small amount of amniotic fluid from around the baby."

The image her description paints slices a knife across my jugular. "No."

"Gio—"

"No," I repeat, louder this time. "I'm not letting anyone put a needle in your stomach." Just the thought of someone doing that to her has me itching to kill. The doctor who came to collect a blood sample last week to check her HCG levels barely made it out alive, and his needle was minute compared to the one I'm imagining. "I don't care what they promise or how safe they say it is. It's *not* happening."

Before I can pace out my anger, Valentina grabs my hand and holds me still. "They do it with ultrasound guidance, so they see *exactly* where the needle goes. It's quick, but..." Her words trail off to silence.

"But?" I ask, my brow arched.

She considers lying, but the combined scents of our arousal on the sheets scrunched around her ass stop her. She knows I can force the narrative, so she chooses honesty.

"It's not without risk. There's a tiny chance of miscarriage... and infection."

"To you?" The fear gripping my throat makes it difficult to speak. "Is the risk of infection to you?"

She sheepishly nods. "That's why they only recommend it when there's a valid reason." I shake my head when she murmurs, "This is a valid reason. I can't carry this child for nine months and then hand it to Valeria."

"You won't have to."

"You don't know that. There's no prerogative with cases like this. It all falls on which family the judge deems the better fit."

"Which will be mine."

She acts as if I never spoke. "We could both lose custody if Valeria wins the popularity contest she's been priming for her entire life. I'm—"

"Worth a million times more than whatever her strongest point is."

You have no idea how hard it is not to strip her bare right now and fuck her as raw as the emotions in her eyes are shredding me. The only reason I don't is because she needs this. She needs to shed the dead layers of skin Valeria's lies coated her in.

Eventually, Valentina discloses the true cause of her unease. "If you don't want to do the amniocentesis test, we need to play nice." She drags her shaky hands down the front of her dress, ridding her palms of sweat. "That's why I invited Valeria to my mother's birthday dinner."

I jackknife back so quickly I mentally book a chiropractic appointment. "You did what?"

She doesn't reply. She doesn't need to. Her silence paints the entire picture.

"That's fine. I'll tell her she's no longer invited. I doubt she's even started getting ready yet. She's infamous for being late."

Valentina slows my stomps to the door with a confession. "She's already here. She is getting ready down the hall."

I turn on my heel like a dog detecting fear. "You invited her into my home without considering how I would feel about that?"

She stands her ground, and as much as I hate admitting this, I'm glad. "Don't do that. Don't tell me I have as many rights here as you do, then strip away the privilege when it doesn't suit you. Either I have a voice here, Giovanni, or I don't. Which one is it?"

I love her gall. It proves what I've always known. Every man in this house would fall on his knife for her and then kneel at her throne. But it doesn't hide the truth. "She hurt you."

"Because she's hurting, Vanni. Gosh. How can you not understand that? This is hard on her, too, and since I'm the easiest person for her to take it out on, I'm subjected to the brunt of her wrath."

"It is only hard on her because she's not getting her way."

My hands twitch to spank her when she rolls her eyes. "Hello, pot, meet kettle."

I don't understand her metaphor, so I ignore it. "You don't know this woman, *dolcezza*. You don't know what she is capable of."

"Because you're not letting me form my own opinion. You've kept my head in the clouds so much the past three weeks I can't think straight."

"There's a difference between being distracted and placing yourself at risk."

Valentina slants her head, aligning our eyes. "I'm not distracted."

"Yes, you are."

Her laughter is as brittle as her words. "With what?"

I stalk closer, my steps purposely slow. "With me." My nostrils flare when I breathe in deeply to suck in the scent of her rising arousal. "That isn't a bad thing, *dolcezza*. Especially when it keeps you out of trouble."

Valentina's throat bobs harshly when she spots the determination in my eyes. It will take a tank to evict us from this room before I have her pliable under my touch... and that's exactly what arrives when a knock sounds at my door a second later.

33

VALENTINA

The dining room of the Caruso manor glows like an amphitheater dressed for the opera. Crystal chandeliers scatter rainbow hues across polished floors, and the long table covered with used silverware and smeared porcelain plates gleams beneath them. My mother's laughter rings across the room like a gentle melody, and for the first time tonight, I let myself breathe.

My mother's birthday celebration is going better than I'd hoped. Even Valeria arrived early and has played the role of family friend and Caruso business associate to perfection. Her sophistication and graciousness have had my aunt searching the many gilded frames on these walls numerous times this evening, seeking her portrait.

Her amicable nature wasn't what I pictured when I confessed to Giovanni that I'd invited her. I had hoped the extension of an olive branch would free her from the mud the IVF clinic threw on us, but I didn't think it would actually work.

Valeria has far more at stake than I do. She's already clutching at straws to keep the interest of a man who doesn't look at her the way he does me, and in eight cruel months, the final thread may unravel.

I hate myself for saying this, but god, I hope Giovanni is right. This pregnancy was unexpected, and I offered to have a termination when I thought of it as more of an object than a living thing, but the thought of carrying a child for nine months and then handing it to someone else to take care of is worse than a knife to the heart.

I won't survive it.

That's why I'm trying to build a relationship with Valeria. It would be easier if Giovanni were on board with my plans. I knew he'd oppose, so I prepared for an argument. Mercifully, I was saved... No. *Rescued* from reneging on my invitation when his father appeared at our door.

Giuseppe is the head of the Caruso family. When he requested permission to escort me to the dining room, Giovanni didn't argue. It makes me wonder if his father's influence is resolute enough to tug Giovanni toward an amicable playing field instead of one shrouded in darkness.

I cling to that thought like a lifeline while straying my eyes across the guests enjoying an after-dinner drink.

Mom is radiant tonight. Happiness paints her cheeks with more color than they've had in months, and when Giovanni's father greeted her by taking her hand and pressing his lips to her skin, the hue stretched to her chest.

Several times tonight, I've caught her eyes sparkling as brightly as the chandeliers, and her breath has hitched more than once. I know my aunt sees it too. Her grin is wicked, and her gaze forever darts between Giuseppe and Mom like a gossip reporter hunting for its next scoop.

She'll corner Mom later, I'm certain.

She lives for gossip like this.

I lean back in my chair and then angle my body closer to Giovanni. He sits beside me with his hand resting on my thigh. Every time his thumb brushes my skin, warmth blooms through me.

He's quiet tonight, but I don't question it. We've never had a discussion with our clothes on, and I'd rather not test out how much I'll hate our first one while in the presence of our parents.

"They're getting along well," I whisper in Giovanni's ear before nudging my head across the table to my mother and his father across from us.

The table is a masterpiece. White linen is stretched across a setting that can seat fifty, and hundreds of candles flicker on the faces of those dearest to my mother. I invited only my aunt and Valeria, but it appears Giuseppe took this celebration as an excuse for a Palermo reunion. There are over thirty guests I've yet to meet.

Giovanni's nod causes his pricey aftershave to overpower the scent of the roasted meats and jeweled salads we consumed. "I haven't seen him like this since Mamma passed."

There's no malice in his tone. No anger. Still, I can't help but ask, "Does that bother you?"

His lazy smile as he shakes his head sends a low, steady pulse throughout my body and makes this gathering feel more like a funeral than a party.

It's been hours since I've been beneath him, but it seems more like a lifetime.

I've never been so eager to be the first to leave.

Earlier, I made out that I hate how well his attention pinches my smarts. I lied. I love how carefree his doting has made me, and that the world doesn't seem as scary as it once did. I guess this is where I'm meant to say it was the hormones talking during our argument. I would if I didn't think it was the cheat's way out.

Eager to fix my rights, I ask, "Should we do the cake?" Even though I'm asking a question, I don't give Giovanni a chance to respond. "We should do the cake."

With a quick adjustment of his position, which announces he's aware of the cause of my eagerness, Giovanni signals to the head butler to fetch the cake.

I'm not solely requesting we tick off the last item on our agenda tonight because I'm a horny wench endeavoring to make up for years of abstinence in a month. My mother also looks tired. She's putting on a brave front, but the more the festivities continue, the wobblier her steps become.

I brush my lips against the edge of Giovanni's mouth before gathering my mother from across the room and placing her at the king's spot, as per Giuseppe's silent offer when he pulls out his chair for her.

Although Mom's relieved sigh is silent, I still hear it. I was right. She's exhausted.

"Just a few more minutes, Mamma. The cake is the last item on the agenda. Then you're free to go. I promise."

She pats my hand and smiles up at me. "Thank you, *tesoro*. Tonight has been wonderful, but I am exhausted."

"Don't thank me. I only told *him* your approved date."

Her eyes gleam with a sparkle I haven't seen before when she follows the direction of my gaze. As if he can sense my mother's presence as well as Giovanni can mine, Giuseppe cranks his neck to face us the second Mom's eyes land on him.

When she mouths her thanks, he dips his chin, bowing out of a shower of praise with a gratitude I'm certain my mother has never witnessed.

The cake arrives like a crown jewel, carried on a silver tray by a butler dressed in a tuxedo, and everyone moves in close. Tears prick my eyes when the attendees break into the familiar melody of "Happy Birthday." I'm not being emotional solely because they sing it in Italian. It's because this time last year I was told it would be Mom's last birthday.

I'm so glad she proved the doctors wrong.

My mother must be feeling the same heavy sentiment. After brushing a tear off her cheek, she blows out the candles in one graceful breath and then giggles as if she's years younger when the guests cheer, "Hip hip hooray!"

I glance at Giovanni when his father warns my mother of the consequences of the knife hitting the base of the cake tray, while drifting closer. "You have to kiss the closest boy. That is the rule, Concetta. And we both know how much you love following the rules."

Giovanni's smile is there, but it's tight, like a mask stretched too far. That is, until he spots my gawk. Then his smile turns genuine, and it makes my pussy ache.

I'm about to join him, craving his closeness, but Aunt Maria cozies up to my side, thwarting my wish.

"Tell me you see that too, *tesoro*?" Her eyes snap to my mother, who's glowing like a woman half her age and in love. How do I know this? She looks exactly how I did while putting on makeup hours ago. "I swear, Valentina, if Giuseppe isn't careful, she'll faint from excitement before he gets anything good from her."

"Stop." I gag to hide my grin, but my lips curve anyway. It's good to tease and gossip. It feels normal. "Her cheeks are heated because she's tired—"

"Of sidestepping all the duds who chased her after she let that god go."

Absentmindedly, I accept a dessert plate from someone on my right. My mind is too fogged trying to decipher my aunt's riddle to offer my thanks, let alone name the person who handed me a slice of my mom's favorite dessert.

The chocolate fudge cake with raspberry filling and ganache frosting smells so divine that I pick at it while prying for more information. "What do you mean? They were only friends, right? Giuseppe is years older than Mom."

"With age comes experience," my aunt practically croons. "And who are you to talk? Giovanni is ten years older than you."

I talk around swirls of chocolate frosting melting on my tongue. "How do you know that?" I've shared many things with her and Mom during our daily visits to the hospital, but since Giovanni is in attendance with us, I keep most of the conversations centered on Mom's prognosis and upcoming radiation schedule. "I've never mentioned his age."

"The walls in this town whisper." I slap her hand away when she snatches a raspberry drizzled with a sweet nectar and crushed almonds off my plate and pops it into her mouth. "And I'm always listening."

After bumping me with her hip, she shadows closely behind Mom and Giuseppe when he guides her out of the dining room. They can't be leaving. Since we're not guaranteed a set amount of time, my mother never leaves without first saying goodbye. Giuseppe is most likely directing her to the closest bathroom since most guests washed down their meal with half a dozen glasses of wine.

Even though my heart sings a happy serenade when it detects Giovanni's closeness a second before his torso warms my back and his lips find my neck, my tone sounds firm when I say, "If you eat a single morsel of my dessert, I won't be held accountable for my actions." Unladylike, I shove a forkful of cake into my mouth and talk around it. "There are plenty of leftovers"—I nudge my head to the table housing more slices of cake than there are guests hovering in close to collect a slice—"over there."

I sense his smile more than I see it. "I'm good." His prickles graze my skin when he drags his lips down my neck to pepper my skin with kisses. "I'll have my favorite dessert later."

A delicious shiver rolls down my spine. It has nothing to do with the bursts of flavor activating my tastebuds. It's from recalling why he calls me sweetness. He said I'm the sweetest dessert he's ever tasted and that he'll never settle for second best, so *dolcezza* was the perfect nickname.

I breathe deeply while trying to remember that not every second in Giovanni's life must be devoted to me. God, he makes it hard. Just his lips on my neck and the heat of his body pressed against mine have my hips naturally gyrating.

With his mouth sucking my skin, marking me, he slides the hand he curled around my waist lower. It suspends briefly at the swell of my midsection—compliments to a three-course meal, not a baby—before it inches even lower.

I draw in a needy breath when his fingertips skim the apex of my pussy.

Another inch and he'll be stroking my clit.

Since half the guests are still lining up for cake, and the other half are too enamored by the sickly sweet dessert, I sweep open my thighs. Not a lot, just enough for Giovanni's hand to slot between them for the briefest second.

"Fuck... you're wet." His voice melds through my veins like liquid ecstasy. "Perhaps I should take you to the coat closet and have my way with you as I'm sure my father is wishing he could do with your mother."

Bringing our parents into this should immediately dispel my horniness. It doesn't. Don't ask me why. I'm as lost as you.

"Why don't you?"

The heavy ache between my legs builds when he angles his head so our eyes meet. I don't know what he sees, his eyes are too dark to reflect, but as fast as he snuck up on me, he dumps my half-eaten cake on the table, curls his hand around mine, then makes a beeline for the closest exit.

As we're about to break through the swinging doors the servers have used all evening, the doors burst open and a tall, brooding man passes through them.

A collective gasp booms around the room before the stranger's natural arrogance suffocates it of joy.

"Sorry I'm late." He moseys in like he owns the place. "I seemed to have misplaced my invitation."

He barely gets a foot inside the dining room when the hand not curled around mine shoots out to grab his arm.

Giovanni's hold is firm enough for the man to wince, but he tries to hide it with a friendly greeting. "Giovanni. It's nice to see—"

"Leave. *Now.*" No matter how much I attempt to keep Giovanni with me, he goes right up to the stranger. "Or I'll escort you out... unbreathing."

Every head turns our way when the man's laughter echoes through the suddenly silent room. He must have a death wish. I could hear the actuality in Giovanni's tone, and I've known him for only a short time.

"Why would I leave, Vanni? This is a family event." His shrug is as arrogant as his expression. "And I'm family."

He scans the people gawking at him, as if seeking assistance. I'm confident he'll continue going it alone, so you can imagine my shock when a loud "Daddy!" bellows across the room.

Valeria pushes back her chair so fast it screeches against the floor. I do nothing but stare.

Daddy? This stranger is her father?

My pulse stutters as confusion makes a mess of my thoughts.

Valeria throws her arms around the stranger's neck and greets him with a hug. "I thought you said you couldn't come."

He doesn't return her level of affection, and it makes the air even more humid.

When Valeria climbs down, she places herself between Giovanni and her father, which leaves Giovanni no choice but to either free her father from his clutch or risk hurting her to get to him.

My worries must be circling in his head, because he frees Valeria's father from his grip, but not without a stern shove. "Last warning, Tommaso. Leave. Now."

"Tomasso?"

It dawns on me that I mumbled my comment out loud when my mother's shocked gasp shrills into my ears. She's standing at the main entrance of the dining room, and her hand is covering her mouth.

The color Giuseppe worked so hard for tonight drains from her cheeks as her eyes dart between Valeria and her father.

Then her eyes find me, and they're overcome with panic.

"Valentina." My name sounds foreign since it's hacked with fear. "We need to leave."

I blink, stunned. "Mom, what's—"

Quicker than I can question her swift change in demeanor, she races around the room, clamps her hand around my arm, and then drags me toward the exit. "Don't ask. Just move." Her command is as deafening as the crack of a whip.

As she yanks me toward the door, the room stills. Nobody moves. Not even Giovanni. He knows I won't tolerate anyone disrespecting my mother, so he has no choice but to watch her drag me out of the festivities or risk losing me for good.

My heels skid on the polished floor when I endeavor to slow Mom's steps. My fight and Tommaso's mocking chortles only increase her determination. Her grip is ironclad as she drags me through a maze of chairs and startled faces with Giovanni hot on our tail.

"Mom, please stop. You're hurting me..."

My confession tears out of my throat with a sob, but her resolve remains firm.

"Mom, please…" I can't tell the difference between the pain of my request and the ache rocketing up my arm. That's how hard she is gripping me.

"Concetta!" Giovanni's shout slices her strides in half, though it doesn't wholly end them. "You need to listen to her. You're hurting her. Your daughter. Your flesh and blood. You're fucking hurting her." A mix of anger and unease blazes in his eyes. "Let her go, or I'll—"

I miss his threat when white-hot and merciless pain explodes through me with the tenacity of a bomb. It spears my abdomen and ripples the air with a scream I can't hold back.

As my knees buckle, my hands dart down to clutch my stomach. My nails bite through the silk fabric, but it has nothing on the agony shredding through me when bright crimson droplets paint the tips of my fingers.

Looking down, my heart shatters. Blood seeps into my dress and spreads like a stain of betrayal. My vision blurs with tears when a long trail careens down my thighs before it pools on the marble floor under my heels. As the chandeliers blend into the white halos dancing in front of me, I fight to stay upright.

They're so pretty they make death less scary, and I nearly succumb to the blackness calling me to it until the voice from my dreams ramrods through chaos.

"Valentina!"

Giovanni catches me in his arms and pulls me into his chest. His heartbeat slams against my ear when he races us past the priceless antiques that adorn the hallways of his family compound.

"Don't fall asleep," he demands between stomps. "You can't fall asleep, okay? Stay with me. Keep your eyes on me."

Pain overtakes every joyful spasm he's given me when he gallops me down the front stairs and sprints for the SUV with Matteo behind the wheel and Dante holding open the back passenger door.

The faces of the guests who followed his sprint blur as he carefully places me on the back seat. No amount of tenderness can diminish the terror on my mother's face, Valeria's wide eyes, and the calm-as-death nature of the man behind them, though.

Valeria's father is unfazed by the dramatic event occurring, and although the pain could be making me hallucinate, it appears as if he's smiling.

As the tangy aroma of blood swamps my tonsils, my body convulses. The pain is excruciating. I've never experienced anything close to this level of hurt, and I wouldn't wish it on my worst enemy.

Though it doesn't make my desire to be my mom's guardian angel any less stringent.

"Gio... Gio..." If this is my final day on earth, I don't want to leave until I'm confident Giovanni isn't angry at my mom. She needs someone like him on her side, and I don't want her unusual freakout to make things weird between them. "My... mom..." The world spins so fast I can't hold on. I'm seconds from passing out. "She... She..."

"Your mom is okay. I promise she'll be fine. It's crucial that you concentrate on you now, *dolcezza*. Can you do that for me? Can you put yourself first for a change?"

My fingers clutch his shirt as the darkness creeps in. "I... I..."

My vision fractures as the lights dancing across his handsome face fade. I try to cling to the honesty in his words when he promised Mom would be okay, but the fight becomes unbearable crazily fast.

The agony in the lower half of my body is horrific, but it has nothing on the pain slicing through my head. It feels like my brain is too large for my skull and that it's seconds from seeping out of my ears.

"Valentina, open your eyes."

Giovanni shakes me when I fail to obey his command.

I try to tell him I'm okay. It's peaceful here and pain-free. But the same blackness swallowing all light and sound entombs my words in my throat.

"Valentina!"

The last thing I hear before I'm swallowed whole is Giovanni's broken plea: "Stay with me, Valentina. *Please.*"

Then nothing.

34

GIOVANNI

Matteo hasn't even brought the car to a stop before Dante leaps out of the front passenger seat, flings open the door next to me, then assists me in lifting an unconscious and severely bleeding Valentina out of the back. Blood is everywhere. Between her legs, in her mouth, and trickling from her nose.

I crash through the hospital doors like a hurricane roaring through a glass factory. Valentina is flopped in my arms, and that terrifies me more than the amount of blood she lost during the commute to San Giorgio's. She's always felt vibrant and alive. Now she's limp like a fragile doll and cold against my chest.

"Help!" My beg bellows over the sound of doctors being paged. "Please, someone help!"

My lungs are burning from how fast I ran from the dining room to the convoy of SUVs my family is never without. I can barely feel it. Pain doesn't matter. Nothing matters except getting Valentina the help she needs.

When nurses rush forward with a gurney, I hesitate. Letting go feels like I'm surrendering the last thread of hope stitching her to my life.

If it weren't for the violent sloshes of blood splattering my shoes, I'd never hand her over.

My arms barely open before she's rolled away on a gurney and swallowed by fluorescent lights and starched sheets.

The emptiness of her no longer in my arms hits harder than any physical blow I've faced.

"What happened?" a nurse questions while cutting off Valentina's dress. She's already snapped gloves on her hands and covered her hair with an ugly bonnet.

"She... ah... she collapsed." I don't recognize my voice. It's weak and submissive. *Nothing* close to how it usually sounds. "She was standing... Then she clutched her stomach..." My teeth grind. I can't finish explaining what happened after that.

Another medical professional joins us. His composure brims with urgency. "Are there any medical conditions we need to know?"

A hundred different responses flash through my head, but not a word leaves my lips. My mind is a blank slate, wiped clean by the panic slowly killing me.

Mercifully, not everyone turns mute when overcome with fear.

"She's pregnant."

I turn so fast my neck muscles crack. Concetta stands at my right. Her face is pale, and her wet eyes are wide with guilt.

"How far along?" the doctor asks.

"I don't know," Concetta replies, shrugging.

When she peers at me, hopeful I'll fill in the gaps in the timeline, I offer nothing but silence.

Valentina and I agreed to keep the pregnancy a secret until she reached the safe zone. Although she's close to her mother, and I was confident she'd eventually crack under the weight of the guilt she unnecessarily placed on herself, she never tattled. I'm confident in this because I haven't left her side in weeks, and I monitor all her calls and messages.

Yeah, yeah. Save your lecture for when my woman isn't bleeding to death. When she's safe, you can do your worst, and I won't retaliate. I doubt I'll feel it. Nothing could hurt more than the pain tearing me in two right now. Not a single fucking thing.

"What?" Concetta's one word scrapes out of her throat like gravel being dragged over bitumen. "A mother knows these things." Her voice is strong now, and unashamed. It reminds me that there's strength in confidence.

I am Giovanni Caruso.

I don't bow for anyone—except her.

"Do whatever it takes to save her. I don't care what it costs." My brothers spread out behind me in silent support when I put decades of sacrifices on the line. "I'll give you everything I have… every last cent."

Before the doctor can reply, a male nurse enters Valentina's cubicle. His expression hardens with distraught the moment his eyes land on Valentina's beautiful face. He knows her. Not intimately. He'd already be dead if that were true.

After cursing under his breath, the nurse's eyes find mine. I'll give credit when it's due. His glare could melt ice. He's either an extremely confident man or stupid. I'm itching to kill, and his glare makes him a prime candidate to face my wrath.

The fear blooming out of him when I return his silent hatred doesn't weaken his accusatory tone when he diagnoses Valentina's condition without viewing the monitors screaming in alarm.

"It's most likely a hemorrhage from multiple gravidities or OHSS." His eyes are back on me, full of silent accusations. "I told them this was dangerous. Inserting sperm directly into a surrogate who is on gonadotropins can be fatal if the pregnancy isn't monitored by trained physicians. That's why we inseminate the eggs *after* they've been retrieved."

I'm lost. Completely and wholly fucking lost.

"The patient is on gonadotropin?"

"She was." The male nurse shifts his eyes to the head doctor, who asked the question. "I'm uncertain if she still is."

The doctor nods before appearing like a shadow at my side. "She needs immediate surgery. Best-case scenario is that we're looking at an ectopic pregnancy or pregnancies, but I'm afraid it could be OHSS."

"OHSS?"

"Ovarian hyperstimulation syndrome. It's a severe condition where the ovaries swell and cause fluid buildup in the abdomen and lungs. If it isn't caught early, it can also cause blood clots and kidney failure."

My fury collapses under the weight of my fear. "She could die?"

My fists curl so fast my knuckles crack when the male nurse mumbles under his breath. "All because you care more about an heir for your *legacy*"—he air quotes his last word—"than a living, breathing person. I only gave Valentina information on the clinic so she could help her mother, not for her to get trampled by a plan too stupid to be logical."

He looks like he wants to spit at my feet. I might let him if he'll take some of his attitude and apply it to saving Valentina's life. Even with nurses and doctors probing and prodding her, she hasn't moved an inch.

"You should be ashamed of yourself." He glances past my shoulder to someone entering the ER from the main entrance. "Both of you. If you had just let the clinic remove her eggs and inseminate them the right way, all of this could have been avoided."

Hate so black it singes the earth between my feet roars through me when I crank my neck back. Valeria is barely a foot inside the ER waiting room. Her face is ashen and marked with tears.

Her unvoiced remorse does little to cool my fury when she mouths, *I'm sorry*, two seconds before she races back through the double doors faster than a bullet leaving a gun.

My head screams at me to take off after her and rip her to shreds, but a question too fragile not to fracture my psyche concretes my feet to the floor. "There's little chance we can do anything for Valentina's baby, but if you could choose, who should we save?"

Not even confirmation that my child is also Valentina's sees me hesitating. "Valentina," I say, my voice rough with emotions. "Save Valentina. *Always.*"

The doctor nods before he reenters the cubicle, where the male nurse is frozen in shocked silence. He didn't anticipate my reply, and the instant Valentina is safe and conscious, I'll find out why. "We'll do everything we can, *Signor* Caruso."

He waits for me to nod before he wheels Valentina behind the flapping plastic doors of the operating room.

35

GIOVANNI

Every time a nurse passes the waiting room, my heart rate spikes as fast as my chin jerks up, and I brace for news that never comes. Time stretches cruelly and endlessly as I bob my leg like a crack addict overdue for a fix.

I don't even know how I got to the waiting room. One minute, I was in the ER. The next, I was seated on a hard plastic chair with my elbows on my knees, and my head in my hands.

Anger burns in my chest, but underneath the rage is a fear so potent it's the equivalent of acid in my veins. I'm fucking terrified. What if the doors open and good news doesn't walk through them? I won't survive the agony my father has endured over the past thirteen months.

Not hearing Valentina's laugh again or feeling the movements of her curves under my hand when she quivers in ecstasy *will* kill me.

If she's no longer in this world, I won't be either. There are no rewrites for my story. No part two. I'm the fucking penguin with his perfect fucking pebble.

It's only given out once.

Finally, the doctor who wheeled Valentina away hours ago appears. His expression is calm, but his eyes are stormy. I reach him in less than a heartbeat, and my brothers rise with me like a force ready to fight the injustices of the world.

"She's stable." His confession releases the pressure valve in my chest. "We controlled the bleeding by removing one of her fallopian tubes and are managing the complications of OHSS with medication."

"Where is she?" Concetta asks, reminding me that she's here.

I'm not avoiding her on purpose. I'm just too caught up in my worst nightmare to drag anyone else into the mess. I thought I handled pressure well. Tonight has proved me a liar.

The doctor glances at Concetta and smiles. "She's in recovery."

My throat burns when Dante reminds me it wasn't solely Valentina's life on the line tonight. "And the pregnancy?"

Remorse blisters through the doctor's eyes. It discloses everything.

While not all is lost, things don't look good.

Grief claws at my chest, but the sheer relief that Valentina is alive soothes its wounds. "Can I see her?"

"Soon," the doctor answers, alerting me that I asked a question.

Silly me.

"I *want* to see her," I correct.

"Soon," he repeats. "She's still under anesthesia..." His words trail off when I arch a brow. I wasn't asking permission to see Valentina. I'm telling him I want to see her. Those are two very different things.

His throat works hard to swallow before he briefly nods. "Okay. But only one visitor at a time. She needs time to recover."

My brothers nod in understanding. I stand my ground.

"Two." I curl my hand around Concetta's shuddering one before tugging her forward so she stands next to me. I was furious she didn't immediately heel to Valentina's request for her to stop. Then I remembered who she was dragging her away from. Tomasso is a worthless piece of shit. He'll trade his own daughter for some coin, so there's no way I'd let him anywhere near Valentina. Concetta must be of the same belief. Although I would have handled things differently, a parent doesn't have the same crutches as a partner. "Two visitors this time."

Again, the doctor surrenders. "Very well. Follow me."

It takes only one glance at my brothers for them to move forward with correcting the injustices that occurred tonight. I'll join them the instant Valentina is out of the woods. She comes first.

She will *always* come first.

It's business as usual for the Caruso realm when Matteo leads the pack of wolfhounds out of the hospital while shouting, "It's party time, boys!"

Excluding the steady beep of monitors, the room Valentina is recovering in is quiet. Tubes snake from her arms and under the sheet, and a heart monitor shows the safe rhythm of her pulse. I move to her side and take her hand in mine. It's warm now. *Thank fuck.* For hours now, I've been suppressing the urge to go on a rampage. It was close to bubbling over, but one brush of her skin against mine and the viciousness of the tornado consuming me downgrades from catastrophic to an EF3.

"I'm here, *tesoro*," her mother whispers from the other side of her bed as her thumb strokes her left hand. "I'm not going anywhere, so you take all the time you need to rest. It's my turn to take care of you."

Valentina's eyelids flutter, and I swear a ghostlike smile twitches on her mouth when I correct her mother's promise. "It's *our* turn to take care of you."

Hours later, in the silence of the ICU room Valentina was recently moved into after recovery, Concetta uses the alone time to interrogate me. We had a dozen nurses and doctors between us in the recovery unit, so this is her first opportunity. "Did you know Valentina was planning to sell her eggs?"

Too shocked to remain tight-lipped, I shake my head. She said she knew Valentina was pregnant because a mother knows, but I didn't know motherly instincts stretched this far.

"Did you?"

Her eyes lock with mine, and they shimmer with unshed tears. "I suspected," she says softly. "She didn't tell me. I found a prescription for gonadotropin the first night she didn't come home from her interview." She returns her eyes to Valentina, who now looks like she's sleeping instead of fighting for her life. "I wasn't snooping. I just needed to know you were okay." Her hand tumbles when she runs it down Valentina's cheek. "I wanted to ask you, but I didn't want you to feel ashamed." A broken sound escapes her. It's jagged and bitter. "I also didn't want to explain how I knew what gonadotropin is administered for." With six short words, she underhandedly announces who her daughter got all her good qualities from. "Desperate times call for desperate measures." A huff rattles in her chest as she returns her focus to me. "If only they were interested in fifty-five-year-old, overcooked menopause eggs, then maybe this could have been avoided."

Laughter whistles from my nose. It's unexpected, but it lowers my agitation a ton. I hate what Valentina has gone through and what she still has to face, but if she hadn't gone to the clinic on that specific day, I could still be scrounging the streets of Carlisle, trying to find her.

Concetta cuts off the peculiar sensation bombarding me by reminding me I still have a minefield to tiptoe across before I'm close to putting this chapter of my life to bed.

"Who was that lady earlier? The one in the ER? I know she was at the dinner party, but anytime I went to introduce myself, she scuttled off."

Not wanting even a snippet of frustration to hinder Valentina's recovery, I guide Concetta to the corridor outside her room before answering. "That was Valeria Giuffrida."

"Giuffrida," she whispers, as if testing the name out to see if it's a good fit.

When her brows furrow, stumped, I ask, "Do you know her?"

Her headshake isn't overly convincing, so she adds words to the mix. "It's probably for the best. I would have hesitated slogging her with my bat if she were the daughter of someone I know. Now my conscience is clear."

Before I can assure her a clear conscience isn't needed for someone like Valeria Guiffrida, the doctor who saved Valentina's life joins us in the corridor. I owe him everything, and the way he walks like his head is shoved up his ass announces he knows this.

He can strut. If he asked for my soul right now, I'd hand it over without blinking.

"*Signor* Ca—"

"Please, call me Giovanni."

He hesitates, then bobs his head. "Giovanni... We ran an urgent blood workup to check the function of Valentina's kidneys and found something concerning in her bloodwork."

My recently cooling temper peaks, but I leave the floor to him, realizing sometimes muscle isn't needed in cases like this. Strength is.

The doctor's expression hardens. "She had a high dose of strychnine in her system. In the past, strychnine was administered to treat human illnesses, but today, it's mainly used as a pesticide to kill rats. Symptoms of strychnine poisoning usually overcome a patient within fifteen to sixty minutes. If you hadn't gotten her here as fast as you did..."—he exhales slowly like his following words are as hard for him to deliver as they are for me to hear—"she wouldn't have made it." He glances toward Valentina's room as a professional mask slips over his face. "I need to order additional tests. As you saw, strychnine poisoning causes extreme negative health effects, so I need to make sure we didn't miss anything."

"Wait." My commanding tone freezes him halfway into the room. "How was it administered?"

I've heard of strychnine before, but only when running a street dealer out of Palermo for mixing it with LSD, heroin, and cocaine to make the hit faster for his customers.

Faster *and* deadlier.

Palermo had a record number of drug-related deaths that year.

The doctor flips through Valentina's chart before scanning her notes. "It was ingested."

Ingested? He must be mistaken. "That's not possible. I ate the same things Valentina did. We shared the same plate, for fuck's sake, and I feel fine. Am I angry? Yes. Furious? Fucking oath I am. But do I look like a man who was recently poisoned?"

My pulse pounds in my ears as I replay the night in my head. There were some incidents where the itch to kill trekked through my veins, but they were more jealously based than foiling an attempted murder. A handful of the serving staff were too admiring of Valentina's curves. I took care of the main culprit, and Dante handled the rest.

Suddenly, my jealousy lifts enough for clarity to seep between the cracks. "The cake. She didn't want to share her cake." I whip around and lock eyes with Concetta. "Who gave her the cake?"

Her brow furrows. "What?"

"The cake, Concetta!" My roar startles the nurses behind the nurses' desk, but I don't have time to apologize. I'm barely holding on by a thread. "Who handed it to her?"

The crowd pressing in closer, curious to see if Concetta's knife would touch the bottom of the cake plate, obscured my view. I remember that moment with clear precision because the guests cheered when Concetta's knife scraped the steel, and then she tilted her head so my father could kiss her cheek. It was an innocent, playful gesture. Except it wasn't because some fucking prick used the distraction to poison my future wife and the mother of my children.

Concetta's lips tremble when she admits, "It was the woman I asked about earlier. Valeria."

The name shunts me back three places, and then a memory surfaces in the ripple of my balk. There was a flash of color behind Valentina when I scanned the crowd. I wasn't staring in admiration. It was in recognition. Valeria's dress was the exact shade as Valentina's. It appeared to have been made from the same roll of silk.

Fury roars through me, hot and merciless. Valeria did this. She tried to kill Valentina, and she may have succeeded with our unborn child.

Every negative thought I've suppressed over the past three weeks rolls through my head until there's only one left:

Valeria tried to take Valentina from me, and now she will lose *everything*.

I'm already devising the worst death imaginable when Concetta ups the stakes. "My sister... she ate some of Valentina's cake. That's why she isn't here. She said she wasn't feeling well and that she needed to lie down. Your father offered her the guest room on the main floor."

"I'll send someone to check on her." My promise doesn't weaken her worry in the slightest. She's torn, unsure if my family's quest for revenge ranks higher than her sister's life. It doesn't, because anything that hurts Valentina hurts me, and my family refuses to make the mistakes of our ancestors.

I feel as conflicted as Concetta when my call to the compound's landline goes unanswered. I try again, but each attempt achieves the same result.

That's wrong.

That's dangerous.

The compound never goes silent... except when we're at war.

My heart rate spikes until the rapid incline of my pulse pounds in my ears. Bad shit is going down, and I'm miles from the action.

That would have been inconceivable only months ago.

As turmoil rages through my veins, I glance through the small window in the door of Valentina's room. She's swamped by a hospital bed and beeping machines because Valeria forced her into a fight she didn't choose. Leaving her while she looks so vulnerable would feel like ripping my heart out with my bare hands. I can't do it. I refuse.

I aim to calm the tremor in my jaw by evaluating the facts instead of letting them railroad me. My brothers most likely shut down communication within seconds of me deploying them to clean up the mess. I did the same thing before tossing Valeria at Valentina's feet.

Without evidence, there's no chance of conviction. My family has lived by that motto for decades.

Furthermore, only a fool would go against us now. We're the strongest we've ever been. A fucking atomic bomb couldn't take us down.

I remind myself of that on repeat while storing my phone in my pocket and walking toward Valentina's room.

My conscience is clear. Then Concetta grips my arm like I'm the only buoy in a turbulent ocean. "Please, Giovanni..." she begs, her lips quivering. "Maria has been our rock these past few months. She held us together when everything was falling apart."

She isn't playing with my emotions like a fiddler does a fiddle. Valentina has mentioned numerous times that her aunt has been their only solid support throughout all this. But it doesn't alter the facts.

"I can't leave her."

"I'll stay with her. I won't leave her side for a second." I'm not close to siding with her until she adds, "Valentina won't survive losing her aunt. She'll blame herself." She strays her watering eyes to her only child. "Just like she blames herself for my cancer diagnosis."

Again, she isn't making shit up to force me to prioritize her sister over her daughter. Her words are so gospel I'm about to walk out on the woman I swore to never abandon.

"I'll go make sure Maria is okay..." She exhales sharply, relieved. She shouldn't. "But if I find out Valentina woke to an empty room..." My glare finalizes my threat.

Concetta hears my warning loud and clear. "I won't leave her side. She comes first."

"Always," I confirm.

The guilt that pummels into me when I enter Valentina's room to brush my lips against her mouth is as brutal as a shot of methanol.

Every instinct in me screams to stay. To sit beside her and hold her hand until she wakes up.

But her mother is right. Losing her aunt will gut Valentina, and that isn't something I can sit by and watch.

"I'll be back as soon as I can."

Concetta's quick head bob hides the fear surging in her eyes when I tear out of Valentina's room and race for the closest exit.

36

GIOVANNI

Harsh blue and red ambulance lights streak the stonework of the Caruso compound when I pull down the long driveway at a speed too fast to be safe. I slam on the brakes, kicking up gravel, before I exit my SUV with my gun in my hand and the engine still running.

The scent in the air isn't suitable for a family residence.

It reeks of controversy.

Relief batters me when I recognize the generous frame of the person the paramedics are wheeling down the front stairs. Valentina's aunt is strapped to a gurney. She's pale and clammy but breathing. Dante is following closely behind her. He's also pale but uninjured. Shockingly.

After storing my gun, I stride toward the paramedics and say in a commanding tone, "Take her to San Giorgio's and make sure they know she's a Caruso."

The driver nods without pause. His loyalty will be well rewarded.

While waiting for them to load Maria into the ambulance, I pull out my phone and bring up the number of the phone I organized for Concetta's room weeks ago. It's the "free" iPhone she's never questioned.

Not wanting the loud ring setting all women over fifty seem to have to wake Valentina, I send a text message instead of calling.

ME:

Maria is conscious and fine. Being transported to San Giorgio's now.

Her reply is delivered fast.

CONCETTA:

Thank you.

She must type at the speed of lightning, because before I can request an update on Valentina, another message pops up.

CONCETTA:

The doctor said they're keeping Valentina under sedation until he's confident they didn't miss anything. That gives you plenty of time to grab Valentina a change of clothes... and perhaps the baseball bat from my apartment! 😉

Her suggestion re-sparks the darkness inside me. She knows what's coming, but instead of shying away from it like she did a relationship with my father in her late teens, she wants to be a part of it.

I like that almost as much as I'm obsessed with her daughter. If she's no longer afraid of what my family name means, she won't object when I gift it to her daughter.

ME:

Consider it done.

When my phone whooshes, announcing my text has been sent, I

store it back in my pocket and turn to face Dante. "What the fuck happened? When I tried to call to get someone to check on Maria, my calls went unanswered. I thought we were under attack."

The instant our father became unwell, we became primed for our enemies to make a move. It would be the first internal mafia war since the Cosa Nostra was almost wiped out, but only a fool believes loyalties won't be tested when he's got everything to lose.

Dante rubs the back of his neck while muttering, "It's complicated."

"Complicated?" He did not just fucking say that to me.

Like a man not in fear for his life, Dante jerks up his chin before shifting his narrowed eyes to his right. My teeth meet forcefully when I follow his gaze.

Valeria is in the foyer of my family home, milling around like a fucking guest. Her composure screams the fragility of a porcelain doll with a large crack down its face, but that's it. That's all she is. Upset but relatively uninjured... and somehow still breathing.

My blood pressure spikes.

How the fuck is she still walking after everything she did?

My brothers were meant to handle this, yet here she is, breathing in the air she tried to permanently snuff from Valentina's lungs.

The rage I've been struggling to contain all day is too much. I move before thinking. Dante shouts for me to stop, but I don't hear a word he speaks. The fury burning me alive is too deafening.

Valeria flinches when I storm toward her, and a ton of excuses tumble out of her red-painted lips. "I didn't know." Her hands rise to protect her face like my punishment will only involve my hands. I'm not going to smack her around like her father did her entire childhood.

A bullet is much more effective.

When I yank my gun out of its holster, she talks fast. "All I did was ask the IVF nurse to place your sperm inside Valentina. That's it. I didn't want to get fat taking hormones for egg production, and you weren't interested in the old-fashioned approach, so I picked someone I thought would remain a random. Someone I assumed you'd have no interest in. It just helped that she had a similar name. But that's all I did, Giovanni. I swear."

Her tone is drenched in as much honesty as it is desperation, but I'm done playing nice. "Valentina was poisoned." I crowd in closer until my shadow replicates the darkness I'm about to shove her in. "With the cake *you* gave her."

Her eyes widen as sheer panic slides over her face, her mask ripped away. "I didn't know he was going to do that." Her crackling whisper can't hide the truth in her statement. "I swear to God, Giovanni. I had no idea. He just asked me to give her the cake."

An icy chill rolls down my spine as my wish for vengeance doubles. Good, because I have too much adrenaline to disperse for only one hit.

"*He?*"

That one word kills Valeria better than a bullet ever could. She looks panicked. Rightfully so. She knows I'll be digging more than one grave tonight.

"Who is *he*, Valeria? And why would he want to hurt Valentina? The only person stupid enough to think they'd get any benefit out of her death is you..." My words trail off as the answer to my question wounds me like a bomb exploding in my face.

Two weeks ago, in this very fucking compound, I cut all ties with Tommaso when he delivered Valeria to me already injured. That wasn't my request. I said I wanted eyes on her, but he took it upon himself to split her lip, bruise her eye, and give her a bloody nose.

I told him it was the last straw. If he couldn't follow orders, he wasn't the right fit for the Caruso name.

His mocking laugh rang in my ears for hours. "You don't have a choice," he said, like he had every leg to stand on. "My grandchild makes me family. There are rules not even you can break when blood is involved."

And that's when I made a fatal mistake. I told him the truth, straight from my heart to his ears. I told him Valentina wasn't carrying Valeria's child. She was carrying her own.

My confession turned his leverage to dust. It stripped him of any power he wrongly believed he held, and now Valentina is paying the price for *my* mistake.

My chest is splitting open, but it doesn't douse the rage burning through me.

If anything, it feeds the flames.

Tommaso poisoned Valentina.

He tried to kill her to punish me.

To control me.

And now he and his daughter will die for his stupidity.

My focus drifts back to Valeria when she snivels, "I'm sorry, Giovanni. I didn't know he'd do this when I told him there was no chance you'd pick me over Valentina, especially since she is carrying your child. I swear, I didn't."

I crouch down and look her in the eyes. "You think this ends with an apology? That I'll let you walk because you said you're sorry?" I fist my gun so firmly my knuckles go white. "Your father just declared war on *my* fucking family... for you!"

"No." Her usually stern expression deteriorates as tears spill down her cheeks. "This has never been about me. Not our contract or the baby. It's always been about what *he* wants. I didn't have a choice. I've *never* had a choice—"

"I don't care! Valentina almost died. So now you, and everyone in your family, will learn what happens when you come for what's *mine*." Her snivels ramp up to full-on sobs when I slowly inch back the trigger.

"Giovanni..." This plea doesn't come from Valeria. It comes from Dante, who is standing at our side with his arms folded across his chest. "There's more to this than you know."

"I don't give a fuck."

"You might not, but Valentina may." He steps closer, placing himself in the firing line. "You also know what Valeria is saying is true. You may not like it, but it doesn't make it any less honest."

"You're on her side?" My words spit from my mouth. "She tried to kill the woman I love."

"No, she didn't."

In sync, Dante and I rocket our heads to the side. There's no sign of the illness that's been ravaging our father's body for the past year when he assists Matteo in tossing a battered and bruised Tommaso into the foyer of our family home, and then he slams the door shut behind Elio and Nico.

The war I was anticipating earlier is in effect, except the Carusos aren't being brought before the courts. The Guiffridas are.

My father's voice is a vicious snarl when he looks down at Tommaso and says, "That was all *his* doing."

Tommaso's expression is carved from arrogance, but there's something else there now too. Behind the nicks and bruises is a fear he tries to mask with confidence. "There are rules you can't ignore, Giuseppe. My grandchild gives me immunity."

My laugh is bitter. "The grandchild your daughter just admitted can't possibly be hers?" I shift on my feet to face Valeria. "What did you say again? You didn't want to get fat, so you paid the IVF nurse to insert my sperm directly into Valentina."

Tommaso's expression announces his wish to add to the bruises that have faded on Valeria's face, but he continues to play the game with narcissistic tendencies he always utilizes.

"Not that grandchild." He locks his eyes with mine, then gleams like blood isn't smeared across his teeth. "The one in Valentina's stomach."

I stagger back as if he swung at me with an axe, but he isn't the only one skilled in acting. "Accusations like that will get you killed... slowly *and* painfully."

My father's voice breaks through the drumming in my ears. "It isn't an accusation." Blood dots Tommaso's chin when my father proves age doesn't weaken a man's protective instincts. He kicks Tommaso in the stomach, folding him in half. "It took Concetta's reaction to Tommaso's arrival for me to locate the final piece of the puzzle." His following confession sideswipes me. "Valeria isn't Tommaso's only daughter. Valentina is his daughter, too."

"What?" That didn't come from me. It came from Matteo, who's forming a protective wall in the entryway with the rest of my brothers.

My father's demeanor is so calm anyone would swear he was discussing the weather. "When Valentina was born, a much older and ill-advised midwife ganged up on her younger and more vulnerable patient. She told Concetta that a father's name must be on the birth certificate, no matter how horrid he was, or their request for asylum in the United States would be denied. Concetta was so fearful he'd find them quicker in Sicily than he would in the US that her handwriting was barely legible when she placed his name on Valentina's birth certificate. Valentina's surname was registered as—"

"Raimondi instead of Raimondo," I fill in as the fog slowly lifts.

My eyes shoot to Valeria as my father continues unraveling the massive net holding my family hostage. "Everyone missed the truth because Tommaso went by his mother's maiden name until his thirties. He didn't want anyone to know he was associated with the man who used to beat his mother to a pulp every night, even with him not doing a damn thing about it." He spits at Tommaso's feet, disgusted. "You were a grown man for half their marriage, yet you watched your mother be beaten every fucking night."

When Tommaso doesn't attempt to refute his claims, bile rises in my throat. I shouldn't be surprised by his cowardice. The apple didn't fall far from the tree. Tommaso turned out the same as his father—violent, manipulative, and rotten to the core.

As my father's anger eclipses the leadership that brought our family great power, his tone lowers. "He changed his name when he found out at his father's funeral that the Guiffridas had ties with several influential families. The most notable..."

"The Carusos," I say with him, the haze fully lifted.

My father nods. "That was a month *after* Concetta fled the country." When his anger gets the better of him, his boot lands in Tomasso's stomach for the second time tonight.

Tomasso only smirks.

Valentina's pregnancy makes him believe he has the world at his feet. He thinks it ties him to the Cosa Nostra for life.

I've yet to reach the same conclusion.

He didn't lie when he said there are rules that protect him, but those same rules will cause his demise.

"You poisoned her," I say, eyes locked on Tommaso. "You tried to kill your own daughter, and the woman I love, to punish me."

Fools who think they have immunity are always the fastest to catch.

The loose skin under Tomasso's jaw wobbles when he jerks up his chin. "I didn't know she was my daughter at the time, but since your father can't keep his nose out of where it doesn't belong, I was gifted a lifeline not even you can take away."

Idiot.

He just showed his hand, and he's holding nothing but jokers.

"You got that, right?" I ask, stalking closer to Tomasso, my steps deathly quiet.

"From every fucking angle," Nico replies on behalf of the family.

With comms down to keep this in-house, my brothers had to record Tomasso's confession on their phones. Their footage is all the evidence I need to receive a full pardon for killing him.

When I pinch Tommaso's forehead with the barrel of my gun, his breathing spikes. He still tries to play it cool, though. "You can't kill me. I have immunity."

"*Had*," I correct. "If you'd done your research before trying to weasel your way into the Cosa Nostra, you'd know that term became null and void the instant you went after the spouse and child of a sanctioned member." I whack my chest with my fist to highlight who I'm referencing. "It doesn't matter how high up the chain you are, all spouses and children are protected under mafia law, which means I can use any force necessary to ensure the threat is neutralized. Including death."

Tommaso's throat works hard to swallow as he stares at my father, seeking the truth.

I know the exact moment it dawns on him that I'm not lying. His pupils widen and the fascinating scent of fear seeps from his pores.

"She'll never forgive you if you kill me. I'm her fath—"

I pull the trigger, splattering the sparkling marble tiles of the foyer with his brain matter.

Then I turn the gun on his eldest daughter.

37

VALENTINA

I wake with a groan. My body feels like it's been stitched to the mattress, and it takes effort to peel my eyes open. When I do, the fluorescent light above my head is too white and bright, and the godawful scent of scrubbed-clean stainless steel filters into my nose.

Even disoriented, I know where I'm waking up. I've spent the equivalent of months in rooms just like this. It's different this time, though. I'm not on the pull-out bed. Mom is. She's curled up on the narrow mattress. Her expression is peaceful, and her chest is rising and falling in a slow rhythm that announces she's asleep.

An array of emotions smacks into me. I'm glad Mom is here and that she's safe, but where is Giovanni? Did he leave? Did he—

"Scoot over," interrupts a deep timbre that makes every muscle I own clench at once.

Giovanni.

Seconds later, the mattress dips under his weight, and his arm slides under me. Carefully, he rolls me onto my side so I face away from him. He shuffles in close until his chest is solid against my back and his breaths are warm at my neck.

I flare my nostrils and breathe him in. He smells like soap, cologne, and something darker, like how cigarette smoke clings to your skin even after you shower.

His familiar scent grounds me, but it also reminds me of why we smell so different. My thighs are still sticky, and the hygienic smell isn't solely from the equipment around my bed.

My skin smells just as sanitary.

I stare at the wall, trying to process what's happened, but the question I want answered more than anything slips out spontaneously. "The baby?"

Giovanni's arm around me stiffens for the quickest second before his stressed words batter my temple. "We don't know yet. It's too early." He angles his head so I can see the truth in his eyes when he adds, "But no matter the outcome, nothing changes. It will always be us." His voice is steady now, like iron beneath velvet. "Worst outcome, we'll try again. It won't be until you've recovered, but we don't have to rush." His husky laugh is unexpected but highly required. "My father's illness seems to have left town the instant his eyes landed on your mother."

You can hear the smile in my words. "Maybe he was dying of a broken heart?"

"Maybe." I'm highly skeptical his smile reaches his eyes. He's tense, like he's worried I'll run like I thought he would the instant I realized the blood seeping into my dress was coming from my vagina.

"Is everything okay?"

Giovanni's slow exhale trickles through my hair. "You collapsed because you were poisoned."

"Poisoned? Who would do that?"

The tension exuding from him coils like a spring. "Tomasso."

I blink in rapid succession.

That isn't the name I was anticipating.

"Valeria's father?" I hear Giovanni's nod instead of seeing it. "Why would he do that? That doesn't make any sense… unless it was for Valeria."

"I thought the same." His fingers trace circles on my arm. His touch is both soothing and terrifying. "But it wasn't about Valeria. It was about control and an influence he had no claim to. He wanted leverage, and when I took that from him, he took it out on you instead of on me."

Fear weaves through my veins like ice. I thought I'd only have to get around Valeria to save my heart from being stomped in eight months' time. I had no idea I'd have to take on her entire family.

When I involuntarily shiver, Giovanni inches closer. "He won't hurt you again, Valentina. I promise you that. No one will ever hurt you again." He waits for my shudders to slacken before he says, "But I need you to know that I couldn't guarantee that without the steps I had to take tonight. I had to remove feelings from the equation to make sure *you* came first." His body vibrates with anger. "This was the second time he's tried to kill you, so I couldn't let him off scot-free."

I freeze, and then tug at my ear, certain I heard him wrong. "What?"

The only other time my life has been in jeopardy was when I was nestled in my mother's womb. That tormentor also went by Tomasso, but that name is as common here as Chris is for the rest of the world.

With the pieces too haggard for me to slot together, Giovanni cuts them up into manageable pieces. "Tomasso isn't just Valeria's father, Valentina. He's yours too."

"No," I deny, shaking my head. "You said Valeria's last name is

Giuffrida. That she only used her deceased grandmother's maiden name to save face at the IVF clinic. You must be mistaken..." My words fade as a memory surfaces too fast for my woozy head.

My mother wasn't dragging me away from Giovanni like she was suddenly unsupportive of our relationship.

She was dragging me away from the monster in her nightmares.

The once-safe room suddenly feels suffocating, and the rhythmic beep of the heart monitor is too loud. They shriek in my ears as if they're counting down to a truth I'm not brave enough to face just yet.

I can't help but push, though. "What did you do?"

"Don't ask questions you don't want the answers to, *dolcezza*."

I pay no attention to the warning in Giovanni's tone. "Did you kill him?"

"Val—"

"Answer me. Did you kill my father?"

I choke on a sob when he answers nonchalantly, "Yes. I killed him."

My mind spirals as I fight to grip reality. My father isn't a nice man. *Or should I say wasn't?* But that doesn't mean I wish he were dead. I'd never met him. He could have changed. Twenty-five years is a lot of time for improvement, and he could have done it for me...

A faded memory smacks my inner monologue into submission. Children are molded by their parents' actions. The way they're treated, loved, and supported shapes their future. They learn by example, and only a sturdy foundation of security and love ensures they go into adulthood with good intentions.

Valeria's vindictiveness and her it's-all-about-me mantra prove her childhood didn't have the stability mine did. My mother protected me—both back then and now.

The sheer terror on her face when she dragged me away from my father wasn't manufactured. Fear like that cannot be made up.

She was genuinely terrified, and I can see how Giovanni may have felt the same way when he was confronted with the truth.

An unfamiliar emotion loosens the heaviness on my chest. Is it grief or relief? I truly don't know. If I had to give an answer, I'd lean toward the latter.

Whatever it is, Giovanni feels it too. "If you want to run, Valentina, I understand. But before you do, remember there will be consequences when I catch you." His heavy pause steals my breath.

He didn't kill my father to hurt me.

He did it to protect me.

"And I won't delay my chase for even a second. Injured or not, I'll be hot on your tail within minutes of you fleeing. You can run from me, Valentina, but the outcome of my chase will *always* be the same. You are mine, so when I catch you, I get to—"

"Fuck me," I fill in, whispering.

I'm still bewildered, but I also understand. My father was a horrible man. He was only kind to my mother until she fell pregnant; then it went downhill—fast. He would have killed me years ago if my mother hadn't been brave enough to run, and my grave would have been right next to hers.

I don't doubt that.

Giovanni is everything my father never was. He's fierce, loyal, and extremely protective. Not just of me, but also of my family. My *true* family.

I crank my neck until I see Giovanni's dark and tormented eyes. His decision wasn't easy for him to make. He will stew over it for weeks to come. Possibly even months, and the knowledge clears away the sludge of his confession.

"I'm not going to run," I whisper. "*Yet.*" The tic in his jaw weakens until it matches the beat of my heart monitor when I add to my confession. "I like being chased by you... because I know you'll always catch me."

"Always," he agrees before he drags his index finger down my nose.

The gentleness of his touch and the soothing nature of his promise lengthen my blinks. My muscles spasmed so much today, you'd swear I haven't slept in a year.

"Get some sleep, *dolcezza*." He pulls me back until my body is cocooned by his. "We'll talk more in the morning."

Giovanni rubs my arms soothingly, but I can't sleep. My guilt is too firm. "If I had just listened to you, your unborn child's life wouldn't be in limbo."

"*Our* unborn child."

He firms his hold when the confidence in his tone causes a sob to rumble up my throat. Then he tells me everything. How Valeria refused to take the hormones necessary for egg retrieval because they can cause some patients to gain weight, and the one-hundred-thousand-dollar payment she paid the nurse at the clinic to switch our files. He even mentions how Luca was more an advocate of my rights than a co-conspirator.

When Luca unearthed the "apparent" mishap at the clinic, he wanted to come forward, but Valeria convinced him Giovanni wanted the procedure done as it occurred. Understandably, he was too fearful to go against a man as powerful as Giovanni.

That all changed when he saw me on my deathbed.

"Does that mean?" I take a breather when my voice cracks. If I cry, my mother will wake. She has a knack for knowing when her child is hurting.

As much as I love her, I don't want her comfort right now.

Giovanni's presence is more than enough.

It's overwhelming in the best and worst ways when his fingers brush my cheek before sliding down to cradle my stomach. His touch is gentle and reverent, and when he speaks, the world stops spinning.

"It means this"—he cradles my stomach before his thumb moves in slow circles over my skin—"is ours. As it has *always* been."

As his words ring on repeat in my head, everything fades until it's just us and the God-honest truth.

I'm finally home.

EPILOGUE

VALENTINA

Six months later...

Pleasure spreads from the center of my core and sprouts outward until it tingles in my toes and the roots of my hair with one teasing lick of Giovanni's tongue. He draws my clit into his mouth as he slides two fingers inside me. I clamp the walls of my vagina around him, welcoming the invasion. It feels so good. Having him inside me in any way is pure heaven.

A needy moan parts from my lips when he furls his fingers and milks the sweet spot inside me. My noises are desperate and needy, and they spur on Giovanni.

He eats me for a few hungry minutes before he adds brightness to the stars blistering in front of my eyes.

"Mmm, I smell so good *in* you."

The very second his nose hits the opening of my pussy, I shudder. My climax is brutal and fierce. It shakes my limbs from head to toe and wholly obliterates me.

I teeter between semi-consciousness and unconsciousness when Giovanni's hot breaths batter my aching pussy. "One more."

The bunched-up sheets make a mess of my hair when I shake my head.

That's my third orgasm this morning. I've got no gas left in the tank.

When I say that to Giovanni, he peers up at me and sardonically raises a brow.

"I... Oh, God." The change-up in my sentence is from Giovanni's determination to prove me wrong. He kisses, licks, and sucks at my pussy until pleasure coils in my stomach and then releases.

I cry out as a climax slams into me as brutally as a tsunami crashing to shore.

I've barely emerged from the clouds when Giovanni hooks my ankle and drags me down the mattress. Dark hair spills over my shoulders when he flips me over, then arches my back until his fat cock sits in the seam of my ass.

"Mmm," he murmurs again when I grind against him. "Tempting, *dolcezza*. Very fucking tempting." With his hand wrapped around his cock like a protective barrier, he notches the head of his cock into my ass. Not a lot. Just the tip. "But since your pussy will be out of commission for weeks in two short months, I think I'll save your ass for another day."

"My ass will be out of commission then, too. Remember?"

My clit feels his groan when he wipes the swollen tip of his cock with the damp towel he usually cleans me up with, before he slowly enters me. My moan tells him how much I love it when he goes slow. His gentle side is a rare treat I think will become more frequent when our child arrives in a little over two months.

One of our little sesame seeds held on for dear life. It made it through an attempted murder, two operations, and severe hyperemesis gravidarum. And for every setback, Giovanni was at my side, supporting me.

The doctors warned him I'd most likely miscarry before reaching twelve weeks, yet his support never waned. He was adamant that even if I was diagnosed as infertile, he wasn't going anywhere. His stance made me fall in love with him more than I ever thought possible.

He worships me, both in and out of the bedroom, and I can't wait to see how much our dynamic improves when we become parents.

It's done wonders for Dante, so I don't see it being much different for Giovanni.

A familiar tingle builds low in my core when Giovanni reaches between my legs and finds my clit. He toys with my clit and rocks in and out of my overstuffed pussy.

"You feel so good, *dolcezza*."

I try to reply, but I can't. It's too surreal. Not just for my body, but for my heart as well.

Our coupling was so fast and chaotic it should have crashed and burned within weeks, but here we are, months later, still living the dream.

I'd pinch myself if I weren't afraid of waking up.

It isn't solely Giovanni I'm terrified of losing, but also my mother and Giovanni's father.

Mom beat the odds as well. As of last month, she's officially disease-free. Dr. Russo calls it a miracle. I know better. It's because of him. My mother is alive because Giovanni moved heaven and earth to save her for me, and I will forever be in his debt.

Don't mistake what I'm saying. Even if Giovanni was as poor as dirt and unable to rub two nickels together, I'd still be here.

Love isn't about money and possessions. You could have all the money in the world and still want to burn it to the ground.

Both my father's and Giovanni's father's lives are proof of this.

Valeria did everything she could to make our father happy. She sold her soul. But it still wasn't enough. The more she gave him, the more he wanted. It was a vicious cycle that made her a shell of the woman she could have been if her mother had protected her as my mother did me.

Twenty-eight years of wrong teachings will take more than six months to correct, but if anyone can do it, I believe Giovanni and I can.

Giovanni isn't close to forgiving Valeria, but the fact that she's invited to the baby shower my mom and aunt are hosting today is a step in the right direction. And it will continue to improve the more we replace negative influences in her life with positive ones.

Giuseppe's story is a little different from my father's. He had money, power, and the loyalties of his sons. He just no longer had the love only a spouse can provide.

The loneliness of contemplating a life without his other half ate at him—literally.

Science says you can't die from a broken heart. Giuseppe's illness proved otherwise. He was withering to nothing, preferring to contemplate death rather than to continue living without love.

Then an old flame re-sparked, and he found a new reason to live.

I won't lie. Having hyperemesis gravidarum comes in handy when your middle-aged parents forget the purpose of a dining table.

You're meant to eat at it.

Don't look at me like that. Giovanni ate at my aunt's table, and anything after that can be excused by baby brain.

This, though. I'll never forget this.

A connection like the one I have with Giovanni doesn't have an expiration date. It's like canned food. It lasts forever and will survive any storm.

I genuinely believe that, and I truly believe in him, my dark knight who is screwing me to near unconsciousness.

I rock against Giovanni, taking another two inches. My grinds are cruel. I want him to lose control, and I want him to lose it now.

"Fuck... *dolcezza*," Giovanni roars, his hand slipping on my hip. We've been going at it for hours, so every inch of our bodies is covered with a sheen of sweat. "It just gets better and better."

Butterflies take flight in my stomach as several indicators of another orgasm present. I love how obsessive he still is. How possessive. It's like his thirst will never be quenched and I'm his only source of fluids.

As I sink into the pillow, I shake and moan. Everything is so deliciously tender that when Giovanni's dick throbs in a way that announces his release is imminent, I give him the words he needs to push him over the edge. "I love you, Vanni."

He groans my name as he comes hard, and I surrender to the tingles running rampant through my body. My lungs fail me. I'm reduced to wheezy pants and a mouth that shouldn't be as wet as it is.

Giovanni is just as exhausted. He collapses onto the mattress, taking me with him. Our position is similar to the one when he snuck into my hospital bed months ago, but this time, instead of facing away from him, I face him.

For several long minutes, while he strives to catch his breath, I admire every perfect inch of the man I'll forever class as mine. Even when he's sated, his muscles are primed to move if anyone dares to challenge him, and his eyes are burning with an intensity that makes me feel like I'm the only person in the room. Perhaps even the only person in his world.

My heart stutters when I take in the dark lashes curtaining his eyes, and the five o'clock shadow that's arrived twelve hours too early.

I've seen handsome men before, but Giovanni is on an entirely different scale. He isn't just a handsome man, though. His powerful aura is his armor, and there's warmth hidden beneath the layers of steel that is reserved solely for me.

His eyes tell me this when he notices me staring, as do the words he speaks next.

"I love you too, *dolcezza*. Always."

The next book in Caruso Cosa Nostra is Brutal Betrayal (Dante's story). You can pre-order it now!

Facebook: facebook.com/authorshandi

Instagram: instagram.com/authorshandi

Email: authorshandi@gmail.com

Reader's Group: bit.ly/ShandiBookBabes

Website: authorshandi.com

Newsletter: https://www.subscribepage.com/AuthorShandi